The Colors of Tess Gray

AN ELIZA GRAY NOVEL

J. Willis Sanders

BUGGS ISLAND BOOKS

Printed in the United States of America
Cover art by MiblArt

By J. Willis Sanders

The Eliza Gray Series
The Colors of Eliza Gray
The Colors of Denver Andrews
The Colors of Tess Gray

The Outer Banks of North Carolina Series
The Diary of Carlo Cipriani
If the Sunrise Forgets Tomorrow
Love, Jake

Writing as J.D. James: the Reid Stone Series
Reid Stone: Hard as Stone

The Colors of Tess Gray

loneliness

Inside Denver's home, which he had once shared with Eliza, Tess went to the sliding glass doors. The lake she loved no longer held her attention—not the trees filling with leaves, not the springtime fisherman seeking largemouth bass, not the pair of ospreys circling high in a sky so blue it tempted her to tears.

Five months ago today, Denver had left at her suggestion to take a sign language interpreter job at the Smithsonian in Washington, D.C., where he was probably sleeping with his friend and fellow sign language teacher Akina. Yes, sending him there had been a risk, but that risk was better than him staying here, where a local woman might ruin his chances with Eliza.

Sure, he had called now and then to see how Tess's guitar making and playing was coming along, but without mentioning the night before he left, when they had made love. What a night, one she would never forget, although she knew within her heart that he and Eliza still belonged together.

The aroma of coffee drew Tess from the view of the lake and into the kitchen, where the maker was dribbling its last drops into a mug.

May. Five months. She would be eighteen next month and intended to ask Mama and Papa if she could make the drive to D.C., to see Denver for her birthday. Not only did she want to see what might be happening—or not—between him and Akina, she wanted to see him just for her sake. Five months was a long time without seeing someone she cared about so much.

Then too, she wanted to see how he felt about Eliza by asking him face-to-face. The subject was touchy. No one had seen her since she had left last June, when she had gone to Ohio, leaving Denver nothing but a note that said for him to not contact her in any way.

Tess started to add sugar and creamer to the coffee, but returned the containers to the cabinet and refrigerator instead. Let the bitter taste hide her bitterness for her sister, who had devastated Denver further by sending him a divorce notice on Christmas Day of last year.

Tess added sugar and cream regardless. Nothing could hide her opinion of Eliza, especially when everyone had found out how she was living with a man and his three-year-old son in Ohio. After she and Denver had lost their daughter at her birth, how could she betray him like that?

Tess sipped coffee.

She had asked herself this question for almost a year now, and the answer was always the same: because Eliza was willing to throw away her marriage in order to have a child to love, but without the courage to overcome losing her own daughter so she and Denver could find their way back to each other again, and possibly, to get pregnant again.

In her jeans pocket, her phone vibrated. She swiped the screen to reveal Mama's number. "I'm still here," she said. "I thought I'd have coffee and enjoy the view of the lake before I vacuum and dust."

"Tess?"

"What?"

"I'm your mama. That means I know you go there because you miss Denver. Your papa and I realize how close you two got after Eliza left him."

The admission didn't surprise Tess. Anyone would have to be blind to not see how she and Denver loved being together, whether it was while building guitars or learning to play. Then again, Ivy had seen them kissing goodbye in Papa's furniture shop and had told Mama and Papa.

"My feelings don't matter, Mama."

"Because you think he and Eliza belong together. Do you love him?"

"I just told you my feelings don't matter."

"What about *his* feelings? Does he love you?"

The question made Tess hesitate. Although he had mentioned the possibility of them being together, he hadn't said anything about it since he had gone to D.C. Knowing him like she did, always the thinker after the emotion of a situation passed, he probably thought their closeness had come from losing Eliza.

"Are you there, Tess?"

"If he does love me, he hasn't said so. I'm not eighteen yet. If he comes back after my birthday next month, I hope we can date like normal people."

"Good, your papa and I approve. Denver's a wonderful man and you're a wonderful daughter, unlike Eliza. How she could hurt him so terribly by divorcing him, I'll never know." Mama paused. "Willow called while ago. She said Mark called and was asking about you."

Tess rubbed the knot forming between her eyebrows. Mark had been dating Willow when Denver and Eliza got married, and he had come to the wedding with Willow. He had remarked to a then fourteen-year-old Tess about how she and Willow resembled each other with their auburn hair, including how Denver's hair was brown, unlike his sister's. At the time, Tess had thought Mark was kind of cute but too old for her. Little had she known how Denver's age, nine years her senior, wouldn't bother her in the least when they started having feelings for each other.

She turned her attention back to the phone. "I'm not interested in Willow's old boyfriend. You can tell her that when she calls again."

"Are you coming home soon? That guitar you're making won't build itself. I've never known you to take so much time with any of your papa's rocking chairs or footstools, or his outdoor furniture."

"Building guitars is different. It takes more time than furniture because you have to get the sound right."

"Well, are you coming home?"

"I'm going to dust first." Tess ran a finger along the bar, which came back clean. She had kept the house in great shape since Denver had left, and she would keep doing so in case he came back unannounced. No, he wouldn't do that, not if he and Akina were getting along.

Mama huffed into the phone. "If you take as long dusting as you do with that guitar, you'll be there until next year. Don't dust a hole in anything. I already told you I know you go there because you miss Denver."

Tess ended the call and heated the cooling coffee in the microwave. Mama wasn't usually so short with her, but this thing between Eliza and Denver had the entire family on edge. None of them had ever believed the loss of Denver and Eliza's daughter would lead to their separation, much less their divorce. Whether here at home in Clarksville, or at any of the places Eliza and Denver had traveled to for her art shows before she got pregnant, anyone who saw them always remarked on how perfect they were together, evidenced by how they looked at each other, with nothing but love in their eyes.

The microwave dinged. Tess sipped coffee.

And now that love was gone.

No, she didn't believe that when Eliza had left, she didn't believe that when she had sent Denver the divorce papers, and she didn't believe it now. To allow herself to do so would be giving up on love.

Tess poured the coffee in the sink and washed the mug for next time. In Denver's room, she pulled back the covers, undressed completely, and crawled into his bed. Holding his pillow close, she imagined the aroma of his aftershave, imagined their last night together, imagined how she had never known such physical pleasure, mixed with the agony of knowing she loved a man who was in love with his wife who had divorced him.

On the nightstand, Tess's phone vibrated in her jeans pocket. A swipe of the screen showed Denver's number, which sent a tiny thrill of anticipation along her shoulders and neck, where he had kissed and caressed on that night five months ago. She swiped the answer icon. "Well, well, how's things at the Smithsonian, you bozo?"

He shared a soft laugh. "Hi, Tessy, how're you?"

"Don't *Tessy* me, *Denny*."

"Stop your teasing, unless you really think I *am* a bozo. Do you? I never quite know where I stand with you."

Tess paused. Do it or not? What the heck, he needed a reminder of what had happened in his bed last December. She spread her auburn hair on the pillow and covered everything but her nude shoulders with the sheet, pouted her most sultry pout and took a selfie and sent it to him. "Take a look at that and see if it tempts you."

"Is it a photo of that guitar you've been working on since forever?"

"Not even close."

"Are you at my house?"

"No hints."

"Okay, give me a minute." Seconds passed. "Who the heck is in my bed? I recognize those yellow sheets."

"Uh-huh, you really *are* a bozo if you don't recognize me in all my naked splendor. Maybe I should drive up there and remind you."

"I recognize you." Denver grew quiet, likely ogling the selfie.

"Sorry about that," Tess said. "Should I send one without the sheet?"

"And make me get a ticket driving to Clarksville? No thanks."

"It's about time you gave me a compliment. How're things going up there? Are you and Akina working hard?"

"Pretty much. A lot of people visit the Smithsonian. Even if a group doesn't include a deaf person, we're instructed to translate the tour guide's words anyway."

"Now, Denny, I didn't mean *work* work. I meant homework."

"Nope. We keep stuff cleaned up as we go. Akina's a great cook. We take turns in the kitchen."

Tess blew a raspberry.

"What's that for?" Denver asked.

"Not *work* work, you bozo. I mean pleasure work."

"Oh, you mean are Akina and I sleeping together like we did back in Ohio before I fell in love with she who shall not be named?"

Tess grinned at their nickname for her dumb sister. "It's about time your lightbulb went off. Well?"

"Nope. Akina's a great friend and that's it."

"Any hot dates?"

"You spoiled me the night before I left."

"I can live with that. You realize I'll be eighteen next month. We can get married without asking my parents."

Denver shared that same soft laugh. "Always the tease. In case you were wondering, I do miss you."

His sincere admission brought the surprise of tears to Tess's eyes. Yes, they were close, and she hoped they always would be. "I—" No, regardless of how much she loved him, she couldn't admit it and ruin the possibility of him and Eliza getting back together.

"Frog in your throat, Tessy?"

"I—" Tess swallowed. "It's good to know I'm missed. I miss you too. I—"

"Yeah?"

Tell him something, anything—except how she wanted him again, right here in his bed, like right *now* right here in his bed. "Did I tell you about that used clunker Papa bought me for getting my driver's license?"

"You sent me a picture of you smiling while standing beside it. It looks like a nice car to me."

"You know me, the exaggerator. Yes, it's nice. Mama and Papa still believe in being frugal. Some of their Amish ways stayed with them after they left Ohio."

"While yours have zipped off to my bed. Do you nap in it often?"

Tess regretted sending him the photo. She didn't want him to think she was some kind of pervert. "I'm at home. I bought some yellow sheets just to mess with you."

"And you wait in bed for me to call?"

Tess sniffled. "I think I'm catching a cold."

"Uh-huh. Are your mom and dad and Ivy doing okay?"

"They're good."

"How about Ethan? I'd call him, but I'm afraid he'll mention she who shall not be named, and I don't feel like talking about her." Denver coughed. "Maybe I'm catching a cold too."

"What's up anyway?" Tess asked. "Did you call just to check up on me?"

"I was wondering what you're doing for your birthday next month. Eighteen's a big deal."

Tess hesitated. She better make an excuse so she could surprise him when she drove up. "I'm still working at the bed and breakfast. My birthday's on a Saturday, so I'll be there."

"That's no fun."

"You could drive down and take me out."

"Don't tempt me." Denver paused.

What was he thinking? If anything, Tess hoped he really *was* thinking about their last night together in his bed. "Denver?"

"Yeah?"

"We're close, right?"

"How can you ask that when you helped me so much after Eliza left? Between just being there for me, and having Lily's headstone made, including that plaster cast of her hand and footprints, along with keeping me sane by joining me in bed the night after Eliza sent those idiotic divorce papers, we're more than close and you know it."

Hesitant breaths whispered into the phone. As much as Tess hoped he was about to tell her he loved her, she didn't want that to happen. Along with not wanting anyone else to ruin any chances of him and Eliza working through their problems, she didn't want to ruin them either. Still, just imagining him saying those three words to her instead of Eliza brought tears to her eyes again. "I better go," she whispered.

"Me too." Those same hesitant breaths again. "Tess, I ..."

Why couldn't he just say it so she could say it? "Denver, you know you can tell me anything, right?"

"I know. Hey, Akina just got up and it's my turn to cook breakfast. Catch you later, okay?"

"All right. Bye."

Saved by Akina, Tess ended the call. No matter how they might feel about each other— Tess shook her head. How often did she have to remind herself of how Eliza and Denver belonged together?

What an idiot she had for a sister. Not only had she married a guy who was perfect for her, she had divorced him. Whatever she was doing in Ohio with that man and his son, it better be worth losing her husband over.

Eliza

Having finished the breakfast dishes, Eliza found Josh and David in the chicken coop. Josh was going to see Anna today, and Eliza wanted to know if they all could go.

She watched Josh show his son how to take an egg from beneath a hen without disturbing her off her nest. David preferred chasing chickens to touching them, although he did love fried chicken. She went to him to wipe a smudge from his forehead with her apron. "Come here, Mr. Mess. You can get dirtier quicker than anyone I know."

He stood still until she finished. "Can you get an egg without making the chickens squawk, Mama?"

Smiling at his preferred name for her, she kissed his cheek. "Why would I do that when you're learning how? Besides, I'm the one who fries the chicken you like so well."

"Don't forget the mashed taters and gravy." David went to the door. "I'm gonna dig in the poop pile for fishin' worms so we can go later."

Eliza followed him out, Josh behind her. "That boy sure knows how to keep me busy," he said. "If it isn't fishing, it's reading to him. If it isn't reading to him, it's carving him toy trucks and tractors out of wood." He turned from watching

David dig in the chicken manure pile out by the side of the garden, where they let it age before applying it as fertilizer. "How long before you start painting with those supplies I gave you at Christmas? Since the weather broke, you can sit outside and do it."

Eliza considered Josh's narrow face and sharp nose. The man ate little, likely because of the stress from his wife's nearly year-long stay in a long-term care facility. It was so hard to believe, her being hit by a dairy tanker while walking to a neighbor's house for flour. Josh tended to drink from a small brown bottle at times, likely from stress too. At least he didn't overdrink like Denver had for the months before she left him.

"I'll think about painting soon," she said.

"Don't forget teaching David too. He'll turn five next year and go off to school, and you'll miss him then." Josh paused. "I haven't told you in a while, but I hope you know how much I appreciate you staying with us after Anna's accident. It's hard enough working a farm as it is. I couldn't begin to do that and take care of him by myself."

Eliza noted how he hadn't mentioned her adopting David. He had asked her about it at Christmas last year, but he had never broached the subject again. She had taken his request to mean while Anna was still alive, when he likely had meant after she died.

At the manure pile, David, wearing jeans and a blue T-shirt, dropped a wriggling worm into a can. His dark hair stuck up in a cowlick at the crown of his head.

Eliza loved the boy beyond reason. Yes, she would adopt him if Josh asked again. Still, the question of her long-term future here sometimes teased itself into her mind, either late at night or, as she watched the sun set over the rolling Ohio hills, when she thought about Denver.

Had she made a mistake by leaving him? Before they lost their daughter, she never doubted her love for him. That night though, the night she had left him, still stuck inside her mind like a cocklebur on a pants leg: difficult to remove and painful if it bored through the cloth of the protective cloak of denial she had wrapped around herself. Yes, she would always love him, but to stay married to him when she couldn't stand the thought of ever sleeping with him again—much less making love to him—meant she had made the right decision of leaving him. Better to live here with Josh and David, where no one made such demands of her.

"Do you mind if David and I come with you to visit Anna?"

"I hate to take him there. He always asks why she's so thin."

"If you don't mind me saying so, you're thin yourself."

"Because I work so much. Anyway, I take after my papa—he was thin too."

"What about your mama? I never met either of them before they died."

"She was average size, maybe a bit more. She still made lots of Amish recipes after Papa died and she left the Amish."

Eliza recalled their conversation about this. What a shame for Josh's mama—and now Josh—to blame the Amish for his papa not getting the medical treatment he needed for his cancer. Josh had also left the Amish after Anna's accident, saying if she had been treated for mumps as a child, she wouldn't have lost her hearing and would've heard that truck coming.

He ran his fingers through his brown hair. "I better water the garden, or all those seeds and plants we put in last week will never grow. He left for the spigot on the house and turned it. Several sprinklers sprayed the dark rows of soil.

With his fishing worm can, David ran to Eliza. "Papa got me wet, Mama."

Eliza knelt to brush dried chicken manure from David's jeans. Over his head, she saw Josh take a swallow from a small brown bottle and return it to his pocket. She hadn't smelled alcohol on his breath so far today, but he usually didn't take his rare swallows so early.

Patting her hands free of the dirt, she stood. "Did you find enough worms to go fishing?"

David nodded. "When can I learn how to paint? Papa says you'll teach me?"

"Would you rather paint than go fishing?"

He screwed his face into a frown. "Well …"

"'Well' what?"

He ran to the manure pile and dumped the worms from the can, covered them with manure and ran back, puffing hard. "Now they can—" He took a breath. "Now they can wait for us."

He took Eliza's hand, and she led him to the house. As they passed Josh at the spigot, David grinned hugely. "Papa, Mama's gonna paint."

"That's good to hear. Go on inside, okay? Eliza will be there in a minute. He's a great son," Josh said, after the door closed behind David. "Some people say boys don't mind their parents, but he always does."

"What did you want?" Eliza asked.

"I'll go ahead and visit Anna while you two pai—" Josh took his phone from his pocket and looked at the screen. "It's Anna's nurse." He swiped the screen. "This is Josh. Is something—" His eyes widened. "Really?" His eyes went to Eliza. "It's … well, it's so hard to believe. Yes, I'll come right now." He dropped the phone into his pocket and hugged Eliza. "Anna's waking up!"

Eliza didn't care to say anything negative, but Anna's coma may have left her unable to move and in need of months in a rehabilitation center. "Josh, what exactly does 'waking up' mean?"

Josh's grin fell. "Aren't you happy for me and David? I'd still like you to stay until she's back to normal again."

"You realize that may be a while yet. What did the nurse say exactly?"

"Anna's mumbling in her sleep."

"Is that all?"

"Isn't that enough? She hasn't made a sound since the accident."

Eliza didn't know how to take the news. Taking care of David was one thing. Taking care of a woman who would need serious medical care was something else. "I'm happy for you and David. Do you want to tell him yet?"

Josh blinked once, twice, and a third time. "What would I do without you? I should think before I get so excited. I would hate to make David think Anna will come back home like normal. We'll keep this between us until she's doing better." He took his keys from his pocket. "I better go."

Eliza watched him hurry to his pickup. Thank goodness she had been able to make him see logic instead of emotion. She hoped Anna would make a full recovery for his and David's sakes, but she would have a long, hard road to recovery.

"Mama?" The screened door squeaked open. "I saw Papa leave. Is he going to see Mama?"

"That he is. Are you ready to paint? We can sit under the oak tree by the barn and paint the flowers your mama planted on that end of the garden."

David answered by zooming inside. "C'mon, Mama! I'll help you carry everything!"

Denver

Reading the Sunday comics on Akina's sofa on a lazy afternoon, Denver stopped to poke her bare foot near his elbow. "Who's turn is it to cook supper?"

Stretched out beside him, her head at the other end of the sofa, the rest of the paper opened before her, she looked over it to return the poke to his foot. "That depends on what you want." She turned a page. "Do you miss Clarksville yet?"

"I miss my grill. Steak in a pan sucks."

"Mmm-hmm, and it's too expensive to eat out on our meager salaries." Akina yawned. "You didn't answer me about Clarksville."

"Forget Clarksville. I told you how my mom and dad left Willow and I enough life insurance to take care of us for a long time." He stood and stretched. "Sheesh, do you ever feel like you don't want to do anything?"

Akina's dark eyes peered over the paper again. Her hair was longer in Ohio, when they had taught sign language together at Jon's school. She now had a pixie cut, which made her oval face even cuter. "You know I've figured you out since you got here in December, right?"

"How so?"

"You always say that about not wanting to do anything when you're thinking about home."

Denver dropped to the sofa. "I don't remember telling you that."

"You usually bring up home after you say it." Akina raised the paper. "Let me read this article. Then we'll decide about supper."

Denver looked around the small apartment: nothing more than two bedrooms, one bathroom with a tiny shower and a vertical washer-dryer combo, and a galley kitchen without a window. It was like living in a sardine can with no view of any trees or sky.

Akina crossed her ankles. She wore blue sleep shorts and pink T-shirt—no bra. After his last night with Tess, and no sex for five months, being around Akina was torture. He patted her foot. "Do you ever think about … you know?"

"It's hard to read when you do that."

Leaning back on the sofa, Denver clasped his hands behind his head and closed his eyes. What a mess his life was, even after coming here to teach sign language and get his mind off of his troubles with Eliza.

Tess.

Now there was someone he needed to get his mind off of. As much as he tried to stop thinking about her, he couldn't, and he needed to because she was young and had her whole life ahead of her. On the morning he had left her, they had talked about dating when she turned eighteen. The last thing she needed was to tie herself down to him, nine years her senior, with marriage and kids.

Then there was his job.

As much as he enjoyed sign language, translating for tour guides was boring except for when a deaf person signed with him.

Along with the mundane nature of his job, which he worked at six days a week, he hadn't toured D.C. on his own or with Akina yet. The day he left Clarksville, he and Tess had mentioned her coming up and doing that together.

Sure, he missed Clarksville. He even missed Eliza when he allowed himself to think about her. Still, if Tess came up, he could see where things stood between them.

To get his mind off of Tess, he turned sideways on the sofa and took Akina's feet into his lap to massage them.

Akina wiggled her toes. "You're pretty good at that. I'd do yours but they stink."

"I can wash them."

"Are you a foot guy now? You never did that when we had our fling in Ohio."

Denver rubbed her calf. "Oh, I'm an everything guy. You should know."

"Denver?"

"What?"

"Are you sure you want to do what I think you want to do?"

"What do you think I want to do?"

"If my hair were still long, I'd think you want to pretend I'm Eliza."

Denver shoved Akina's feet from his lap. "Wrong."

"Have you thought about going to Ohio to see if she's really living with that guy and his son?"

"Ethan wouldn't lie about it. Besides, I signed the divorce papers in March. I'm officially a free man."

"You didn't tell me that. Wait a minute." Akina dropped the paper on the coffee table and sat facing him. "I thought divorces took a year?"

"Contested ones do. Like I told you, Eliza made her choice. I didn't see the need to fight the divorce when she didn't want me anymore."

"March," Akina said, her eyes narrowing. "Was that when you hardly said anything for a week?"

"Yeah. No matter how much I've told myself it's over since she sent me the divorce notice in December, it's still hard to believe."

Akina leaned close to rub his shoulder. "Me too. When you and Eliza met, it was instant chemistry." She took her hand away. "Do you have any idea how long you'll stay here and what you plan to do after?"

"Get on with life. Maybe find someone who won't rip my heart out. Maybe have a family like I've always wanted since I met Eliza."

"Anyone and anywhere in particular?"

"I love Clarksville. Regardless of this thing between Eliza and me, her family has been great. Including Willow, they're the only family I have now."

Akina's lips twitched with a quick grin. "I liked meeting Willow at your wedding. She didn't like Jan one bit. Do you have anyone in mind to spend your life with. I'm sure it isn't Jan."

"Ain't happening, she's still a city girl. I like the outdoors too much for her." Denver patted Akina's knee. "What're you doing for the next sixty years?"

Akina slapped his hand away. "I like having my own way too much. Unlike you, any guy I marry has to keep the toilet seat down, his laundry in the hamper instead of around it, and not mind my bras and panties hanging on the shower rod to dry."

Denver paused. Akina wore some extremely sexy bras and panties—thongs too—and taking them off the shower rod every night before a shower teased him into fantasizing about taking them off of her. He patted her knee again. "I guess I'll have to find a hometown girl who doesn't mind all that and is as good in the sack as you were in Ohio."

Akina licked her lips. "We did have some great times there, didn't we?"

"What's sex anyway? It's been a while."

"For me too, but you're still on the rebound. Like too many couples, they equate sex with love, and it's anything but."

Denver stood and stretched. "Want to go out for supper, my treat?"

"And make me change out of my PJs, no thanks." Akina took the paper from the coffee table. "Go ahead. I'll have a sandwich or something."

In his room, Denver put on socks and shoes. He took his bike from the corner and carried it downstairs to the street. Watching traffic, he slipped between two cars spaced far apart. Thank goodness weekend D.C. traffic didn't fill the roads like it did during the workweek mornings. One wrong move or one inattentive moment could get a rider injured or worse.

At the bistro five minutes away, he opted for a steak and cheese and a bottle of water, secured the bag on the bike's rear rack, and rode toward the National Mall, using the Washington Monument's 555-foot height as a guide.

Nearing the famous cherry trees, which had bloomed in April, he parked the bike beside one and ate his meal while watching the sun shimmering on the surface of the tidal basin, fed by the Potomac River.

To his left and right, tourists strolled the sidewalk, some holding hands, some not. The scene reminded him of his and Eliza's walks on the shores of Buggs Island Lake, during their honeymoon at the cabin in Occoneechee State Park.

He finished the sandwich, washed it down with water, and crunched the crinkly plastic bottle in his hand. His life sucked worse than he had ever thought possible. He hated being alone. He hated being single. He hated the feeling of loss. Worse than that, he hated feeling like he would never be a dad.

No, what he hated was feeling like he would never be a dad to his and Eliza's children. Along with loving her, being a dad had been his dream since their wedding. They spoke of it often, between her art shows, in hotel room after hotel room, until she had showed him the pregnancy test results. Of all the times they had smiled together, they had never smiled that big, making love right away.

Denver rubbed his forehead. He understood how losing Lily had devastated them both, but to the point of divorce?

The light breeze gusted, rustling the leaves overhead and sending waves lapping near his feet. Behind him, footsteps of more people passed—people likely in love or married like he and Eliza had been.

The footsteps stopped. "Denver?"

Denver turned to face Leah Hite, the girl from Clarksville he had taken out on the pontoon boat to watch the Lakefest fireworks last year, after Eliza had left. He gave her a quick hug. "Hey, Leah. It's good to see you."

"You too." She placed her hand on the shoulder of a girl of about fifteen. "This is my sister, Lisa. We're seeing the sites."

Denver said hi to Lisa, a brunette with curly hair and cute dimples like Leah. "Nice to meet you, Lisa. What have you seen so far?"

"Not much. It would take a week to see everything."

"We went to the National Gallery of Art this morning," Leah said.

"I haven't been yet," Denver said. "I don't guess my ex-wife has any paintings in there."

"We stayed in the section with the Italian artists mostly."

Lisa nudged Leah's arms with hers. "Leah thinks those old Italian guys are hot."

"Shut up."

"You know you do."

"Whatever." Leah faced Denver. "How's it going? Will you come home anytime soon?"

Denver said nothing. What a question, one he didn't know how to answer. "I'm not sure. I might drive down for Lakefest and to visit my in-laws."

Leah linked her arm with his and led him away from Lisa, who was taking pictures of the tidal bason with her phone. "I know I apologized for coming on to you last year, but I am sorry about that. I'd love to start over and see if you're worthy of me."

Denver noticed her half-smile. "Tease away. How do I know you're worthy of me?"

"What if I come back next weekend and we find out? It's not like I've seen much of anything here."

"I don't know. You might attack me again."

Leah slapped his arm. "Now who's teasing? Seriously, I'd like to have a date or three and see if we have more in common than ripping each other's clothes off on your sofa."

"Until Tess showed up at the sliding glass doors and rescued me, you mean."

"Shut up. You were pulling my clothes off just like I was pulling yours off."

"Your memory sucks, Leah. We were mostly just kissing."

"Yeah, but they were great kisses." She let go of his arm. "I really would like to see if we're compatible. Think about next weekend and give me a call."

Lisa strolled over. "My pervert sister told me how hot you are, Denver."

Denver faced Leah. "Oh really?" He faced Lisa again. "Exactly how is she a pervert?"

Leah shoved Lisa down the sidewalk. "See you later, Denver. Let me get this blabbermouth back to our hotel room before she ruins all of my surprises."

As they left, Denver laughed, which felt great after wondering where life might take him. Maybe he and Leah could be a match after all, which would leave Tess to pursue her young life like she should.

singing

Tess finished showering the sawdust from her hair. She had spent several hours sanding the rosewood back of the guitar she was working on, and the stuff tended to float everywhere. Hair blown dry, she dressed in jeans and a green blouse. As she sat on the bed to put sandals on, someone knocked on her door. "Tess, your papa said someone's singing at the restaurant tonight. He thought you might want to show off the first guitar you made and maybe generate a sale."

Tess opened the door to reveal Mama. "How does Papa know a guitar is involved instead of some other instrument?"

"Someone at the grocery store told him. The singer's local and plays guitar. A woman plays the electric bass and sings too. They use recorded drums as backup."

"Maybe I'll grab a bite and see who they are."

Mama left. Tess closed the door and took the cased guitar from beneath her bed. She had quit her job yesterday, intending to help Papa more with his furniture business. Her boss hated losing her, so she wouldn't mind her stopping by.

Tess opened the guitar case. Somewhat plain, with a spruce top, mahogany back and sides, and a rosewood fretboard instead of ebony, the guitar still sounded great because of the custom-carved bracing that supported the top and back. She checked the tuning, adjusted two strings, and strummed all six. The back vibrated against her stomach while the neck thrummed within the palm of her left hand. Definitely a sweet-sounding guitar.

She started to get the instruction book from her dresser but didn't. Not only had practicing for the past five months help keep her mind off of Denver, it had shown her she was a pretty decent player. She held a G chord and raked the flatpick across the strings, followed by several rising and falling scales and ending with an instrumental song she had written. Not bad, not bad at all. Satisfied, she cased the guitar, slung her purse over her shoulder, and stopped in the kitchen, where Mama, Papa, and Ivy were sitting down to supper. "See y'all later."

"Good luck," Papa said.

"Maybe you should play with those people," Mama said. "You play as well as anyone I've heard on the radio."

"Thanks, Mama, but I'm not all that great."

"I think you are," Ivy said. "You sing pretty too."

Tess's cheeks warmed. She didn't know anyone had heard her singing in Papa's shop when no one was around. "Thanks, Ivy, but if I sang around anyone eating, they might throw up."

On the way to Clarksville, Tess sang along with a soft rock station on the radio. Maybe Ivy knew something about singing after all, because Tess didn't have any problem with staying in key with the woman singer, even changing to tenor during the chorus.

She turned into the side street where the bed and breakfast was located. Cars filled the parking area beside the sidewalk. How did people play and sing in front of a crowd like this? If she had to do it, her nerves would shake her apart.

She parked in the spot about half a block down the street and walked back to the vine-covered outside eating area. Most of the tables were taken, with people either eating or waiting for food. At a wooden counter, she told the greeter she didn't have a reservation. The greeter said to take any table left, so Tess did.

In the far corner of the area, a guy with dark hair was facing away, leaning over to adjust his sound board. He turned around, said, "Check, check" in one of two mics, and went back to the sound system.

Tess rolled her fingertips on the table. The guy was Willow's old boyfriend, Mark. When did he start singing and playing the guitar? Well, if he was good enough to play here, he must be okay.

A woman, maybe in her twenties, came from the side-entrance to the bed and breakfast. Holding her stomach, she said something to Mark, who said something back. Still holding her stomach, she left to get in one of the parked cars and drive away. Mark stepped to one of the mics. "I'm sorry everyone, but my bass player isn't feeling well and had to leave."

Several people looked at each other, disappointment in their expressions. Tess stood. What better time to sell a guitar?

She worked her way through the tables to Mark's side. "What's up, Mark?"

Mark tilted his head to one side. "If I know you, I should be able to remember you from all that auburn hair."

"It's been a while. I'm—"

Mark's mouth fell open. "Noooo, you're Tess, right?"

"That's me. I see you lost your bass player."

"And singer. I hope you don't mind me saying so, but you sure grew up gorgeous."

"It's my hair. Willow said you liked her auburn hair too. Just don't call me Aubie like you did her. That's a dumb nickname."

Mark rubbed the dark stubble lining his jaw and chin. Tess noted his blue eyes and dark eyebrows, which gave him an intense look. He lowered his hand. "I better pack this stuff and get out of here."

Tess took a sheet of paper from a music stand. "Is this your set list?"

"Yeah, not that I'll get to play it."

"Soft rock, huh?"

Ignoring her, Mark turned off the sound system. Tess took his electric/acoustic guitar from its stand and took her own flatpick from her pocket.

As Mark started to turn off the guitar's amp, she cut loose on an G scale and ran it into an E minor scale. A few tables away, a couple clapped. Mark turned around. "No way, you play the guitar?"

"Just don't ask me to sing. If you can play the bass, I can help out. I know all the songs on your list."

Mark turned the sound system back on and slipped the bass guitar strap over his shoulder. At the mic, he winked at Tess and then faced the audience. "Good news, everyone. A friend's gonna help me out tonight. Please give a hand to Tess Gray."

Tess waved. "Hey." She leaned close to Mark. "Thanks for putting me on the spot."

He pointed to the first song, made famous by Linda Ronstadt in the seventies, *Blue Bayou.* "How about it?"

"That's sort of draggy, isn't it? I mean Linda's great, but this crowd needs to work up an appetite." Tess pointed to one of the last songs. "How about that?"

"You know *Hotel California?*"

"What key?"

"B-minor, like The Eagles played it. Let me bring up the drum track." Mark pushed a button on the sound system several times. "Press that foot pedal by the mic when you want it to start." Mark moved to his mic. "Go ahead, Tess. Let 'er rip."

Tess took a step forward, auburn hair flowing over her shoulders as she started the song. Lights hanging overhead shimmered on her green blouse. She finished the opening and hit the pedal, which started the drum track. Several people in the audience clapped, one man even yelling, "All right now! That's what *I'm* talkin' 'bout!"

Grinning hugely, Mark eased to the mic and sang while Tess kept the rhythm going. The bass thudded into her back from the speakers. The guitar resonated in her ears. When Mark started the chorus, the thrill of making music with something drew her to the mic, where she sang tenor harmony to his lead. Several people stood and clapped. Heads bobbed to the rhythm. Toes tapped the wooden floor decking. Hands patted tables.

Taking the lead break, Tess jerked the guitar neck upward. Her fingers danced along the frets. The pick blurred through the strings. So this was how it felt to be a musician instead of playing in her bedroom or in Papa's shop. Talk about *fun*.

They ended the song to a huge applause. Mark stepped close. "Despite being a minister's son, I gotta say it—holy crap, where did you learn to play and sing like that?"

"I thought I was okay, but not great. Was it really that good?"

"You smoked it, Tess, I mean you *really* smoked it. We better play *Blue Bayou* and let the crowd settle down so they can eat."

Tess played the intro into the song. Mark sang a verse, and several couples came to the floor to slow dance. As much as she enjoyed playing, she wished Denver was here so they could dance like they did in that restaurant in the mountains last year.

Mark finished the verse and moved closer. "Wanna sing the chorus? You've got a great voice."

Tess went to the mic and sang, but her voice almost broke on one line. When would Denver come back to her, if ever?"

The song ended. The dancing couples clapped and returned to their tables. Missing Denver, Tess didn't feel like playing but did. She couldn't let Mark down, and everyone seemed to really enjoy her playing and singing.

Several songs later, Mark placed the bass into a stand. "Let's take a break." They sat at a nearby table. "Want something to eat?" he asked.

The aroma of a steak caught Tess's attention. "I'll have a salad. I thought about crab dip, but all that bread might fill me up."

"We can share." Mark waved to a waiter, who came over and took their order. He then faced Tess. "How long have you been playing?"

"About a year. I've been practicing a lot the last few months."

"I would've guessed a lot longer than a year."

Tess stood. "I started building guitars last year. When I heard someone was singing here tonight, I came with the idea of a little shameless self-promotion. Wanna see one?"

"Sure. If your guitars sound as great as you do, I'm definitely interested."

Tess left for the guitar and came back. She uncased it on the table and gave it to Mark. "This is my first one. The finish is a little rough, but I mainly wanted to get the bracing right." She sat. "You were with Willow at my sister's wedding. Denver helped me build it. We had a few accidents starting out, but we finally got this one together."

Mark strummed the guitar. "Whoa, you did a great job." He held a G chord. "It frets nice too."

Tess enjoyed the compliments, both about her playing and singing and her building the guitar. "I like the guitar I was playing with you. I need to research the body style and the electronics and make one."

"It's pretty cool," Mark said, returning the guitar to the case. "You didn't try it, but the switch and one of the knobs lets you change tone from acoustic to electric, with variations between them. It's great for different styles of music."

The waiter returned with crab dip and two sweet teas. Tess set the guitar case by the mics and came back. She liked talking guitars with Mark, and he wasn't hard on the eyes at all.

Mark placed his hands together. "How about a short blessing? You know, since I'm a minister's son."

"Let me. I've got a lot to be thankful for." Tess bowed her head. "God, thank you so much for all your blessings, especially for the blessing of music. And please bless this food too, amen." Thinking how she wished Denver were here to share the meal, she tore a piece of the crusty bread from her half of the loaf, slathered crab dip on it, and enjoyed the delicious combination.

Mark did the same, washing it down with tea. "You might not have seen me at the funeral. Are Denver and Eliza doing okay?"

Tess clenched her teeth. The last thing she wanted to talk about was Eliza. "I guess you haven't heard. My stupid sister divorced Denver. That's why he's building guitars with me, to get his mind off of her."

"That doesn't make her stupid," Mark said, his voice low.

"It does in my book." Tess tore another piece of bread from the loaf. "Denver did everything he could to help her get over losing their daughter, and she just left him in the middle of the night. You don't do that to someone you love."

"That's pretty bad. Is he seeing anyone else yet? When I was dating Willow, I met Eliza when Willow invited me to supper. Denver seemed like the family type."

"He is. You know he lost his parents a few years ago. From everything he says, they were great."

"Then he wants kids. I guess Eliza was too hurt to think about that." Mark drank tea. "Is he seeing anyone?"

Tess swallowed crab dip. "Not that I know of."

"How about you, are you seeing anyone?"

Pausing for tea, Tess was tempted to ignore the question. Instead, she decided on a test. "Is that your way of asking me out?"

Mark pointed at her guitar. That depends on how much you charge me. Do I get a discount for how well I kiss?"

Tess snorted laughter. "Save your money. You'll need it for bail when you get arrested for dating a seventeen-year-old."

Mark's eyes widened. He sat back in his chair. "Durn, I thought you were at least twenty. You sure look twenty. Are you sure you're not twenty?" His eyes darted down and back up.

Tess shook her head. "Some minister's son you are."

"What do you mean?"

"A woman—especially a well-endowed woman—prefers a man who looks her in the eye."

Mark's cheeks reddened. "You got me. Talk about the sins of the flesh."

Tess noticed her boss speaking to diners. She came over. "I had no idea you could play and sing so well, Tess." She faced Mark. "You do realize she's a lot better than—"

"You're reading my mind," Mark interrupted. "Sheila's been talking about quitting anyway."

"Sounds like a good opportunity, Tess. I pay well for great music. See you later."

Tess faced Mark. "Exactly how well?"

"If you can be here two weekends from today, you'll find out."

She aimed a knife at him. "You do know I worked my butt off tonight."

"Half the night. Let's finish this food and get back on stage. If you finish the second set like you did the first, I'll make sure you get paid."

Behind Tess, a couple was talking about how great she sang and played. She enjoyed hearing it, but she had a question for Mark. "Look, I don't mind playing some but not all the time. I'm getting my guitar business going, and I help my papa with his furniture business. Are you okay with letting me know ahead of time?"

Mark tipped his glass toward her. "A good work ethic, I like that." He drank and set the glass down. "I play about twice a month, sometimes more depending on the money. Sheila and I are starting a website, and we're getting a lot of hits. If it keeps growing, I can make money from it too."

"But are you okay with me not playing every time?"

"It's only twice a month." Mark leaned over the table. "I was paying Sheila a third. What if I pay you half?"

"Half of what?"

"If you help me with the website, I guarantee you'll be impressed."

"Sheesh," Tess said. "Why can't you just tell me a number?"

With his fingertip, Mark wrote a three-digit number on the table. "How does that grab you?"

"That's hundreds?"

"And that's just for playing small gigs. I get more for that here."

The amount tempted Tess. She pictured fancier guitars, more intricate inlay, more exotics woods. She offered her hand. "I'll be here in two weeks."

Mark pumped her hand once and released it. "Very, very cool. Now I get to hang around with you until you turn eighteen so we can go out."

Tess sipped tea. She wouldn't date Mark or anybody else when she loved Denver, who needed to bring his behind home.

disappointment

On the front porch, Eliza put a stuffed toy horse on the railing and returned to her chair. Beside her, with a variety of water colors on a table between them, David squinted at her. "Can't we paint an elphant, Mama?"

"El-*uh*-phant. I know it's hard to say, try again."

"I can say horse. *Horse.* See?"

"Uh-huh. We can't paint an elephant because you don't have—"

"Wait a minute." David pattered inside and pattered back. He stuck two toothpicks into the horse's mouth. "He's an el-*uh*-phant now."

Eliza covered a smile. David had brought more joy to her life than she had ever thought possible. She placed a sheet of paper on his small easel and one on her large easel. "Dip your brush in water and touch the paint with it. What color do you want your horse to be?"

"Elphant, Mama. He's gonna be gray, like in my book." David wet his brush, dabbed it into the gray watercolor, and smeared it across the paper.

Eliza did the same thing, enjoying the fresh morning air before the heat of the day set in. With that sensation, a vision of her and Denver paddling the canoe on the lake crept into her mind. They loved going out early, when pairs of ospreys and bald eagles would circle the sky in their search for fish. Then they would paddle home, have breakfast, and more often than not, one of them would slip up behind the other to nuzzle a neck or kiss a cheek, which would have them making love minutes later. Their passion sometimes kept them wherever they were, be it the kitchen, the living room, or in the bedroom. It made no sense for her to remember such times with melancholy when the physical act, like when she had tried to kiss Denver that last time, had made her run to the bathroom and vomit.

"Mama, you're not painting."

Eliza shook her head. She had been holding the brush to the paper, leaving a gray smudge and nothing more. "I guess I was daydreaming."

"'Bout what?"

David's question gave Eliza pause. The logical result to her and Denver making love, not only for pleasure and to express their love, was to have a family. Her epiphany caused a sudden ache for motherhood deep within her heart, of dreams left to smolder, of that single hope fading with each day she was away from Denver.

"Mama?"

"What, David?"

"I see boys and girls in town. Some of them have a brother or a sister. When can I have a brother or a sister?"

"You know your mama is sick, right?"

"I know."

"Mamas can't have children when they're sick."

"I saw a cow have a calf one time. She *sounded* sick."

"This is different." Eliza put the paint brush down and smoothed David's hair from his forehead. "We have to be

34

patient. If you're meant to have a brother or sister, God will see to it."

David stopped painting. "Papa said he hates God."

"Your papa's upset because your mama is hurt."

"I don't hate God. He brought you here when I needed a mama."

"He brought me here when I needed a special little boy like you too."

Dabbing his brush in paint again, David stopped to look her way. "I'm not *really* your little boy."

"No, not really."

"Do you ever want a little boy or little girl? If you do, they could be my brother or sister."

Eliza couldn't mention the obvious: that for her to have a child meant she had to have a husband, and she had left hers.

As she started painting again, Josh drove up in his pickup and parked. Walking to the porch, he lowered his head as if something were bothering him. With Anna's recent turn for the better, he should be happy. She put the paint brush down and stood as he climbed the steps. "Is something wrong, Josh?"

He went inside. She followed him to the kitchen, where he dropped to a seat at the table. "I can't believe people can be so cruel."

Eliza sat too. "What do you mean?"

"A nurse didn't hear Anna mumbling. A person bathing her said she heard her."

"What do you mean she *said* she heard her? Did she hear her or not?"

"Anna's doctor ran some tests, and there's no change. He asked the person about it. At first she said she heard Anna. Then, when the doctor pressed her about it, she admitted to feeling sorry for me and making it up."

Eliza wanted to tell Josh the woman wasn't cruel, just overly thoughtful. Still, to give false hope *was* cruel. "Did they fire her?"

"They moved her to an area where no patients are in a coma. I see you and David are painting. That's a bright spot in my day."

"Do you want breakfast since you left early to check on Anna?" Eliza went to the stove to put a pan on a burner. When she turned, Josh was taking a drink from a brown bottle. He took another bottle from his pocket, took two pills from it, and washed them down with more alcohol. Eliza turned away, not wanting him to know she had seen him. "Would you like eggs and bacon?"

"I'm going to bed. I can't seem to get more than a few hours of sleep for a while now."

Eliza put the pan away. Maybe those pills were sleeping pills, but he shouldn't take them with alcohol. "Wouldn't you like to sit out on the porch with David while he paints? The fresh air might help you go to sleep."

"I suppose." Josh followed her to the porch and took a seat beside David. "Hello, Son. What are you painting?"

"Hey, Papa. Mama says it's a horse but I say it's an elphant." He pointed. "See his long teeth? That's poofticks—" David giggled. "I mean toothpicks. I stuck them in his mouth."

Smiling softly, Josh rubbed David's back. "Aren't you smart?"

"He is," Eliza said, returning to her chair. "I've never been around a three-year-old who could speak so well and who knows their colors like David."

"That's 'cause you teach me, Mama."

"You two sure get along well," Josh said. He leaned back in the chair and closed his eyes. Within no time, he was softly snoring.

David touched a finger to his lips. "Shhhh, Mama. Papa's sleep."

"I see that," Eliza whispered. As the horse took shape beneath her paint brush, she considered Josh and Anna, including how he likely still believed Anna would come home one day.

She dropped the paint brush and picked it up. Did Denver still believe in their love, in her, and in her coming home one day? Ethan had told her how Tess had called not long after Eliza had left, and how Denver was seeing some woman. Yes, he might do that to get over losing his wife. If so, where would that relationship go?

Eliza dabbed the brush in brown watercolor and returned to the horse. Simply thinking about Denver sleeping with another woman didn't bother her, while imagining him making love to another woman did.

And what about Ethan saying Tess had a crush on Denver? Young girls had crushes all the time, but could she have feelings for him—*serious* feelings? Then again, Tess would be eighteen soon, the age Eliza was when she had met Denver, and Eliza knew all too well how she had been drawn to her future husband, including how she had thought of him making love to her before it had ever happened.

She glanced at David, whose eyes were narrowed in concentration as he painted. Her old life was gone now. She would live day by day, loving this wonderful little boy for as long as she could.

As far as Denver, he could date whoever he wanted, and if that person were Tess, maybe she could make him happier than some other woman. After all, she had told Eliza how seeing her and Denver together had made her see what real love was, so maybe she could have that with Denver.

Eliza bit her lower lip.

Like imagining Denver making love to another woman bothered her, imagining him making love to Tess was worse—a betrayal even.

David rinsed his brush in water, then dabbed it in white watercolor to paint his elephant's tusks.

Eliza put her brush down.

Betrayal.

No doubt, Denver thought she had betrayed him when he got the divorce papers. Since that was the case, who was she to let the thought of him making love to anyone—even Tess—bother her?

But it did.

D.C. date

About half a block away from Akina's apartment, Denver opened Leah's car door. "Thanks for parking down here."

Wearing jeans, a pink blouse, and tan flats, she got out. "I'd prefer we keep our date private too. After what you told me, about how Akina knows Tess, I wouldn't put it past her to tattle on us." She gave Denver a quick hug. Seeing as how he hadn't held a woman since the morning he had left Tess, Leah felt great in his arms. Better get that under control. Take it slow. See if they were compatible. Go from there.

Leah ran her fingers through his hair. "I like your hair a little long like this, just starting to curl over your ears." Her eyes, brown with golden flecks near the centers, met his. Brunette curls, hint of freckles across her nose, full lips that kissed so great that time on the sofa.

Denver pulled away. "Whoa, I think we better see some sites before we end up in the back seat of your car."

"Or in my hotel room." Leah palmed his cheek. "I'm sorry. We already said sex isn't the best way to start a relationship. Where do you want to go?"

"I haven't thought about it. You?"

"Let's walk to the Washington Monument. I don't feel like being cooped up inside a stuffy museum on a gorgeous day like today."

"Great. We can get there in about twenty minutes."

As they strolled the sidewalk, Denver noted how Leah liked the outdoors, a plus in her favor. The last type of person he needed to date was one like Jan, who considered dirt an alien life form with a virus ready to attack.

Cars and busses passed on the busy street, leaving hints of bitter exhaust. Other people—families, couples, and singles—remarked about sites they planned to see or simply kept quiet. One family, consisting of a couple and their four kids, were arguing about something to eat.

Leah made a face. "Ugh, why can't parents keep their kids under control?"

"Kids that age get tired of walking," Denver said. "They look to run from about five to ten."

"Who wants that many kids so close together?"

"I'd like a couple one day." Denver stopped at a crosswalk and waited for a car. "You?"

"One's enough for me, and no time soon."

The car passed. They crossed to the other side of the street.

Although Denver and Eliza had talked about having two kids, they had considered three. Still, one would be fine too.

A block further, Leah stopped at a restaurant with outdoor seating. "Can we get something? I didn't have breakfast."

"Sure, I can eat."

They took a seat. A waitress brought them menus and asked what they'd like to drink. Denver ordered sweet tea with lemon. Leah ordered a Bloody Mary, saying she needed something to wake her up. The waitress left, and Denver faced Leah. "It's a little early for alcohol, isn't it?"

"I plan to make you drink half and take you back to my hotel room. Are you willing?"

"Well …"

Leah shoved his arm. "Look at you, thinking I'm serious. I just like a Bloody Mary once in a while. Is anything wrong with that?"

"Not at all," Denver said. "You know I like a glass of wine from when we went out in Clarksville."

The waitress brought their drinks. Denver ordered a BLT and a side salad. Leah ordered spaghetti and meatballs, a salad, and garlic bread. "Oh, wow, I love spaghetti. Do you?"

"Sure. Do you like pizza?"

"Just plain cheese."

"Really? I like them loaded with everything, even anchovies."

Leah stuck out her tongue. "Fish on a pizza? Gross."

Denver looked away. A plain cheese pizza? Strike one for compatibility. Well, he could always order his own pizza if they went out for it sometime. He sipped tea. "Do you like fish at all? Fresh striper or crappie fillets from the lake are great."

"It's okay. How do you cook them?"

"I like it fried, but broiled or grilled is healthier."

"Not healthier for me," Leah said. "If anyone makes me eat fish, I want it fried so I don't have to taste it."

Denver drank more tea. Strike two. He tried to eat healthy instead of gorging on oily foods.

Leah sipped her drink. "The last time I was at your place, when Jan, whoever she is, interrupted us, you never told me who she is. Did you really jilt her for your wife?"

"I remember you saying you asked around about me. You know how Eliza and I lost our daughter. Do you know anything about her art?"

"That's right. When my sister and I were here last weekend, you asked if any of your wife's paintings were in the museum we went to. Is she that good?"

Denver didn't care to get into everything, but if he and Leah were going to see each other, she might as well know the entire story of how he met Eliza when he taught her sign language in Ohio, her background as a deaf Amish artist—self-taught at that—and how Jan was her agent for her art shows.

When he finished telling Leah, she leaned back in her chair. "Wow, talk about baggage. Since Jan stopped by on the night we were about to fool around, I assume she doesn't have any hard feelings about you leaving her for Eliza."

The waitress brought their food, giving Denver time to sort out an answer. "When Eliza and I met, it was instant chemistry. The sign language teacher I was working with at the time knew it right away. Then, when we went to pick up Eliza's paintings for her first art show, Tess saw it too, in how we were looking at each other."

Leah crossed her arms. "Denver."

"What?"

"Are you sure we should be seeing each other?"

"Why?"

"If you and your ex were that good together, you should try to work it out."

"She made her choice. Besides, I signed the divorce papers in March."

"Is she living in Clarksville? I'd hate to see her when we're together."

Denver clenched his teeth. Here it was, another thing he didn't care to talk about. He needed to clear the air and be done with it. "She's living with a man and his son in Ohio. She doesn't call her family or me, so there's no chance we'll get back together, much less see each other."

Leah touched his hand. "You still love her, don't you? I can see it in your eyes and hear it in your sad voice."

"I—" To keep from answering, Denver drank more tea.

Leah took a bite of spaghetti. "Your silence says it all, Denver." She stood. "Maybe I should go. I can't compete with a woman you're still in love with."

Denver lowered the glass. "Please, Leah, don't go. Whatever Eliza and I had is gone. That's why I'm seeing you, to move on with my life."

"If you're sure." Leah sat. "I just don't want to start having feelings for you and get hurt."

"I don't want to get hurt either. I've had enough of that to last a lifetime. That's why I want to take it slow. Believe me, if I ever tell another woman I love her, it'll be the real thing."

Leah returned to her meal, and so did Denver. He ate mechanically, hardly tasting it for thinking about another woman he had sometimes felt like telling he loved—Tess. Although Eliza had been his best friend before she left, Tess was his best friend now, including a great lover: playful, sensual, and fun to the point of making him forget Eliza, which was a huge accomplishment. The one night they had spent together was pure magic, and it would take a long time to purge it from his mind, regardless of Leah or any other woman he might date.

Sandwich and salad half-eaten, he sipped tea while Leah twirled spaghetti on a fork. After swallowing it, she wiped sauce from her lips with a napkin. "Tell me about you and Tess. Why were you two in the clothing store at the same time when we met last year."

"Her family was out of town and she locked herself out of the house. Being a relative, I let her stay with me."

"Was this before or after your wife left you?"

"After."

"You know Tess has a thing for you, right?"

"Well, you had a crush on me in high school."

"A crush is one thing. Showing up at your house when we wanted to be alone is something else. Personally, I think she intends to replace her sister. Aren't you attracted to her?"

"Jealous?" Denver asked, trying to deflect the truth, which was how he was *extremely* attracted to Tess.

Leah stuck her tongue out. "Jealous my foot. I'm with you and she's not. And don't think you're gonna get out of answering my question of if you're attracted to her or not."

"Oh sure, I'm attracted to her. I slept with her the night before I drove up here for my job. Then, as soon as I got in the door to Akina's apartment, I slept with her too. I'm just a dog when it comes to women."

"Oh, stop it," Leah said, rolling her eyes. "If you were a dog with women, we would be in my hotel room right now." She finished the Bloody Mary and stood. "Pay the waitress and let's get out of here. I need to walk that spaghetti off."

Denver did so, noting how Leah didn't offer to pay for her own her food. He didn't mind paying, but offering would've been nice.

Ten minutes later, at the base of the Washington Monument, Leah looked up at the top. "Do we really have to climb up there?"

"Put it this way," Denver said, "it's good exercise for if we ever sleep together."

Leah's arched eyebrows raised. "I like the sound of that. Are you rowdy in bed? Do you get all loud and sweaty? Do you just go until you can't go anymore?"

"Is this the pervert in you that your sister warned me about?"

"I like sex, sue me." Leah took his hand. "Let's walk and talk about it."

Denver let her lead him along. If she liked sex that much, he wanted to know just how promiscuous she might be. Sure, he liked sex too, but he had only slept with Akina, Eliza, and Tess, and he didn't have to worry about any sexually transmitted diseases with them—*or* pregnancy.

Leah stopped in the shade of several trees and sat at the base of one. "Have a seat and tell me about your sex life."

Denver sat. "It's pretty boring. I've been with a total of three women and that's it."

Leah plucked a piece of grass. "I slept with a woman once," she said, not looking at Denver. "I didn't like it much."

Denver's mouth threatened to fall open. "I never expected that, not after you said you had a crush on me in high school."

"People experiment, Denver. I tried a threesome one time too. Now *that* was fun."

"Really?" Denver was tempted to leave. "What about diseases and stuff? When you have sex with one person, it's like having sex with everyone that person has had sex with, and so on and so on. That's risky and you know it."

Leah's cheeks reddened. "Why not call me a slut and be done with it?"

"Am I telling the truth or not?"

"These were people in college. I knew them well enough to not take any chances."

Denver picked a stick up from beside him. "I'm not into that stuff. If I'm with someone, that person's got to be with me and me only. If I thought she wanted to do that kind of thing, I couldn't be with her."

"Did I say I was doing that stuff now?"

"No, but you said you liked it."

"That was years ago and only for fun. I understand what it takes to be in a committed relationship now." Leah lowered her head. "I'd be willing to get tested for STDs if we decided to sleep together."

The idea lessened Denver's anxiety about Leah's past. At least she was taking it seriously now. "I'm glad you said that. When the time comes, I'll do the same for you."

Leah lay down in the grass. The sun filtered through the leaves and dappled her face with light. She reached for Denver. "Lie down here with me. I really like being with you."

Denver did so. Leah snuggled into his shoulder. "I like how you think about stuff. A lot of people don't do that. I didn't for a long time, but I guess I had to grow up." She propped herself up on her elbow. "Can I kiss you? I've been wanting to all day."

Denver slipped his fingers into her curls and pulled her to him for a kiss. Regardless of the softness of her lips, all he could think about was kissing Tess on their last night together, when they had made love. No matter how much he tried to get her out of his head, even by dating Leah, all he wanted was to go home and see where they stood.

He kissed Leah's neck below her ear, ran his tongue to where her neck curved to her shoulder.

No. Tess had her whole life ahead of her. Yes, he cared for her—sometimes called it love—but she deserved better than him, better than tying herself down to him, better than the simple life he wanted, of a wife and kids and loving each other until the whole world almost disappeared.

He sat up. "Sorry about that. I got carried away."

Leah sat up too. "I'll say. Were you ...?"

"What?"

"It doesn't matter. Lie down and let me snuggle you and nothing else."

Denver did so again. Leah had his number but not quite. She probably thought he was thinking about Tess just now, when he really was thinking about Eliza.

hope

Sitting with David at the end of the garden, where Anna's wildflowers formed a waving blanket of blue, red, and yellow in the breeze, Eliza adjusted the wide-brimmed hat she had bought for painting in the sun. Beside her, in one of the folding lawn chairs she had also bought, David pointed. "Look, Mama, a yellow butterfly."

"That's why we're out here," Eliza said. "If we're quiet, it might land so we can paint it."

David raised his head. His narrowed eyes peeked from beneath the brim of his own hat. "But I like it yellow."

Eliza waited until the urge to laugh had passed. "I meant paint it on the paper, not paint it a different color."

True to her wish, the butterfly fluttered to a blue cornflower and settled to sip nectar, working its wings back and forth as if they were the pages of a book opening and closing, opening and closing.

David dabbed his brush in blue watercolor. "Do the flower first, right?"

"That's right. Then paint the butterfly like it's flying near the flower so the yellow and blue don't mix."

Instead of painting, Eliza watched David. Each night she knelt by her bed to thank the Creator for bringing him into her life, filling with her new bits of happiness each day.

She dabbed her brush in blue paint and started painting the cornflower.

But Josh was another case altogether. He rarely showered, sometimes going more than a week. When he left the Amish, he shaved his beard. Now it grew again, gray mixed into the bristly growth. His breath offended terribly as well. She had bought everyone new toothbrushes, leaving them in the bathroom as a reminder, but he hadn't used his.

And that wasn't all.

She had found three empty bottles of alcohol in the trash and one bottle of sleeping pills, all from this week. Although both types of bottles were small, especially the sleeping pill bottle, she needed to tell him he could harm himself if he continued taking them so often.

The butterfly fluttered away, circled the flowers, and came back to the original one again.

How was Denver doing with her gone now for a year? In the months before she had left, he hadn't taken take care himself much better than Josh.

The memory of Denver on the dock, passed out from drinking beer, burst into Eliza's mind. He must've been hurting like Josh was hurting, from losing his wife he loved so much. If that were so he should've told her. Yes, he may have thought physical love could show emotional love, but she needed support and understanding after losing their daughter, not his suggestions of sleeping together.

Eliza continued with the flower, using another brush to add a hint of green on the inner petals, which weren't fully opened.

David took a clean brush from a jar on the table between them and wet it with water, dabbed it in yellow and touched it to the paper, just above the flower. "Mama?"

"What, sweetheart?"

"Papa's sad all the time. He doesn't read to me anymore. He smells bad too."

"He's hurting from your mama being sick. When people hurt like that, they can forget to take care of themselves."

David lowered his brush and faced Eliza. "If he's hurting, should he go to Heaven like Meemaw? Then he won't hurt no more."

"He loves you and your mama. It would hurt him more to leave."

"But mama could go too. Then they could be happy and not hurt anymore."

The idea surprised Eliza. "Wouldn't you miss them?"

"I …"

"What, sweetheart?"

"I think I would be happy after a while."

"Why's that?"

"'Cause they would want me to." David raised the brush again, dabbed paint, and lowered it. "If I went to Heaven, I would tell God to help Papa be happy 'cause I'm happy."

Eliza said nothing. David was too young to understand how much it hurt to lose a child. She would never get over it, never be happy like before, never feel whole again instead of feeling as if her soul had been ripped from her body, leaving her an empty shell except for her time with this sweet little boy.

As she started to paint again, Josh parked in the driveway, returned from seeing Anna. Eliza waited for him to open the truck door, to shuffle toward her and David. Instead, Josh flung the door open and ran toward them, where he kneeled beside

David. "Son," he said, his voice breaking, "your Mama's waking up. Thank God. Thank God."

Eliza stood. Josh had already experienced the false hope of Anna mumbling. If this were another one, he shouldn't tell David. "Josh, are you sure? Maybe we should wait and see what's—"

He grabbed her shoulders. "It's a miracle, Eliza. God is working a miracle."

"But—"

"No buts. Anna is waking from the coma."

David slid from the chair and hugged Josh's thin waste. "See, Papa? I told you not to hate God."

Josh picked him up and spun him around. "I should've listened, Son." He put David down and faced Eliza. "I know you think I should be more cautious, but it's real this time. She opened her eyes and I called the nurse. She called a doctor. By the time he got there, Anna had closed her eyes again. The doctor pinched her arm, and she opened her eyes again. She closed them right away, but he said her opening them is a good sign. If she starts waking for longer, and by someone shaking her shoulders or calling her name, it means she's coming out of the coma."

"That *is* a good sign. Do they know if she'll fully recover?"

"Not yet. They'll have to run tests after she wakes and can communicate. It's a good thing we learned signs, isn't it?"

Eliza sat again. "I'm so happy for you." She was tempted ask about the recovery time and how it would affect how long she might stay here.

"I see what you're thinking," Josh said. "The doctor said Anna will need rehabilitation before she can come home. Don't worry about going anywhere. If you're willing to stay, we'll need your help for a while yet."

David went to Eliza. "You gots to stay, Mama, okay?"

"Don't worry," she said. "It sounds like I'll be here a long time yet." She picked up her brush. "Finish your picture so you can show your mama. She'll love a visit when she's able."

"I'm going to take a nap," Josh said. "Maybe I can sleep now."

The grass rustled beneath his feet as he walked away. David faced Eliza. "I don't know, Mama."

"What don't you know?"

"In my dreams, Mama says she wants to go to Heaven."

"Dreams don't always mean what we think they mean."

"But she said it."

"Let's paint anyway. Maybe your butterfly will make her want to stay with you and your papa."

Brushes dipped and dabbed paint. The butterfly circled away and came back. A bumblebee hummed within another bloom. Warm and sultry, a breeze blew over a pasture from across the road, bringing the sour aroma of cow manure.

Eliza didn't know whether to believe Josh or not. Yes, the doctor seemed sure, but David wasn't sure at all. As Eliza knew, hope was a fleeting thing—something that could either fill a heart with joy or leave it as dry and empty as a field of corn in the fall, husks withered and clattering in the wind. Regardless of all that, if Anna came home one day, it might be time to make plans for a future that didn't include living in Ohio.

Eliza stood. "David, I need to go in for a few minutes."

He stopped painting. "Okay, Mama."

Inside, Eliza found Josh in the kitchen, slicing a tomato at the counter. He faced her. "I thought I'd have a tomato sandwich. It feels good to have an appetite."

Eliza sat at the table. As much as she hated to consider leaving David, she needed to word her request in such a way as to not make Josh suspicious, or he might think she would leave before Anna was back to normal. And too, she wanted to eventually reconnect with her family, to explain how Ethan was wrong about her living here. No doubt they would be upset about her leaving Denver, but she wanted to move back to Clarksville one day. Even if she never married again, which she had no intention of doing, she loved the area and the lake. Since that was the case, she would enjoy a house on the lake, and since she was painting again, she could earn the money to buy or build a nice home, snug and cozy instead of large and rambling like Denver's house.

Josh returned the mayonnaise to the refrigerator and sat across from Eliza. "Josh, I was thinking about driving home and getting some of my painting supplies. Can you stay with David a few days so I can do that?"

"Aren't they still in your husband's house? You haven't seen him in a year."

Eliza hadn't told Josh about filing for divorce. She didn't want him to think she was available, back before it seemed as if Anna was going to either die or stay in a coma. "I'm sure he'll let me get whatever I need."

"When do you want to go?"

"There's no hurry. Maybe in a month or so."

Josh took a napkin from the holder and wiped his mouth. "That'll be fine."

Eliza stood. "Let me get back to David. He sure loves painting."

Eliza sat beside David again. How would her family treat her when she went back? More importantly, how would Denver react? Ethan said Tess had a crush on Denver. She was almost eighteen. If Denver were attracted to her, and if Mama and Papa allowed it, would he date Tess? Eliza shook her head. They wouldn't dare do such a thing. Denver was probably dating whatever woman Tess had said he was.

Still, the idea that Tess wanted Denver nagged Eliza. Thinking about it was one thing, while seeing it was another. For some strange reason, imagining him in the arms of another woman didn't bother her, but imagining him and Tess together—hugging, kissing, even making love—made Eliza want to scream.

She picked up her brush. When she went back, she would find out exactly what Denver was up to, and it better not be with Tess.

visit

In his bedroom, Denver closed his suitcase, glad his boss had let him leave early today. He wanted to get home and surprise Tess and see how things were between them. More and more he missed her, even to the point of disregarding his own belief that she was too young to marry or tie herself down with kids.

First things first: call the bed and breakfast for two prime rib take-out meals for him and Tess, ask her over to talk, and see how it went from there. Since he was leaving on a Saturday afternoon, the traffic should be lighter, allowing him to time everything for about eight tonight. He would stop around seven to call the order in, pick it up at seven-thirty, and call Tess and head home.

It took forty minutes to clear the D.C. traffic. Whistling as he drove, Denver turned the radio on to find a soft-rock station. Yep, have a great meal with Tess, talk about her turning eighteen, ask what she'd like to do on their dates, tell Absalom and Oneita, hope they were okay with it, and see how things went after that.

Fredericksburg, Virginia passed an hour later, followed by Richmond in an hour and ten minutes. Next came Petersburg, where he lost thirty minutes due to a long-haul truck accident, which backed traffic up for a mile.

In Emporia, he stopped for a bathroom break, a soft drink, and to fill up with gas. Back in the pickup, he almost dropped the drink.

Emporia? He had taken I-95 in Richmond instead of I-85, putting him forty-five more minutes behind schedule. Leaving the gas station, he hit highway 58 West. How could he be so stupid?

In South Hill, he pulled over to call in for the take-out order. Lucky him, the restaurant had some prime rib left.

When the lights of Clarksville sparkled on the lake as Denver crossed the business bridge, he glanced at the dashboard clock. Nine o'clock sharp. Late but not too late.

At the restaurant, he had to park in the overflow. The restaurant must have live music tonight, although he heard none as he jogged to the front porch. He paid for his meal and walked across the front porch—to stop in his tracks.

Over by the stage, Tess sat at a table with a dark-haired guy, his back facing Denver. Was she dating someone?

Smiling, she raised her hand and ran her fingers through the guy's hair.

Denver clenched his jaw hard enough to bite through a fishhook. Huh, all this time she had acted like she cared about him, saying they could date when she turned eighteen, even making love to him on the night he last saw her. What a betrayal, one he had never expected.

In his pickup, he called Leah. "Hey, this is a surprise," she said. "Did you miss me after our date last weekend?"

"I just picked up two prime rib meals from the bed and breakfast. How would you like to go catfishing on the pontoon boat tonight?"

"It's kind of late, isn't it?"

"Catfish bite better at night, how about it?"

"What about mosquitos and bugs?"

"I've got spray. C'mon, it'll be great."

"Can we snuggle? You know how I like that?"

"I'll throw a blanket in the boat and we can snuggle all you want. Can you be at my place in thirty minutes? I've got to pick up some bait."

Leah said she would. Denver ended the call and drove to the grocery, where he bought a refrigerated container of earthworms, a chilled bottle of red wine, and some plastic cups and utensils to eat with.

At home, he bypassed the house and its darkened windows and eased down the gravel path to the dock by starlight. He should've plugged in the LED lights. Maybe when he got back.

In the road by the house, gravel crunched. Leah rounded the corner. "I can't see to walk."

Denver took a flashlight from a compartment on the boat, shined it on the path, and Leah came to the dock. He turned the light off and kissed her, which she returned. "Mmm-mm," she said. "Maybe we should— No, we said we'd take it slow, so none of that." She climbed into the boat.

Denver took the ropes from the cleats, cranked the motor, and headed out onto the lake.

* * *

Tess took her hand from Mark's hair. "Ugh,"" she said, grimacing, "what a spiderweb. I guess it was in those vines over the stage area."

Mark stood. "We better end this break. A few people are leaving. They must not know we're gonna play another set."

Tess stood too. "Be right back. Gotta run to the ladies room."

At the mirror, Tess checked her hair for spider webs and found none. As the door closed behind her, her phone vibrated in her jeans pocket. "Hi, Papa, what's up?"

"Did you know Denver was in town?"

"He didn't say anything about it, why?"

"I went to the grocery for some ice cream and saw him leave the parking lot."

"That's strange. I thought he would let us know he was coming."

"Me too. We haven't seen him in six months. How's the music going?"

"It's great. You should bring Mama and Ivy sometime."

"I will. Are you going by Denver's on the way home?"

"I think so. I'd like to see why he hasn't called."

Tess slipped the phone back in her pocket. After not seeing her for six months, Denver had come home without calling? That wasn't like him at all.

She joined Mark, who started a drum track for the next song. Although she played, she didn't feel like it. All she wanted was to see Denver and find out why he hadn't told anyone he was coming home.

Especially her.

* * *

Done with helping Mark load his sound equipment in his van, Tess drove home. The LED dash clock read 11:45, pretty late to see Denver. She turned in at his road. But not too late to find out why he hadn't called people he supposedly loved to let them know he was home.

At his driveway, instead of pulling in she hit the brakes. Beside his pickup sat Leah's car. Not only that, all the lights were off in the house, meaning he and Leah were—

Tess killed the engine and got out, started to key the paint down the driver's side of Leah's car but didn't. Miss Brunette Bimbo might do something like that, but she wouldn't.

In the car again, she drove home. What she *would* do is grab Denver by the collar in the morning after Leah was gone and find out what the heck was going on.

At home in bed, Tess rolled over and over. What a jerk he was. He had all but promised they would date after she turned eighteen, and that's all she had waited for since December.

Then again, late at night, or while building her latest guitar, she had considered how he and Eliza belonged together. Regardless, one way or another, Leah sure wasn't going to get him.

* * *

Denver checked the time on his watch. 2:15 and he and Leah hadn't caught anything. Good thing. If they had, he would be tempted to put it in the back seat of Tess's car and let it stink it up.

Leah left the seat across from him and sat beside him at the console. "I know I wanted to snuggle, but I need a bathroom. If you haven't noticed, I'm not a guy who can take a whiz off a boat into the lake."

Denver took a five-gallon bucket from behind the seat and gave her a roll of toilet paper from a compartment beneath his seat. "Have at it."

Leah took the toilet paper. "This is moldy. Besides, I need to do more than pee."

Denver took the toilet paper from her and dropped it in the bucket." Can't you hold it? I want to catch at least one catfish."

"No, I *can't* hold it," Leah said, crossing her arms. "It's also not romantic to do that where you can see me."

Denver got up to reel the two lines in and pull anchor. He returned to the seat and cranked the motor. When it came to the outdoors, Leah wasn't much different than Jan.

As soon as he tied the boat to the dock, Leah hopped out. "Will you come on before I go right here?"

He gave her the key. "Go ahead. That opens the sliding glass doors at the deck."

"I can't see. Where's that flashlight you had when I got here?"

Denver took the flashlight from the compartment and gave it to her. Although the beam lit the gravel path that crunched beneath her shoes, she could hardly walk for holding her legs together.

Denver followed. What a disaster of a night. Not only had the fish ignored the worms, he had seen Tess with another guy, something he had never thought was possible after they had talked about dating when she turned eighteen.

In the house, after visiting the other bathroom, he went to the kitchen to wait for Leah. He could barely hear the toilet flushing several times. She came out and dropped the key on the counter. "There, Mr. Pee off the durn boat guy. Did any of that sound like I didn't need a bathroom?"

Denver put the keys in his pocket. "Sorry about that. I'm sorry we didn't catch any fish either."

"Well, that prime rib made it all worthwhile." Leah yawned. "I'd offer to stay, but like we've been saying, we need to take it slow." She sniffed her fingers. "And no amount of washing my hands will get earthworm smell off of them." She yawned again. "How long are you staying in Clarksville? We could do something else before you leave."

Denver didn't know how to answer. "I'm not sure."

Leah kissed his cheek. "Okay. Give me a call and let me know when you want to do something."

The front door closed behind her. Denver went to the refrigerator but found it empty. Tess must've cleaned it out. He snapped his fingers. He and Leah had only drunk a cup each of the wine he had bought at the grocery. Might as well empty that so he could get some sleep instead of thinking about how Tess had kicked him to the curb for another guy.

* * *

Blurry eyed from not enough sleep, Tess rolled over. The barest hint of sunlight shone through her curtains. Good, great, fantastic. She could go see Denver and get to the bottom of this thing with Leah before Mama, Papa, and Ivy woke.

On the way to her car, she detoured for Papa's shop for the guitar she had finished two days ago. If Mr. Andrews acted like an idiot, he might see what it felt like to get whacked in the head with a custom-made six-string—or better yet, Leah would find out.

At Denver's house, Leah's car was gone. Good, great, fantastic again. No interruptions for the knock-down drag-out fight about to happen.

Tess got out with the guitar case and banged on the door until Denver opened it. "What the heck do you want?" he asked, rubbing his eyes.

She shoved by him and continued to the living room. "Why didn't you let me know you were coming home?"

In his boxers, Denver shuffled to the sofa and yawned. "Let me wake up. We need to talk."

Tess went to his bedroom for his robe and brought it back. "Put that on. I don't ever want to see you almost naked again."

"You ain't kiddin'." Denver lay the robe across his lap. "I thought you cared about me. The first thing I see when I get back is you running your fingers through some guy's hair."

Tess put the guitar case down. "What are you talking about?"

"I came without calling to surprise you. I got two prime-rib take-outs at the restaurant and saw you with that guy. Pissed me the hell off."

"Don't curse, dammit. You tell me not to often enough."

"You make me mad enough to curse."

Tess sat in the chair. Time to lay it on his sorry behind. "You didn't see what you think you saw, so forget it. What I want to know is how you could sleep with Leah when I thought you cared about me. Talk about being pissed off."

"What are you talking about?"

"Papa called me at the restaurant. He said he saw your car at the grocery store. I came here from the restaurant and saw Leah's car. All the lights were off, so I knew what that meant." Tess crossed her arms. "You make me sick, doing what you did with her in the same bed where we made love."

Denver's cheeks flared red. "We went fishing and that's all. You made me so mad, I called and asked her to come."

"Look at those red cheeks," Tess said, pointing. "You're lying and you know it."

"Forget that, who's your new guy? Is he the one you slept with when you were fifteen?"

Tess took a magazine from the coffee table and threw it at Denver. "You jerk. That was Willow's old boyfriend Mark. I'm playing guitar and singing with him."

Denver threw the magazine across the room. "If that *was* Mark—and I don't believe it for a minute—the only singing you did was in the back seat of his car."

Tess got up, opened the sliding glass doors, and opened the guitar case in the floor beside them. She took the guitar out and showed it to Denver. "People went on and on about how my stupid sister learned sign language in a few months. She isn't the only one who can learn something really well in a short time. This is my last guitar." She pointed. "See the D inlayed in the headstock? See the vines inlayed into the ebony fingerboard? See the Adirondack Spruce top and the rosewood back and sides? See the finish I finally got perfected?"

Denver rolled his eyes. "What about it?"

Holding the neck of the guitar as if were a baseball bat, Tess went to the deck and raised the guitar over her head by the trunk of a huge oak growing beside it. "I'll tell you what about it. I love—no, *loved* you so much, I made this guitar as a present for you, but you can forget it." She slammed the guitar into the tree over and over, splintering the body and twanging the strings until nothing but broken wood hung from her hand. "That's what about it." She went inside and dropped the guitar's remains in the floor. "Take that and shove it. I hope you and Leah are happy, dammit."

wedding

As Tess left the driveway, gravel clattering beneath the car from its spinning tires, Denver got up to look at what was left of the guitar, which was pretty much just the headstock with the D inlaid into it. Could she really have made this for him? If so, and if she really had been playing and singing with Mark, a phone call would clear things up.

In his bedroom, Denver took his phone from the nightstand and called Mark, who answered after a few rings. "Hey, Denver. I haven't talked to you in a while."

"Right. Look, are you and Tess playing music together?"

"We sure are. She's amazing."

"And that's all? You're not dating or anything?"

"I tried, but she reminded me how she's not eighteen yet. I don't feel like getting into trouble for dating a minor. Virginia sure has some weird laws."

Covering his eyes, Denver shook his head. He had messed up, and not just a little. "Thanks, Mark. Sorry to bother you."

"Why did you want to know if Tess and I were dating?"

"A friend wants to ask her out and wanted to know if she's dating anyone."

"Well, I wouldn't want to go back to seventeen again, but I might if I could ask Tess out."

Denver thanked him and ended the call, texted Tess that he was sorry and waited for her answer.

Nothing.

Zilch.

No text tone.

Nothing.

He put on shorts and a T-shirt and went to the deck to put the pieces of guitar in the case and slide it under his bed. In the kitchen, he made coffee. Time for a plan to earn Tess's trust again, which he sure didn't deserve after dating Leah.

Sipping coffee at the counter as the sun rose over the lake, he couldn't think of a single thing. If he went to see her, she would slam the door in his face. Also, Absalom and Oneita would want to know what was wrong, and— No, Tess had probably told them he was back, and that meant they would want to know when he would visit.

Denver put the coffee mug down.

No again. Absalom had told Tess about seeing him, so everyone knew he was back. Time for some damage control.

Denver sat on his bed with his phone to text Absalom how he was here to check on the house, but he didn't. Would Tess tell him about their fight? No, not at all, because she would want to keep their relationship a secret.

Just to make sure, Denver texted Absalom how he was here to check on the house anyway. Absalom replied he understood, and asked Denver if he wanted to come over for supper tonight. Denver replied he had plans, cheeks warming at his lie, but what choice did he have? If he went there, Tess wouldn't want to see him, and Absalom and Oneita would want an explanation.

Denver slipped dock shoes on, put his keys and wallet in his pockets, and went to the front door. Better head to the grocery store since the fridge was empt—

The door opened and Willow walked in. "Going somewhere, big brother?"

Denver closed the door and hugged her. "It's good to see you. I was— Wait a minute, how did you know I was here instead of in D.C.?"

"I called Akina."

"Why didn't you call me?"

"I thought I would surprise you."

"Coffee? I just made some."

Willow followed him to the kitchen. "Sure, then I can tell why I'm here."

Denver filled mugs and gave Willow hers. Same red hair, a shade lighter than Tess's, but curlier instead of wavy like Tess's. "Well," he said, "I know you're not doing something as dumb as getting married like I did, right?"

"Have you heard from Eliza? It's hard to believe she divorced you. I really liked her. You know, like a sister."

Denver swallowed coffee. "Not a word."

"And she's really living with some guy and his son?"

"That's what Ethan said."

"That makes no sense." Willow drank coffee. "As much as she loved you, I have a hard time believing all that."

"Me too. I told you how I almost fainted when I found out."

Silence fell between them. Denver started to ask if Willow wanted breakfast but didn't because of the empty fridge. "Okay, why are you here?"

Willow clinked her mug to his. "I'm getting married in a month. Guess who's going to give me away?"

"You're getting married in Clarksville?"

"If it doesn't bring back any memories of Eliza that bother you, I want the reception at the old manor house at the golf club." Willow took her phone from the purse she had placed on the counter, swiped the screen a few times, and held it so Denver could see. "This is William. I met him in med school. He's a great guy. He reminds me of Dad with his serious side, but he has a fun side too."

"I'm glad for you," Denver said. "At least one of us should have a happy marriage. Where's he from?"

"Would you believe South Hill? Talk about a small world."

"Cool. Will you two work nearby? That way I'll have some family around instead of just my in-laws."

"That's the plan. We hope to buy a house in this subdivision after we get jobs." Willow sipped coffee. "You know I'm inviting your in-laws, right?"

Denver thought she would. If he and Tess hadn't settled things before the wedding, she would ignore him. Fine. He could deal. "Sure, no problem."

"Well … there *might* be a problem," Willow said, hesitation in her voice.

"I don't know how, unless …"

"Figured it out, huh?"

"Don't tell me you're inviting Eliza."

"And Jan and Akina."

"They'll come if they can. Not Eliza, no way. She burned the proverbial bridge between her and everyone here when she divorced me."

Willow went to the refrigerator and opened it. "Why's the fridge empty when Akina said you left yesterday? I was thinking about eggs and toast."

Denver paused. Tell Willow about Leah or not? Sure, since it looked like his relationship with Tess was over before it started.

"I dated someone a few times lately. We took the pontoon boat out fishing last night, almost as soon as I got here."

Willow returned to the bar and sat. "Is she nice?"

"Sure, she's nice. Her name's Leah."

"If she likes fishing, that's something. That one time Mom and Dad took Jan fishing with us, she frowned every time we reeled one in."

"I sure miss them," Denver said, trying not to sound sad.

"Me too," Willow said. "Another reason I came is to try her wedding dress on. If it'll fit, I'm wearing it. Is it still in that cedar chest in the guest room?"

"It is. I wonder what kind of advice they would give me about Eliza?"

"Have you thought about talking to her? Maybe a year apart has helped her put things in perspective."

'Yeah, right," Denver said sarcastically. "Like the perspective to rip what's left of my heart out and stomp all over it."

Willow rubbed Denver's shoulder. "It sounds like you still love her."

"Part of me does. If I ever see her again, I have no idea what'll happen. One thing for sure, she'll know how much she hurt me."

Willow looped her purse strap over her shoulder. "C'mon, big brother. Let me take you out to breakfast."

"Good idea. Then I can get some groceries."

In her car beside his pickup, Willow started it. "Where to?"

Denver fastened his seat belt. "Let's try that place near the elementary school. I heard they serve a good breakfast."

At the restaurant, which was only about five minutes away, Denver and Willow ordered eggs over easy, bacon, whole wheat toast, coffee, and orange juice. Their meals came hot and their orange juice came cold. Denver buttered his toast. "You're really gonna ask Eliza to the wedding?"

"Why not? Maybe you two can talk things out." Willow drank orange juice. "It could happen, right? It's not like she's gotten married."

"Ethan would've called if she had." While eating eggs, Denver thought of another question for his sister. "You want me to give you away. What do you think of letting Ivy be your flower girl?"

Willow swallowed coffee. "Exactly what I was thinking. I'm going to ask Tess to be my maid of honor and Oneita to be my matron of honor. They're the closest thing we have to family."

"What about Absalom? Does he get a role to play in this wedding of yours?"

Willow laughed. "As big as he is, he could be the bouncer. No, it'll just be great having him there like family." She crunched toast and swallowed. "I called Mark about the wedding. He says he and Tess are playing and singing together. He said he would be glad to play at the reception, but I told him I already have a band lined up. I told him to come anyway. Still, I hate how everything will be a bittersweet."

"I know what you mean," Denver said. "I'd give anything if Mom and Dad could be there."

The conversation halted, no doubt because of the somber subject, until Willow looked up from her plate. "Since you're dating Leah, I assume you want to get married again."

"I do. I hadn't thought much about it or having kids before I met Eliza. She and her family changed all that."

"Is there any chance losing Mom and Dad changed that too?"

"I started thinking more about that lately. I don't want to wake up an old man one day without a wife or children or grandchildren. I loved our family before Mom and Dad died. Sure, we could argue, especially when you and I hit puberty and thought we knew more than they did about life. Now I know we were just young and hardheaded. They had already experienced a lot of living before we came along. That included making intelligent decisions, like college and careers before having kids."

Willow returned to her food. Denver faced the double glass doors, where the sun rose higher in the blue sky. Where his life was headed, he had no idea, but he hoped it was in a lot better direction than right after Eliza had left him.

He sipped coffee.

But would that direction include Tess? He hoped so, but who knew what it would take to get there, and what would happen if they never made up? Although Leah was a possibility, he didn't feel that spark of chemistry that he had felt with Eliza.

Eliza?

Didn't he mean Tess?

For a moment he let himself feel Eliza's hand in his, let himself kiss her, hold her, smell the fresh air in her hair when they made love on the deck of the cabin during their honeymoon in Occoneechee State Park, when a shower of red and gold oak leaves fell around them.

That was love—a love he might never feel again.

Tess.

Yes, there had been times when she had been the flame that had ignited his love like that, and he wanted to see if their love could grow to the same proportions as his and Eliza's love.

Denver excused himself and went to the restroom. He unrolled a handful of paper towels and sobbed into them.

God help him. God help him. He was still in love, not only with a woman who had divorced him—possibly to take another man's child as her own and to marry him—but he didn't know if he would ever stop loving her.

He wiped his eyes and blew his nose.

Tess could make him forget Eliza. After all, she did that before he went to D.C., while they made love in the bed where he had made love to Eliza countless times before.

It was funny how that had never crossed his mind then, which was more proof of how Tess could very well be the next woman of his dreams, but only if they could work things out.

Still, Eliza would haunt him for a long time. The key was to forget her, including her not coming to the Willow's wedding or the reception.

possibilities

In the department store fitting room, Eliza buttoned a pair of jeans David was trying on. "You're growing fast, young man. How do they feel?"

David tugged at the waist of the jeans. "They're okay, Mama."

"Good. Let's get your old jeans back on and get some more. Don't let me forget some shirts too, and some shoes and socks and underwear."

At the jeans display, Eliza folded three more pair over her arm and took David's hand to take him to the shirts.

"Well, look who's here."

Eliza recognized Jon's voice. Unsure how he might feel about her situation with Josh and David, she faced him. "Hello, Jon. How are you and your family?"

He patted her shoulder. "There's no need to use such a solemn tone, Eliza. I'm happy to see you."

"I didn't know. I'm sure Ethan has mentioned me living with Josh."

"And this handsome young fellow here." Jon knelt by David. "I'm Jon. Eliza learned sign language at a school I built near my house."

David peered up at Eliza. "You didn't tell me that."

Jon stood. "I'm sure she's got a lot on her mind." He faced Eliza. "On my way to your old home the other day, I saw you and David with easels set up. It's good to see you painting after … well, you know."

Eliza knew Josh meant after her daughter had died. "Josh bought the supplies for David and I for Christmas."

"That was nice of him." Jon leaned close to Eliza's ear. "Look," he whispered, "regardless of what Ethan thinks he heard from the gossips, and how you slapped him, I realize you're under a lot of stress from losing your daughter. I try my best to not judge, but honestly, when I heard you had divorced Denver, I was shocked."

"It's hard to explain, Jon."

"I don't need you to explain. What matters is you're happy." He patted David's head. "I'll leave you to your shopping." Turning to leave, he faced her again. "If you're painting again, will you do any more art shows?"

Eliza didn't answer. She had already thought about having more art shows to earn enough money to afford a house on the lake in Clarksville. If she worked out her differences with her family, she could even live in the same subdivision where they and Denver lived. How that would affect her and him, she didn't know.

"Maybe you should think about it," Jon said. "Collectors at my shows are always asking when you'll start painting again." He grinned. "We know how Jan loves her commissions, but she's an excellent agent. Would you like me to mention how you're painting again?"

"Only if she doesn't tell Denver or my family. We don't get along right now, if you know what I mean."

Jon's eyes softened. "I understand. I'll tell Jan you're thinking about it and tell her to keep it to herself if she wants to earn her commissions." He said goodbye and left, leaving Eliza to finish shopping with David.

At home again, she used scissors to cut the tags from the purchases, put them away, and made her and David a tomato sandwich each. Thank goodness for meeting Jon. If she decided to move back to Clarksville, she could earn enough money to live wherever she wanted. Still, Anna had a long way to go before she could come home, but it would be a good idea to start on paintings to sell.

David took a bite of sandwich. "Mama?"

"Yes?"

"What's divorce?"

"You've got ears like an elephant, don't you?"

David touched one ear. "El-phant ears is bigger than mine."

"I'm teasing. A divorce is when a married man and woman aren't married anymore."

"Why? They're supposed to be like Mama and Papa. They love each other."

Eliza looked away. Out of the mouth of a boy almost four-years-old.

"Mama?"

"Yes?"

"Did you love a man like Mama loves Papa?"

Eliza threw her sandwich in the trash. Yet another question to aggravate her. Although she believed she still loved Denver, that life was gone now. She would never marry again, would never love again. Better to be alone instead of hurting any man who might love her because she couldn't share a tender kiss or caress, and especially because she couldn't even begin to imagine making love to him.

She poured milk for David. "I forgot your milk."

"You didn't answer me."

She sat beside David. "Love is hard sometimes. It's not the same for grownups as it is for a mama and a papa to love their children like you. You're easy to love."

David drank milk. "Why's that? It's easy for Mama and Papa to love each other."

Eliza took a napkin from the holder and wiped his milk moustache. "Just believe me." She stood. "I'll have some milk. Then we'll paint some more."

"Like what? We did flowers and butterflies already."

"What if I paint you?"

"I didn't know you could paint boys. Can you make them look real like your flowers and butterflies?"

"I sure can." Eliza went to the refrigerator for milk and filled a glass. "Finish your lunch. I'd like to paint before your papa gets home from seeing your mama. Then I'll have time to cook supper."

Taking a swallow of milk, Eliza stopped when her phone vibrated with a call. She made sure it wasn't anyone she didn't want to talk to and answered the call from Josh. "Hi, Josh. David's all set for clothes until he outgrows them again."

"That boys grows like a weed in springtime," Josh said. "Anna woke up today for an hour. The doctors say they can start running tests tomorrow to see how much damage the accident may have done to her brain."

"That's good news." Eliza paused. She hadn't considered how Anna might have brain damage from the accident. She went to the living room so David couldn't hear. "What kind of damage do they think she might have?"

"She might not have any," Josh said. "That's what the tests are for. You've been so busy with David, I thought I'd bring a pizza home. Would you believe I've never tried it?"

"Then David hasn't tried it either. Let's start with a veggie pizza. Pepperoni and sausage might be too spicy for him."

"Good idea. Are you planning to paint today? David sure loves it."

Eliza lowered the phone from her ear. Tell Josh about painting to earn money at shows for when she left or not? Not. She would paint and store the finished ones in her room without mentioning why until she was ready to do a show. Anna should be home by then, and Josh would stay here instead of leaving to see her, giving Eliza time to start shows.

"I'm going to start on an oil painting of David."

"Really?" Josh asked with a chuckle. "Do you think he'll stay still long enough for that?"

"He minds well, Josh. He's as sweet as he can be."

"He is that. I'll go so you can get to work."

Eliza ended the call. Yes, whenever she had to leave David, her heart would break like it did when she had left Denver.

She went to the kitchen. "Your papa said your mama stayed awake longer today. Isn't that good news?"

David nodded. "When can she come home?"

"It'll be a while yet. When a person has been asleep a long time like your mama—it's called a coma—the muscles in their legs get too weak to walk. That means the doctors have to help her exercise so she can get strong again."

David finished the last bite of sandwich and washed it down with milk. He looked at Eliza, big brown eyes blinking, and a tear ran down his cheek. "If Mama comes home, do you have to—" A sob caught in his throat. "Do you have to go?"

Eliza hugged him, which made him cry. When he finished, she wiped his face with another napkin. "You'll be four soon, right?"

"Yeah."

"Then you'll be five next year and go to school. That's part of growing up. Part of you growing up—and me—is to let your mama and papa raise you without me here."

"But …" More tears ran down David's cheeks.

"No buts," Eliza said, wiping his cheeks again. "I'll come and see you as often as I can, and I'll always love you."

"But that's not like being here all the time."

"I know." Eliza kissed his hair. "What if I give you my phone number? Then you can call me anytime you want, and that'll be almost as good as me being here all the time."

David wiped his nose with his sleeve. "I guess."

"Good." Eliza stood. "Let's take you to the bathroom and clean you up. I don't want to paint a boy with red eyes and cheeks."

After Eliza wiped David's face in the bathroom with a washcloth, she showed him how to use her phone, including taking a selfie of her and him together. She also told him she would send the picture to Josh's phone so David could look at it whenever he wanted to. This perked him up and made him smile, so they gathered her painting supplies and went outside to the shade of an oak, not too far from the garden and Anna's wildflowers.

She set the easel up facing the flowers, sat David in a chair in front of her, and told him to sit straight, but to let her know when he needed to rest.

With the oil paints mixed on the palette and David still, Eliza touched a brush to a dab of brown for his hair and raised the tip to the canvas.

When David had cried, it was all she could do to not cry too. Losing him would be like losing her daughter all over again, and the thought caused her eyes to sting again.

The colors spread upon the canvas. A butterfly lit on a blue cornflower behind David. Eliza took a clean brush, dabbed it into green, and started on a cornflower's stem.

This painting would take a while. She wanted it to capture her love for David, her love for nature, and her love for her daughter—gone before she even had a chance to hold her and tell her how much she loved her.

Denver.

His moaning sobs on that terrible day had told of his love for their daughter too. He had sounded like a wounded animal on a nature documentary on TV, bawling out its final moments of life before a lion's jaws crushed its throat.

Looking back at those days before the funeral, neither of them had held each other, which she couldn't understand. Then again, at the time, she had never thought of it. Maybe the deaths of his parents had left him raw and aching for them, and the loss of their daughter had opened that wound all over again.

For her, when she and Denver had first gone to the funeral home to see their daughter, the grief of growing up deaf, including the wounds of never being held and comforted by Mama, had forced her into a corner by herself. He had stood beside the white coffin, tears running silently down his cheeks, until he had fallen to his knees to make that pitiful sound of a dying animal.

If only they had comforted each other, had held each other, had at least made the attempt, but that wall of grief had sealed them off from each other until Eliza had left him.

"Mama?"

Eliza blinked. "What?"

"Why aren't you painting? You're just sitting there."

Eliza touched the tip of the brush. The paint had grown thick and sticky. How long had she sat here thinking about her and Denver's grief on that terrible day?

No.

The most important question was what it would take to learn to live with the grief instead of allowing it to rip them even further apart than they already were, including her and her family?

She chose another brush. "I'm sorry, sweetheart. I suppose I was daydreaming about something."

He had slouched while she talked. Sitting tall again, he smiled. "Okay, now you can dream about me."

birthday

Standing in front of her dresser mirror, Tess tied her hair in a ponytail for her birthday supper in an hour. She had texted Denver a few days ago, telling him he better come to avoid questions from Papa and Mama. They had already asked why he hadn't been over to work on guitars or to practice, forcing her to make up stories about him being busy with yardwork around the house.

She tightened the ponytail. Add a touch of lipstick and eyeliner, including Mark coming over, and Denver Andrews would regret sleeping with the Leah that night two weeks ago.

What a bonehead he was, accusing her of dating someone when they had already planned to date when she turned eighteen. Well, not really. On the morning he had left in December, after they had made love the previous night, they had said they would see what happened, or something like that, which was basically the same thing. Now he was dating Leah again, and Tess intended to make him regret it in every way possible, starting with looking so great at her party that he wouldn't be able to keep his eyes off of her.

After applying the lipstick and eyeliner, she went to the kitchen. At the counter making tossed salad, Mama glanced her way. "Don't you look nice. Is that lipstick and eyeliner for Denver?"

Tess didn't want to answer. Mama had already figured out how she and Denver had feelings for each other. Although she had said Papa approved, neither of them had mentioned it since Denver had come back from D.C.

Mama faced her. "I see your thoughts churning in that head of yours. Do you remember telling me how you and Denver had talked about dating after you turned eighteen? That's today, you know."

"I remember. Have you talked to Papa about it?"

"It bothers him because of Eliza, but he wants you and Denver to be happy if you can. Do you think you can? It's a lot to ask, having a relationship with your sister's husband."

"*Ex*-husband, Mama. I know losing Lily was hard for her, but she shouldn't have left Denver and then divorced him. That's not how marriages are supposed to work."

Mama returned to the salad. "Well, just let me and your papa know when you plan to date Denver."

Tess went to the back door. Papa was turning steaks and chicken on the grill. Ivy was placing plates and silverware on the huge picnic table Papa had made, large enough to seat eight people easily.

"Tess?"

Tess turned from the door to face Mama. "What?"

"Denver hasn't come to see us since he came home. Is something wrong between you two?"

"I told you he was busy."

"What about Mark?"

"What about him?"

"You enjoy playing music with him. Do you have anything else in common with him in case Eliza were to want Denver again? I'd hate for you to fall in love with Denver and get hurt like she hurt him."

Tess took a carrot from beside the salad bowl. "Mark and I are just friends."

"But you invited him to supper."

"That's what friends do." Crunching the carrot, Tess went to the door again. Ugh, nosy parents.

The front doorbell rang. "Get that," Mama said. "It's probably one of your two suitors."

Frowning at a remnant word from Amish life, Tess went to the door, where Mark stood with an envelope in his hand, visible through the screen. She let him in, and he gave it to her. "I got you a card. The check from when we last played at the restaurant is in there too."

Tess opened the envelope. The card was the standard for eighteen-year-olds, about growing up and being an adult. The check though, made her eyes pop. "Wow, this will really help buy more guitar materials."

Mark took a folded paper from his pocket and gave it to her. "Here's a list of the electronics for my guitar so you can build one."

Tess took the paper. "Let me put these away, be right back."

Mark followed her down the hall and to her room. She left the papers on her dresser. When she turned to leave, he raised his hand to stop her. "Now that you're eighteen, what's the chance we could try a date and see how it goes?"

The front screened door squeaked open. "Anyone home? It's Denver."

"In the kitchen," Mama said.

Tess pushed Mark into the hall. Although she didn't mind Denver being jealous of him, she didn't want him to get the wrong idea.

Crossing the hall, Denver stopped to face them. His cheeks reddened. He clenched his fists. "Hey, Mark."

"Hey, Denver."

Denver left for the kitchen. Tess hurried after him, Mark on her heels. Denver kissed Mama's cheek. "It's good to see you, Oneita. Thanks for inviting me."

She glanced at Tess. "Tess invited you, not me."

"Yeah, I can tell how much she wants me here." Denver went outside to pick up Ivy, and Tess followed, holding the door for Mark. Denver kissed Ivy's cheek. "Hey, doodlebug. I sure missed you."

"Have you kissed Tess yet?"

"Now, Ivy," Papa said. "Mind your own business."

Denver went to Tess and pecked her cheek. "There you go."

"No, Denver," Ivy whined, "on the lips like I saw one time."

Mark cut his eyes from Tess to Denver and back to Tess again. He went to Papa. "Can I help, Mr. Gray?"

Papa offered his hand. "Call me Absalom, Mark. Nice to meet you. Tess really enjoys playing music with you."

"Yeah," Mark said, his tone flat. "She surprises me all the time."

"You're a professional. Is she any good?"

Mark faced Denver. "What do you think, Denver? Is she any good?"

Denver cut a hard glance at Tess. "I don't know, Mark. I thought *you* might know by now."

"She's *really* good," Ivy said.

Tess was tempted to cross her arms. Men and their testosterone.

Mark left Absalom and went to Denver. "Did you get Tess anything for her birthday? I got her a nice card."

"Was it a thank you card?"

Mark squared off his feet. "Just what are you trying to say?"

"You really should thank her," Denver said, glaring at Tess. "She's great at stringing a guy—I mean a guitar—along."

Tess grabbed Denver's arm. "Let's help Mama bring out whatever she needs us to bring out."

Denver jerked his arm free. "Mark, have you heard Willow's getting married? I'm glad she found a nice guy. There's a lot of jerks around these days who'll take advantage of a girl." He snapped around to face Tess. "Lots of women do that kind of thing too. You never know who you can trust these days."

Mark nodded. "I think I know what you mean."

Papa took several sizzling steaks from the grill and placed them on a platter, then did the same for the chicken. "Tess, go get the iced tea. Ivy, go get the glasses."

Mama came out the back door with a huge bowl of tossed salad. "Get a few bottles of dressing too, one of you."

Tess faced Denver. "You heard the woman, get in here and help."

Mark followed her. "I got it, Denver."

In the kitchen, he took three bottles from the refrigerator. "I see why you won't go out with me. Something's going on with you and Denver. What the heck's wrong with you? He's what, ten years older than you are?"

Tess took the pitcher of iced tea from the refrigerator. "You don't know what you're talking about."

"Yeah, right. I could cut the tension between him and me with an E string."

Tess closed her eyes. How could she get through this stupid birthday and this stupid supper with these stupid men? She opened her eyes. "Look, Mark, you and I are guitar playing friends and that's it. If that's not enough, I can always quit playing and singing."

"I don't want that." He looked into her eyes. "Tess, you're really great. Denver's on the rebound from Eliza. I was at their wedding. If he gets the chance, he'll go back to her in a heartbeat."

Tess paused. She didn't want Mark to know she cared about Denver, especially now that their relationship was up in the air, but she did enjoy playing music, along with making great money. "Mark, what I do with my life is no one's business but mine. I'm eighteen now, so that goes double. I appreciate your interest, but it's not gonna happen. Now, do you want to be friends and music buddies, or do you want to leave and miss out on all that great food outside?"

Mark looked at the bottles of dressing in his hands. "Well, you can't blame me for trying."

"Is that a yes or a no?"

He raised his head. "I'm not dumb enough to turn down grilled steaks and chicken."

Everyone sat at the picnic table. At the last minute, when Mark started to sit by Tess, Denver slipped in ahead of him. "Y'all mind if I say the blessing for Tess's birthday?"

"Go ahead," Absalom said.

Everyone bowed their heads, including Denver. Tess waited until his eyes were closed before she bowed hers. Denver's hand found hers in her lap. She started to jerk away, but the warmth between them drew her to him. What she wouldn't give to be alone with him at his house, to do whatever she wanted with him. She pulled her hand away. No way, not after he had accused her of dating Mark while he was dating Leah, the jerk.

"Dear God, thank You for this family. If not for them, I don't know what I would be doing right now. They helped me through one of the toughest times in my life, and I appreciate it more than I can say. Absalom and Oneita are like my own mom and dad now, and Ivy is like my sister. Tess, as we all know, is a mess, so that means she's very special to me. Thank you for allowing Willow to find someone special too. From our time with Mom and Dad, we both know how important family is, and she's off to a great start."

His hand found Tess's again.

"I only hope I can find someone like that again, to have a family with, to love like I love—" Denver cleared his throat. "Loved Eliza. Thank you for this food. May it nourish our bodies. Amen."

Tess pulled her hand from Denver's. Touched by his words, she forked a huge steak to her plate and started slicing it so he couldn't see her filling eyes.

Oneita forked salad into a bowl for Ivy, poured dressing, and filled her own bowl. "Denver, are you staying home now, or are you going back to your job in Washington?"

"I called my boss the morning after I got here and said I wouldn't be back."

"You didn't tell me that," Tess said.

"Don't you hate it when people aren't honest?" He took a steak from the platter. "I know I do."

"I do too." Tess didn't say the rest: *You butthead.*

Opposite Tess, Mark placed a chicken breast on his plate. "Denver, I've been wondering something."

Denver stopped slicing steak. "Like what?"

"Why you called me the other week and asked if I was dating Tess?"

In the middle of drinking tea, Papa lowered his glass. "I thought you two were only playing music together."

"That's what I thought too," Denver said. "The night I got home, I saw them at the restaurant at a table. It looked like a date to me."

"Really?" Mama asked. "Tess, do you have something to tell us?"

"I think Denver has something to tell us," Mark said. "I told him Tess and I were just friends."

Adrenalin seared across Tess's shoulders. She wouldn't say anything now, but she would the next time she got Mr. Denver Andrews alone. The nerve, knowing she wasn't dating Mark and making all those sarcastic comments anyway.

"I called Mark because of what I saw," Denver said. "Is anything wrong with that?"

Tess squeezed his hand and went inside to wait for him in her room. A moment later, like a good little puppy with a huge ego, he appeared in the door. Look, I know you're mad, but—"

"Shut up." Tess shut the door. "You know I'm not dating Mark and you act like I was anyway? And after I know you're dating Leah, not to mention sleeping with her?"

"I told you we were fishing." Denver offered her his phone from its holder on his belt. "You could call her and see."

Tess ignored the phone. "I wouldn't call that, that, that— Ooooh, I can't even think of a name for her, I'm so mad."

Denver grabbed her shoulders. "Look, the only person I want is you. We talked about dating and now we can. I want to go out with you like a regular couple. I thought you wanted that too."

Tess huffed a stray lock of hair from her forehead. "Admit it, you're sleeping with Leah, and in the same bed we slept in too."

"Nope. Didn't happen."

"Bull. What's so special about her anyway?"

"She's okay. I would even call her special."

"Did you date her in D.C.?"

Denver's eyes darted away and back. "No, why would I do that."

"Liar." Tess took her phone from her dresser. "I still have Leah's number from when I got it off your phone that time." She dialed the number. "Let's see if y'all just went fishing that night. Hi, Leah, Tess here. I hope you're well."

"I'm fine. I hope you are."

"I'm good. Look, Denver told me y'all went out in D.C. It sounds like you had a great time."

Denver snatched the phone from Tess. "Leah? I was just telling Tess how I met you and your sister that day."

Tess snatched the phone back. "Tess again." She turned away so Denver couldn't grab the phone. "What did y'all do? I might like to try it myself."

"Nothing much, really. He sure is a great kisser."

"Thanks for that. Talk to you never." Tess ended the call and threw the phone on her bed. "You. Out."

"Nope. I love you and I'm not going anywhere."

Tess took a guitar leaning in the corner and raised it like a baseball bat. "I already busted one on your tree. How about I bust one on your head?"

Denver's jaw worked back and forth. "You wouldn't. Everybody would hear it."

"Like I give a crap about that." She drew the guitar back. "I realize I've got to deal with seeing you at Willow's wedding, but you better stay away from me, got it?"

Please, Tess, I love you."

She dropped the guitar on the bed. Time to make him beg.

Someone knocked on the door. "Tess," Mama said, "are you and Denver okay? We heard you outside."

"We're talking about guitars, be out in a minute." She faced Denver. "What in the hell do you see in Leah that you don't see in me?"

He sat on the bed. "When I was in D.C., I got to thinking about you. I didn't want to tie you down with marriage and kids at such a young age."

"Whoever I marry, I don't want kids anytime soon."

"I hope you'll marry me."

"And if I don't, I guess you'll marry Leah. Why the durn hurry?"

"At least you didn't say damn."

"Don't tempt me."

"I'm not in a hurry, but I want to get married and have a family. I'll be thirty in a few years, and I don't want to end up an old man without kids and grandkids and a great life with a woman like you. I wanted that with Eliza, but you know what happened."

Tess sat on the bed. "How do I know you didn't sleep with Leah in D.C.? I can't stand the thought of it."

"You'll have to trust me."

Tess stood. "Right, like you trusted me when I told you I was only friends with Mark." She opened the door. "Go eat your steak and try not to choke on it. I'm not sure if I'll slap your stupid back or not."

Denver left. Tess dropped to the bed again.

What a complete jerk, and the worst part was how she would have to deal with him at Willow's wedding.

sleepover

In the kitchen, Denver stared into the open refrigerator. Since Tess had kicked him out of her bedroom a week ago, he didn't have much of an appetite, or much of an interest in Clarksville's Lakefest, going on downtown right now.

He closed the fridge and checked the time on the stove. 11:30.

The food vendors would be serving all kinds of great stuff. A whole deep-fried onion and a roasted turkey leg would hit the spot, despite having to thread his way through the crowds on main street.

He parked in a lot beside the post office and walked to the intersection near the pizza place. The aromas of various foods led him to the onions. As he paid for one, a finger tapped his back. "I'll share my turkey leg if you'll share your onion."

Denver turned to face Leah. "Hey, it's good to see you."

"Are you sure? I wasn't a very good fishing partner that night."

"Hey, you gotta go to the bathroom, you gotta go to the bathroom."

She started up the sidewalk, and Denver walked beside her. "I guess that phone call from Tess surprised you last weekend."

"No joke, especially her saying she'll talk to me 'never.' What's up with her?"

Denver pulled a sliver of onion off, dipped it in horseradish sauce, and offered it to Leah. Maybe he could get her mind off of Tess with food.

Leah opened her mouth. "Mmm, that's great." She offered the turkey leg to Denver. He took a bite and made the OK sign while chewing. Tess didn't know Leah like he knew Leah. She was cute and nice, and she was a local who loved the area like he did.

They continued along the sidewalk, remarking on various crafts sold by vendors, taking bites of onion and turkey until both were gone.

Leah bought a sign at a vendor. "I love this. 'There's No Country Like Lake Country.'" She gave it to Denver. "For you to hang on a tree near your dock."

Denver kissed her cheek. "Hey, thanks."

Leah slipped her fingers into his. "See how sweet I am?"

Denver didn't answer. Instead, he gave her the sign, went to the same vendor, and bought one that said "I'm a Lake Country Girl" and gave it to Leah. "There you go, for your dream lake home one day."

They exchanged signs. Leah, whose head barely came to his shoulder, looked up into his eyes. "I'd kiss you if it weren't for my onion breath."

Denver laughed. "Or for the turkey in my teeth."

Leah pulled him off the sidewalk, out of the way of people walking. "Heck with it." She pulled him down for a long, luscious kiss that made Denver realize how much he missed long, luscious kisses.

"Whoa," he said standing up straight.

Leah slipped her fingers into his again. "How about supper at my place tonight? Then I'll *really* make you say 'whoa.'"

Denver didn't see the harm in supper. "Why not? What's something you like to cook?"

"Well, although I like fried fish from the lake, I love grilled salmon. It's gotta be wild caught, no farm-raised stuff for me. Add some steamed broccoli, some white wine, and banana pudding for dessert, I'm good to go."

Denver licked his lips. "Man, I love banana pudding."

"Great." Leah stood on tiptoe for a quick kiss. "I'll text you my address. Come around seven. That'll give me time to clean up the place and shop and shower and get all prettied up for you."

Denver knew what she meant about showering. Rarely did Lakefest crowds get a chance at a less than ninety-five-degree day, and he had already caught a hint of sourness from his own underarms. "Sounds good," he said. "I need to do some stuff around the house too. Want me to pick up the wine?"

"I've got some in the fridge now." She looked at the sign. "Thanks again for this. I better scoot and get started at home."

"Thanks for my sign too," Denver said. "See you later."

In his pickup, he headed home. Things were looking up with Leah. If nothing else, he could tell Tess about the upcoming date and make her even more angry. Sure, he loved her, but she could be a real hardhead at times.

Still, it nagged him that Leah might think he was leading her on. Nope, not at all. She knew the deal: take it slow, get to know each other, see what happens. Besides, if Tess didn't want him, and if it didn't work out with Leah, someone else would come along.

At home, he vacuumed and mopped, cleaned his bathroom and washed clothes, changed sheets on his bed and chose clothes for tonight—lightweight tan slacks, a yellow Oxford shirt, loafers without socks—and took a shower, shaved, and combed his hair. Dabbing a little aftershave lotion on, he looked in the mirror. Not bad for divorcee with a broken heart—not from one but two women. No, Tess hadn't broken his heart yet, but he had a feeling she would if they didn't make up soon.

He started to dress but stopped to sit on his bed, which used to be his and Eliza's bed.

The day he had received her divorce notice—on Christmas Day at that—he had been at the Gray household, invited over for supper. After the meal, when they went to the living room to open presents at Ivy's insistence, the deputy had come with a large brown envelope.

As bad as the news of the divorce had been, Denver had still thought it could be a mistake. Then Absalom and Oneita had told them how they saw Eliza on the porch of the man she was now living with. Well, with him and his son. No, they just weren't on the porch, he was hugging her on the porch—from the back no less, his cheek next to hers in an intimate embrace that she hadn't allowed Denver to have in a year and a half.

Still, he had thought it was a mistake. Maybe they were friends. Maybe he was grateful for some small thing she had done. After all, she was teaching him and his wife and their son sign language.

But then the man's wife had been hit by a truck and was in a coma. Absalom had called Ethan on Christmas Day to ask why she had sent the divorce papers. Ethan said he had confronted her about gossip he had heard in town, gossip that sounded as if there was more to Eliza's relationship with the man than was proper, especially with his wife in a coma. Ethan had received a slap across his face for his concern, and he had sent a photo of it to Absalom, setting off the rift between Eliza and her family that remained to this day.

As bad as that was, it had floored Denver—literally—to his knees, even to the point of making him think Absalom and Oneita and Tess were Dad, Mom, and Willow, impossible as that had been.

Denver ran his hand across his pillow. Or maybe it was Tess's pillow, where her auburn hair, thick and heavy, had lain while they had made love. The remnant of some sweet scent had lingered on her neck that night—her neck where he had kissed with his face enclosed in the curtain of her hair, soft and lush, like warm summer rain streaming down his face when he had been caught out on the lake in his canoe one time.

He stood.

He missed the closeness of their two bodies together, entwined and joined, sharing each other with moans and kisses and caresses.

He donned his slacks.

More than that he missed Tess's sharp wit, quick grins, and laughter, low in her throat.

He buttoned his shirt.

More than that he missed Eliza's keen eyes, black as night, peering into his while reflecting lamplight. She preferred making love with the light on. Truth be told, he did too, to caress the curve of her shoulders, to watch the rhythm of her hips, to see the dip in her stomach near her navel as she hovered above him like an osprey hovering over the lake.

He put on his loafers.

Would he ever have that again? He liked to think he would. More than that, he liked to think he would have that with Tess.

Standing from the bed to see himself in his dresser mirror, the blurred vision of Eliza and Tess hovering over him set a fire low in the pit of his stomach. It had been seven months since he and Tess had made love, and the yearning for it made him stuff his pockets with his keys and wallet and hurry to his pickup.

No doubt about it, Leah was willing, and so was he.

He went by the grocery for more wine, went by the drug store in case Leah wasn't on birth control of any kind, and drove to her address.

He climbed the condo stairs and rang the doorbell. She opened the door in a towel, wet curls dripping. Denver's mouth watered as she let him in. "You're a little early," she said, waving a hand toward the living room. "I finally got my lake view."

He walked to a pair of sliding glass doors, and she came up behind him. "Were you surprised when you read the text with my address?"

"I didn't think about it."

"I lucked up on renting this place from a high school friend. She's trying a new job in Texas and doesn't want to sell yet, not that I could afford it." Leah looked up at him. "You dress up great, Denver."

He twisted one of her dripping curls around a fingertip. "Your towel is amazing."

Smiling, she padded away, leaving wet footprints glistening on the wood floor. "Let me finish getting ready so we can eat."

Beyond the sliding glass doors, the business bridge into Clarksville loomed to the left, the high, arching bypass bridge to the right. Just this side of the bypass bridge was where he had brought Eliza on the pontoon boat to see her first fireworks show. What a night that had been. They had cruised down the middle of the lake on the way back home, stopping when she had asked him to. Swimming followed, with a light meal of sandwiches and water afterward. Then the boat wouldn't start, leaving them to sleep in each other's arms in an attempt to keep warm from a cold rain that had fallen.

Denver grinned.

During their honeymoon, she had admitted to turning the gas valve off so the motor wouldn't start because she wanted them to have as much time together as possible, preferably without Willow around.

Something chilled his hand. The wine—he had forgotten the wine. He put it in the fridge.

"How do I look?"

Denver turned. Standing in the end of the hall entering the living room, Leah, wearing a yellow, knee-length dress, with thin straps across her bare shoulder, spun around. "Not bad, huh?"

Tanned shoulders. Soft brown curls brushing them. Pink lipstick. Hint of mascara. Denver's heart skipped a beat.

"Whoa, you look amazing."

"As amazing as with the towel? That's what you said about it while ago." She came to him, stood on tiptoe to look into his eyes. Hers, with flecks of gold around centers of deep brown, reflected lamplight from an end table beside the sofa. "Well?"

She wavered in his visions: a blur of Eliza and Tess mixed in. The vision cleared. Neither Eliza nor Tess had freckles. The bridge of Leah's nose was dotted with a faint smattering of them.

Leah dropped to her heels and pointed at her feet. "I'm skipping shoes to pretend we're at the lake."

Denver admired the pink polish, which matched her nails and lipstick. "Hey, sexy feet are cool. Do you lay in the sun a lot? Even the tops of your feet are tanned."

"I use a tanning bed once a week." She moved one of the thin straps off her shoulders. "No tan lines at all."

Denver swallowed. "You mean ..."

"Uh-huh, I tan nude." Leah pattered across the wood floor to the kitchen in the open-plan condo. "Can you pour the wine while I plate the salmon and broccoli? I'm keeping it warm in the oven."

Denver found glasses in a cabinet and poured. "I sort of forgot the bottle I brought."

Leah took a glass baking dish from the oven and placed it on a burner on top, removed the oven mitt and swatted it at him. "I noticed that. I think my towel had the right effect."

Denver couldn't deny that. She had been hotter than hot, and she was just as hot now. He took the wine to a table near the sliding glass doors. Leah followed with their plates. They sat beside each other, facing the lake. Denver started to suggest a blessing, but his guilt at lusting after Leah stopped him.

"You are so sweet," she said.

"How's that?"

"Your cheeks are red. That means you feel guilty for being attracted to me. It also means you were thinking of a blessing but didn't suggest it because of that guilt." Leah bowed her head. "Let me. Dear God, thank you for this day and thank you for this wonderful man here with me. He reminds me of a lost puppy trying to find its way back home. I know he misses his wife, or he wouldn't have married her to start with. Regardless of my feelings, or where this night might lead, please let it start and end with nothing but genuine caring for him as he tries to decide who he really needs to complete his life. Amen."

Denver raised his head. "Wow, Leah, you talk about me being sweet, but that was sweet."

She kissed his cheek. "I really mean it. The thing is, I want you now more than ever, but I don't want any pressure between us." She took a paper from the dress pocket and gave it to him.

He unfolded the paper and read. "You got tested for STDs?"

She touched the paper. "And all the results are negative." She palmed his cheek. "I trust you to be healthy and safe. After all, you've been married, so you would know if there were any problems." She took a plastic something from the same pocket."

"Any idea what this is?"

Denver recognized the closed container. "You didn't start those just for me, did you?"

Leah nodded. "I had my gynecologist call in the prescription when I got back from D.C. Despite talking about threesomes, when I think about you, I want you all to myself. I've thought about it in bed at night." Goosebumps dotted her arm. "See what I mean? Just the thought of us together does that."

Leah admitting how she thought about them together tempted Denver to forget eating and take her straight to her bed. Instead, he picked up his fork. If he really thought about Leah and him together, like when she had admitted it, either Eliza or Tess's face popped into his mind, their eyes closed, heads back, soft moans coming from them. He tasted the salmon. "This is great. What kind of seasoning do you use?"

Smiling softly, like a woman who knew she had him in the palm of her hand, Leah rubbed his shoulder. "It's dill with real butter and lemon."

Denver sipped wine, enjoying the sweet hint of grape at the end. He tried the broccoli, tender and moist. "Despite sounding like a broken record, I'll say this is great too."

Leah picked up her fork. "Good, I like knowing you're satisfied."

Denver continued eating, having no doubt whatsoever at what she had really meant, including how she could do exactly that.

The meal passed slowly, with small talk about Clarksville, more wine, and the delicious banana pudding with perfectly browned peaks of meringue.

Leah got up with their empty plates. "Can you bring the silverware? I'd like to get everything washed before the fireworks start."

Denver did as she asked. "I forgot all about the fireworks."

"Pour us some more wine."

Denver took his bottle from the fridge. "We emptied yours." As he poured, he felt a bit sleepy, an effect of the wine during supper, no doubt. He took the glasses to the table and went back to Leah, to take a towel from a rack and dry the dishes she had washed. "I'll help so we don't miss the fireworks."

Leah placed the last dish in the strainer. "They'll be okay there." She went to the sofa. Denver joined her, sitting at the other end.

Except for the circles of light from the two lamps on the tables at each end of the sofa, the room gradually darkened. Denver and Leah said nothing, simply sat there sipping and gazing at each other. She brought the wine bottle from the fridge and refilled their glasses.

The light from over Denver's shoulder illuminated her lips, now natural instead of pink from wiping them with a napkin while they ate. Didn't matter. Between her lips, her shoulders glowing in the same lamplight, and the soft brown curls falling around her face, he couldn't see anything else.

Leah put her glass on the table beside her, put his glass there too and slid next to him. "Can I unbutton your shirt?"

"It's new, sho—" Denver laughed. "I meant it's new, *so* the buttonholes are tight. All that wine's getting to me."

Leah sat astride him. "I think I can handle a few tight buttons." She unbuttoned his shirt to expose his chest. "Mmm," she said running her finger through his chest hair. "You feel like a big old teddy bear."

Laughing again, Denver stopped. "C'mon now, it's not that bad."

She kissed his neck below his ear, which made him laugh even more. "Sheesh, that tickles, Fleah." He snorted laughter. "I mean Leah."

Leah stood. "I see I need to get your mind on the task at hand to sober you up, Mr. Andrews." She slipped the straps off her shoulders, let the dress fall to her feet, and raised them to step out of the dress.

Black lace, on both her bra and panties, made Denver laugh again. "Hey, I could use you for a fish net."

Leah took off the bra. "What could you use these for?"

Laughing again, Denver fell over on the sofa. "Oh, wow, I'm sleepy."

Leah crossed her arms. "Well, you're not using them for pillows." She put the bra back on. "I guess your tolerance for alcohol is lower than mine. Do you want to sleep out here? I'll make you breakfast in the morning and we can try again."

"Mmm, what?"

"Where do you want to sleep? The bed's a king if you want to share." She pulled him up and put her arm around his waist. "Come on here. The least I can do is offer you a better place to sleep than the sofa."

She took him down the hall to her room, stopping several times when he bumped against the wall, and let him fall to the bed, where he slouched over. "Mmm. Can hardly keep … mmm, keep my eyes ope … open."

"I see that." Leah removed his loafers, pants, shirt, and worked his legs beneath the sheet. "Nice boxers. Too bad there's nothing in them that works at the moment."

She kissed his cheek. "I hope you appreciate this. I've never taken care of a drunk before."

Denver puckered his lips. "Gimme kish."

"Not until you're sober. I'll be back after I straighten the living room and get ready in the bathroom." She padded down the hall.

Off in the night, the first fireworks boomed and echoed. Denver rolled over and pulled the air-conditioned sheets to his chin. As much as he had wanted Leah, just the thought of making love to her had made him think about either Tess or Eliza, but mostly Tess. Eliza was drifting to a place in his mind he had never known, one where anger held her there, within a prison of fear in which he had placed her because he was afraid of what might happen if he ever saw her again. He hadn't noticed that subtle change between love and hate and how it had happened until now. Maybe it was like he had told Tess one time: part of him still loved Eliza but part of him hated her, except now the part that hated her was overriding the part that loved her.

As far as Leah, this was the first time he had pretended to be drunk. As far as an idea of how to get out of making love to her in the morning, he better get to sleep so he could think of one.

Leah padded back into the bedroom. A door closed and shut. He had seen a door to the right when she had brought him in here, so that must be the bathroom.

Sure, she had looked great in black lace, all tanned and curved, and when she had taken the bra off, it was all he could do to not pull her down into his lap again.

What a mess, caught between missing the warmth and familiar touch of a woman and the desire for that woman to be Tess. If he wasn't careful, Leah might have her way with him regardless.

morning

$\mathbf{D}$enver woke to the burning urge to hurry to the bathroom. "All that wine," he mumbled, standing at the toilet. Done with that, he rinsed his yucky mouth with mouthwash and went back to the bedroom.

A hint of sunlight shown beneath the curtains. He faced the bed, where Leah lay on her side, brown curls around her serene features. He should get dressed and get the heck out of here, but he couldn't do that to her after she had made him a great supper.

Her and the bed beckoned. He crawled back beneath the covers. No vision of Eliza or Tess hovered over her face.

"Mmm," Leah said, opening her eyes and stretching. Nude, she went to the bathroom and came back to snuggle Denver's shoulder. "How do you feel this morning, Mr. Wino?"

"Not bad. A good night's sleep helped."

"Do you remember me undressing you and putting you to bed?"

"I think so. I see you left my boxers on me."

She ran her fingertips along his chest, kissed his cheek, and rolled over on top of him. "Maybe I shouldn't have." She kissed his mouth, his throat, his chest, his stomach.

Denver closed his eyes. Sure, he was a weak guy, but Leah's kisses felt great.

She sat up. "Maybe we shouldn't do this."

Denver opened his eyes. "Well, uh—you know, well …"

"You don't agree?"

"I … uh, well."

She returned to his side. "No, we shouldn't. I really like you, so like we said in D.C., we should take it slow." She kissed him again, long and luscious like last night. "And I'd like to see where our relationship goes without sex." She kissed him again. "Know what I mean?"

"Not if you keep kissing me like that, especially looking so great naked."

"True." Leah got up, took a robe from a hanger on the bathroom door and slipped it on. "How about some country ham and eggs and biscuits and red-eye gravy? I bought all that yesterday, hoping you'd spend the night."

Denver didn't get out of bed, too embarrassed to at the moment. "Add some coffee and you've got a deal." To his relief, Leah left. He got up and dressed and went to the kitchen. Leah, her robe clinging to all the right places, was leaning over to get something from the fridge. He looked away. Yep, a weak guy through and through.

She took a package of ham from the fridge. "Make some coffee, okay? It's in the cabinet over the maker. Mugs too."

Denver did so. Minutes later, the aroma of sizzling ham in a pan and coffee dribbling into the carafe made his mouth water. Leah was kneading a mound of dough on a wooden cutting board, forearms knotting. He didn't know she could cook like this, a definite plus in the spouse category.

Biscuits in the oven, she placed four eggs in a pot of boiling water and set the timer. "I hope you like soft boiled eggs.

They're great when they turn out right." She put the carton in the fridge.

As she closed the door, Denver turned her around and put his hands around her waist. "I really appreciate this."

She gave him a quick kiss. "Not too much I hope. I meant what I said about taking it slow, so don't plan on rewarding me with your hot bod after we eat." She shoved him away. "Shoo while I finish everything."

Denver went to the sliding glass doors. Getting to know Leah and all her attributes, he saw no reason why they shouldn't go out more often. Besides, Miss Hardheaded Tess needed to see how she wasn't the only woman he enjoyed being with.

Leah called him to the table. She said a short blessing about being thankful for him and the food and patted his hand. "I'm really enjoying this. I feel domesticated already."

Denver buttered a steaming biscuit. Leah leaned across the table for a slice of ham, revealing cleavage between the folds of the robe. No matter how hard he tried, he couldn't stop looking. Although he was a weak guy, she made it all too easy to be weak, including the fact that he hadn't had sex since Tess, seven months ago. "Leah?"

Buttering her own biscuit, Leah faced him. "Yeah?"

"Since we're gonna take it slow, do you mind getting dressed? I'm dying here."

A slow smile spread across her face. "It's nice to be noticed." She kissed his cheek. "Be right back." She returned minutes later in faded jeans and a white blouse—no bra—and those small, tanned feet with their pink toenails. "How's this?"

Denver's mouth fell open. "Umm … well …"

Leah lifted his chin. "My eyes are up here, you naughty man. Let me get a bra on before our food gets cold."

She came back and sat. Drinking coffee, Denver lowered the mug. "I'm naughty? This from the woman who said threesomes are fun?"

"That was once in college. Besides, not only are you influencing me to be a one-man woman, you're influencing me to take it slow with you."

Denver swallowed eggs, creamy yellow with firm whites. "These are great." He tried a piece of the ham, salted to perfection. "Did you date much in college?"

"Not as much as it sounds." Leah took a bite of eggs. "I guess I make it sound like I slept with lots of guys, but I haven't. I hate for you to think I'm loose."

"Do you mind me asking how many?"

"Just three. Not too bad, huh? How many women have you slept with?"

"Three too."

"Your wife is one, who are the other two? Is one of them … well, I shouldn't say."

Denver wondered who Leah would think he had slept with besides Eliza. "Go ahead, I'm curious."

"You remember how Tess interrupted us last year at your house when we were kissing on the sofa?"

"What about it?"

"You remember how she put that flag on your pontoon boat?"

"What about it?"

"And don't forget how she called me last weekend to see if I went fishing with you, then said she would speak to me *never*."

"What about it?"

Leah turned in her chair to face him. "Don't take this the wrong way, but is something going on between you two? She's gorgeous, I'll admit, but that 'speak to me never' remark means her wit is as sharp as a razor. I'm not like that—what you see is what you get—but you might prefer someone like her—someone who turns on your brain as well as your body."

Leah's admission surprised Denver. She always seemed so confident and self-assured, and now she didn't. "Hey," he said, fingering her hair from her cheek. "Don't talk like that."

"It's the truth. I can't begin to compete with someone like Tess."

"You don't have to. You're great just like you are."

Leah lowered her head. "I don't always feel like it."

Denver lifted her chin. "Where's this coming from, Leah? I never saw you like this before."

"You said you wanted to take it slow. That means getting to know all of my moods."

"I happen to like your moods. I know how it feels to be down from when I was a shy kid in high school."

Leah smiled, mostly with her eyes. "You sure were shy. I dropped my books by you at your locker one day so you'd pick them up for me. You just ignored them."

Happy to see Leah smile again, Denver kissed her—just a slow, soft, sensual joining of their lips. "I'm not ignoring you now. Hey, my sister's getting married in two weeks. Say you'll be my date to the wedding and reception, how about it?"

"The wedding too?"

"If you want to."

"Let me know the time and place and I'll meet you at the reception. I can go for some food and you, but not standing around a bunch of strangers." Leah turned back toward the table, started to raise eggs for a bite, and stopped. "I guess Tess will be there."

"She's the maid of honor."

"Great. With my luck she'll catch the bride's bouquet and you'll propose." Leah took the eggs while Denver swallowed ham, which had cooled. She drank coffee. "Despite how I sound, if I thought you and Tess or another woman would be happy together, I'd be pretty low to not want that."

Denver gave her a quick hug. "Dang. You sure keep rising on the sweetness gauge, don't you?"

Leah cut her eyes at him. "Keep it up. I'll have you back in my bed, and I don't mean for sleeping."

They returned to their food. When they were done, Leah refilled their mugs. They took them to the balcony outside the sliding glass doors, where they sipped without talking.

Denver slipped his arm around her shoulders. What a great woman, one who would be happy for him even if he married someone else. Few people, man or woman, would feel like that.

The sun rose higher in the sky, blue and clear. A pontoon boat passed, leaving a wake that made twin Vs as they left the aluminum floats. Cars came and went on the two bridges, and Denver could barely hear the roll and thump of the tires across the expansion joints in the sections of concrete. Leah's head rose. He followed her gaze to a pair of ospreys circling overhead, distant white dots painted into the blue sky.

As sudden as a summer storm coming down the lake, sadness engulfed him.

How many days had he and Eliza spent like this on the lake, either in the pontoon boat or the canoe? Too many to count, filled with smiles and laughter and kisses and making love late at night after returning home with the sun and fresh air in their hair, cheeks red from forgetting to reapply sunscreen.

Yes, she had parted the bars of Denver's prison of fear in his mind, to peek out and make him believe she could love him again, could consider having a family again.

But with that belief, with that hope, the sting of reality hit him behind the eyes like two frigid ice picks piercing his optic nerves. What was she doing with that man in Ohio, whose wife was in a coma and whose son Eliza had taken as a replacement for Lily?

Denver kissed Leah's cheek.

God help him if he ever saw Eliza again, like at Willow's wedding or reception.

Yes, God help him, because he had no idea what he would do, where it would go, or how it would end.

But he knew it wouldn't end well, and that was cold, hard fact.

Anna

Walking the halls of the long-term care facility beside Josh, Eliza held David's hand. As soon as they had entered the double-glass doors, he had asked about the smell, a mix if disinfectant and wax from the shining linoleum floors. He peered up at her, not knowing what to expect despite Josh telling him how Anna would look different from not being able to eat for so long. "Does she still look like my mama?" he asked.

"Of course she does," Josh said.

At home, although Josh had told Eliza how Anna's hair had grown back after the surgery, which had reduced the pressure on her brain from the accident, he hadn't told David, not wanting to explain something as graphic as surgery to the four-year old.

An elderly man slowly rolled toward them in a wheel chair. Sock feet with red rubber nubs on the soles pulled him along with a hesitant shuffle. Deep lines creased his face, creating chasms of crow's feet in the corners of his eyes. David squeezed Eliza's hand. "Don't worry," she said, "he won't bother you. He's just old like we'll all be one day."

As the man neared, David went to him. "Hi, I'm David."

The man's flaccid lips smiled to reveal pink gums. "Hello, young fella." He offered a wrinkled hand, spotted from a lifetime's worth of sunshine, knuckles swollen and twisted from arthritis.

David shook it once and let go. "How fast can you make your chair go?"

"Not sure. I'm pretty much a turtle these days."

David touched a swollen knuckle. "Do you hurt? My meemaw hurt and went to Heaven. She don't hurt no more now."

The man's eyebrows, gray and prickling this way and that, raised. "That's a nice way to put it, David. You here to see your grandpa?"

"My mama's here."

"I'm sorry to hear that. If she's as sweet as you, you got a fine mama."

Eliza knelt by David and the man. "He's the sweetest boy I ever met. His mama's a fine woman too."

"Glad ta hear it, glad ta hear it. Nice meetin' you, David. I better scoot along for lunch." The man shuffled his wheelchair away.

David waved and took Eliza's hand. "He's a nice man."

Josh patted his head. "You made him happy, Son. I'm proud of you."

"Papa?"

"What?"

"Where's that man's little boys and girls? They should take him fishing like you take me."

"They're grown and working like I do."

"Can't they visit?"

Josh faced Eliza. "He sure can ask some interesting questions."

"He is so sweet, Josh. He talks to people wherever we go in town. Before you know it, they're smiling and talking back."

David tugged Eliza's hand. "Let's go. I wanna feed Mama lunch."

Josh led them to Anna's room. Inside, she lay propped up on pillows, no feeding tube in her nose, thank goodness. She smiled softly, but the left side of her mouth didn't quite rise even with the other side. Holding out her hands, she curled her fingers as if she wanted to hold David, but the fingers of her left hand weren't curling like those on her right hand.

Josh lifted David onto the bedside. He hugged her neck while her thin arms encircled his back, tears glistening in her eyes.

Eliza turned so Anna couldn't see her and so David wouldn't hear. Better keep her voice down too. "Josh, what's wrong with her mouth and hand?"

Josh stepped closer. "The doctors think the damage to her brain caused a stroke."

"Do they think she'll get better?"

"One doctor says no, another says yes, another says maybe. I didn't tell David because I don't want him to think she's hurting."

"How's her rehab going?"

"Not bad." Josh blinked several times, a man seriously worried about his wife. "The doctor that said she won't get better thinks she'll never walk again." Josh blinked again. A tear rolled down his cheek. "A specialist I got a second opinion from says she could have more mini-strokes. He's not too worried about that, but he is about a major stroke. He says she's too weak to survive it."

Eliza rubbed his shoulder. "I'm so sorry, Josh."

A woman came in with a tray of applesauce, green beans, and a small salad. Eliza raised her hands toward Anna. "Time for lunch I see."

Anna nodded slowly. The woman moved a table over the bed and set the tray down. She faced Eliza and Josh. "I wish I knew sign language. It breaks my heart that I can't talk to Anna. She's as gentle a soul as I've ever met. She goes through her rehab without a sound." The door closed behind her.

Josh went to the bed and signed, "Your lunch looks good."

David forked green beans, put them down, and twisted his head around toward Eliza. "Can you sign a blessing?"

Eliza joined them. "I sure can." She signed what David wanted for Anna, who ran her fingers through his hair and then faced Eliza.

"I can do it."

Remembering how Anna had learned many signs from Josh, including many more from a book she had at home, Eliza bowed her head.

A small hand lay on her arm. "No, Mama, you gotta watch."

Eliza raised her head. "I do, don't I? Thank you for reminding me."

He faced Anna, who raised her hands. "Thank you, God. Thank you for my son. Thank you for my husband. Thank you for Eliza." She pointed at the green beans on the fork in her plate, then raised her hands again. "Thank you for droopy green beans." She smiled again, soft and gentle at her own humor.

Josh laughed and so did she, low in her throat. "What a wonderful wife," he signed. "What would I do without you?"

"What would you do without Eliza?" Anna signed. "Without her, my house would be a mess."

David pulled her hands down and raised his own. "No more signs. Time to eat. You come home." Still learning, David's signs were a little slow, but his small hands had formed them perfectly.

As he fed Anna, Eliza motioned Josh away. At her side, he leaned close again. "I was so stupid to blame God for the accident. Even if He takes Anna one day, every minute I have with her is a blessing." He paused to look at Anna and David, who was feeding her applesauce. "That boy of ours is a blessing too. All I want is for him to be happy no matter what."

"Maybe she won't have a major stroke," Eliza whispered. "Maybe that doctor is wrong."

"I hope so," Josh said, his voice low. "If not, they might as well dig a grave for me too."

Eliza empathized with Josh. She had felt the same thing at the cemetery while she lay by her daughter's grave, hugging that small mound of red dirt.

Josh went back to the bed. Eliza sat in a chair in the corner. What a wonderful—

Husband?

Denver.

She had been so unfair to him. He had cried at losing their daughter as much as she, but all she had known was her own pain.

Her black hair fell across her shoulders now, growing several inches since she had left home. She twisted a lock around her finger.

Could she and Denver somehow find their way back to each other again, past the pain, past the heartache, even past her leaving and sending him those divorce papers?

She could find out if she went to Willow's wedding. No, no, not at all. He hated her by now, like her entire family hated her, possibly even Papa, who she had always counted on for a sympathetic shoulder while growing up deaf.

Willow's invitation was in the nightstand drawer by the bed. Tear it up and throw it in the trash when they got back. Tear it into the tiniest bits possible, bits so small and insignificant, even the memory of them would disappear like a December snow melting into frostbitten grass on a sunny morning.

Eliza got up to join Josh, Anna, and David again, raising her hands. "Anna, when you get home, I want to paint a family portrait for you."

"That's right," Josh signed. He faced Anna. "I forgot to tell you, Eliza is teaching David to paint."

"Very good," Anna signed. "He can teach you to paint the kitchen."

Josh laughed. "All right, all right. As soon as you come home and can help."

"And the living room."

"Okay, that too."

"And—"

Josh covered her hands with his and kissed her gently. "I love you, Anna."

Tears filled Eliza's eyes. "I'll—I—"

David looked at her. "What's wrong, Mama?"

"I got something in my eye. I'll go to the car and use the mirror to check."

Ignoring Anna's signs about a mirror in the bathroom, Eliza hurried into the hall, where her flats slapped the linoleum on the way to the parking lot. In the car, she took several tissues to her eyes. What a wonderful love Josh and Anna shared, a love like she and Denver once had shared. It was all gone now, faded like red, orange, and gold leaves in late fall, when a sudden wind clattered them together in the sky.

She had completely ruined her life. All she had left now was her love for David, and when Anna got better and came home, that would be gone too, leaving her with nothing more than an empty heart, no home, and no Denver.

reception

Standing by Denver in the back yard of the old golf club manor house, Leah leaned close. "I should've gone to the wedding. I could've caught the bouquet instead of Tess."

Although Denver had no trouble understanding the meaning of Leah's statement, he hoped she was joking. "Hey, what happened to taking it slow?"

"Just teasing, Mr. Serious. If you can't take a joke, you shouldn't have told me." Leah turned toward Tess. "I love her dress."

Denver said nothing. If he were honest, Tess outshined every woman at the reception, but he didn't want Leah to think she didn't look nice, which she did. Tess, though, looked amazing.

Across the yard, standing in the shade of a huge oak, she wore tiny white flowers woven into her auburn hair. The shining waves fell about her shoulders, bare because of the strapless dress in shimmering green clinging to her hourglass figure. The neckline fell across her cleavage, and a gold pendant, two hearts joined together, hung there from a fine chain. The dress fell to just below her knees. On her feet, open-toed high heels in green matched the dress. Beside her, wearing tan slacks and a navy-blue golf shirt, Mark studied the growing crowd.

"I see you looking at Tess," Leah said. "She's stunning, isn't she?"

Denver turned his back to Tess and looked Leah up and down. "I don't know. Those tanned feet of yours that match that slinky red dress with those spaghetti straps, not to mention the matching nail polish on all your nails, is as hot as hot gets."

Leah shook her head. "My tanned feet don't match my dress. The polish on my toenails matches my dress."

"You know what I mean. Is it my fault I get all confused when I look at you?"

Leah kissed his cheek. "I'll take that as a compliment."

From the side of the house, Willow and William, her new husband, entered the yard to a round of applause. She hurried straight to Denver and hugged him. "You did a great job of giving me away."

William offered his hand. "Can I give her back if she starts nagging me?"

Denver released his hand. "Oh, no, she's all yours now."

William gave Willow a quick kiss. "And I couldn't be happier." He faced Leah. "Willow told me you two were dating. He cupped his hand to his ear. "Do I hear wedding bells in your future?"

From behind Willow and William, Absalom and Oneita joined them. "Congratulations," Absalom said. "Oneita and I can attest to the happiness that marriage can bring."

Oneita, who stood almost two feet shorter than Absalom, looked up at him. "Our marriage is fine except for when this big old bear of a man takes all the covers on a cold winter night. I have to go get my own when that happens."

Absalom wrapped a huge arm around her shoulders and pulled her close. "Tell a tale, Oneita. You just snuggle up to me all the closer." He faced a table filled with food. "Who's ready to eat? I see prime rib over there."

"Go ahead," Denver said. "Leah and I will be over in a bit."

William licked his lips. "That prime rib does look good."

Willow smiled at Leah. "Men—always thinking with their stomachs."

"I could go for some juicy red meat myself," Leah said. She patted Denver's shoulder. "Willow, keep an eye on my date while I fill a plate. He's been checking Tess out, and I would hate to lose him."

As Leah left, Willow faced Denver. "She seems nice, not that you introduced us."

"Sorry about that. I already told you about her anyway."

Willow tilted her head toward Tess. "Is something going on between you two?"

"I'm not sure what you mean." Denver looked across the yard at Tess, whose back was to him.

"That's what I mean," Willow said. "Neither of you have spoken to each other, either here or at the wedding."

"No reason. I've been busy, she's been busy. No reason."

Willow turned to survey the crowd. "I was wondering if Eliza might come."

Denver huffed a hard breath. "You need to forget Eliza and I getting back together. She made her choice and she's got to live with it."

"I guess so." Willow looped her arm under his. "Escort your sister to that table before my husband eats all the prime rib. He's a red meat man like you are."

At the table, Willow filled a plate and joined William at another table. Denver did the same, joining Leah at a table to one side of where the band was setting up and doing sound checks.

Across the yard at another table, Tess and Mark were eating. Tess was sitting with her back to Denver again.

Slicing a thick piece of prime rib, Denver swore under his breath when the plastic knife broke. Tess could ignore him all she wanted, but the first chance he got, even if he had to wait until dark and drag her into the grove of oaks behind the band, he would. They needed to settle the mess between them one way or another—and tonight.

"Do you two mind if we join you?" With a meager plate of food consisting of all vegetables, Jan sat beside Denver.

"Denver," Akina said, sitting between Jan and Leah, "how do we get it into Jan's head that protein is important?"

Denver was glad he had already told Leah about dating Jan. As far as Akina, no one knew about him sleeping with her except Tess. Since both bits of information were safe, he wasn't worried about any revelations tonight.

Leah waved a piece of rare prime rib on a fork. "C'mon, Jan. get with the program. Don't you like a nice hunk of beefsteak?"

"If you mean like my ex you're dating, I sure do. When will you two break up so I can get him back?"

Akina finished a swallow of iced tea. "No way, Jan. My old sign language partner is a one-woman man."

Denver smirked. "Right now I'm a three woman man. It's too bad my bed won't hold four people."

Drinking white wine, Jan stopped. "You wish."

Leah leaned close to Denver's ear. "Darn right you're a one-woman man," she whispered. "The problem is who that woman is."

Denver said nothing. Leah obviously meant Tess again. He kissed her cheek leaned close to her ear. "Hush with that, okay?"

"What are you two whispering about?" Jan said.

"Maybe they're whispering about how Denver left me without a room-mate to pay my rent," Akina said. She aimed a fork his way. "The rest of your stuff's in my car. I'll drop it off later, if that's okay."

"Good idea," Jan said. "All four of us can take this party to that huge lake house and see if we can fit into Denver's bed."

Facing Denver, Leah twisted her lips into a frown.

"Aww, I'm just teasing," Jan said. "Did you two have plans for tonight?"

Leah rubbed Denver's shoulders. "You never know, right Denver?"

He stood. "Right now I'm planning to get some of that banana pudding I saw on the table." On the way, he detoured through the crowd to Tess's table and sat. She whirled toward him. "Seat's taken."

"Hey, Mark," Denver said. "I'm sorry about our misunderstanding at Tess's birthday party. As you might know from playing music with her, she can bring out the worst in people."

Tess's cheeks blazed red. "Didn't I say that seat's taken? I distinctly remember saying that seat's taken." She faced Mark. "Didn't I say that seat's taken?"

"See what I mean, Mark? Y'all have a nice night." Denver continued to the food table and piled banana pudding in his plate. As he did, one of the bandmembers stepped to the microphone. "Good evening, everyone. Congratulations to Willow and William. May everyone looking for love find it like they have. Here's the song for their first dance of the night, *Unchained Melody.*"

At the first words, Denver threw his plate in the trash and hurried to his pickup, parked across the road from the old manor house. Inside, he took a paper towel from a roll he kept behind the seat for cleaning the windows and sobbed into it. Despite being in the pickup, the words of the song made him cry even worse.

What a mess he had made of his life, torn between Eliza and Tess, missing them both, needing their touch, wanting them to come home to him.

He ripped off more paper towels.

Hell no, not Eliza. He was done with her, done with the pain and heartache she had put him through. He loved Tess now, and she would know it before this night was over. They would make plans to date, to tell Absalom and Oneita, to let the entire town of Clarksville know how much they cared about each other.

A tap came at his window. Leah opened the door. "Are you okay?"

"I'm—" Denver couldn't lie. "That song makes me think about Eliza."

"Do you want her back after all this time, even though she divorced you?"

"Look, Leah, what I had with her will never go away. All I can do is try to find it with someone else."

Leah palmed his cheek. "You are such a sweetheart, you know that?"

"A damn fool is more like it." Denver wiped his eyes. "How could I fall in love with someone who would hurt me so much? I trusted her completely. I thought she loved me as much as I love her."

Leah took her hand from his cheek. "Love or loved? If you still love her, how do I know you won't hurt me like she hurt you?"

Denver held her face in his hands. "Look at you, sweet and caring." He lowered his hands. "Eliza and I fell in love over time. If you and I have a chance, it'll take time too. That's why I want to take it slow. There's no guarantees we won't get hurt, but I'm willing to take that chance if you are."

Leah took his hand. "I guess I can do that. Let's start by dancing."

Denver closed the pickup door and walked with her back to the manor house. At least that song had ended, and he wouldn't have to worry about crying like an idiot over Eliza anymore.

As they neared the crowd, the band struck up the song *Hot Blooded*, by Foreigner. Several couples, including Willow and William and Tess and Mark, gathered on the close-trimmed lawn, where they whirled around each other while raising their hands and shaking their hips.

"Wanna give it a shot?" Leah asked. "I'm not much into fast dances."

"Me neither," Denver said. "Maybe when they play the next slow song."

They returned to their table. "Do you want something to drink?" Leah asked. "I see wine and champagne and beer on the drink table."

"I'm okay without it if you are." Denver pointed. "Look at Absalom and Oneita dancing. They look like they're trying to shake the last of their Amish ways out of their behinds."

Leah giggled. "That's nothing. Check out Willow backing her butt up to William. I can tell what they've got on *their* minds for later."

Denver laughed, which felt great after crying in his pickup. He stood. "C'mon here, you hot blooded chick, let's bust a move." He led Leah near Tess and Mark. Time to give her a dose of her own medicine.

The song ended before they could start dancing, and the band played the first notes of *I Only Have Eyes for You*, the song he and Tess had slow danced to at the restaurant in the mountains, where he had taken her for her seventeenth birthday.

Denver slipped his hands around Leah's waist. She pressed close to him, bringing with her the sweet aroma of perfume. Behind Denver, someone tapped his shoulder. "What's the chance I can cut in, Denver?"

Denver faced Mark, who offered his hand to Leah. "I hope this doesn't sound too corny, but where have you been all my life?"

Leah didn't take the hand. "Sorry, maybe later."

Denver turned Leah away, but Mark followed.

"Seriously, if there's another woman here you can compete with, I haven't seen her yet."

A grin teased Leah's lips. "Oh, so you mean you only have eyes for me, right?"

"Pretty much." Mark offered his hand again. "I'll get down on my knees and beg if I have to."

Leah took his hand. "I guess I better, Denver. I can't turn down an offer like that."

Left by himself in the middle of the crowd, Denver looked for Tess. A finger tapped his back. "Jerk."

Denver turned to face Tess. "Jer-kette."

"Well?"

"Well what?"

"Are we gonna dance, or are we gonna stand out here looking like two idiots who hate each other?"

"I'm not sure, not after you've ignored me all night."

"Fine." Tess turned to leave.

Denver grabbed her hand and whirled her into his arms. "I changed my mind."

She joined his rhythm, smooth and slow. Pressing his hands into the small of her back, he buried his nose into her hair to breath in the familiar floral aroma of her shampoo. "Can we stop our feud and make up?"

"Why should I when you brought that brunette hussy here?"

"Cut it out. Leah's a great person."

"Did you propose yet?"

Denver placed his lips near Tess's ear. "Not when I only have eyes for you."

"Bull."

He raised his head to find Mark and Leah, both smiling and talking. "It looks like our dates only have eyes for each other."

"Whatever."

"You need to stop all that."

"Why?"

"Did you forget what I told you in your bedroom at your birthday supper?"

"Refresh my memory," Tess said, almost growling. "All I remember is you and Mark acting like idiots."

Denver popped her bottom. "Stop growling at me. Let's start with this—we both know you aren't dating Mark and I didn't sleep with Leah on the night we went fishing, which is why our feud started to begin with. Do you think you can admit that and forget it?"

"Then what?"

"We date like we said we would."

"And if I don't, I guess you'll keep dating Leah."

"Hey, if you don't want to give us a chance, she will. I told you how I want to get married again and have a family."

"Why her?"

"Why not her?"

"Despite sounding like the proverbial broken record, you and my dumb sister need to get back together."

"That's not happening and you know it."

The song ended, and the band went right into another slow song. Denver lowered his lips to Tess's ear again. "I love you, okay? You make me happy in more ways than Eliza ever did."

Tess lay her head on his shoulder. "You make me so mad."

"Because?"

"Because I have to admit I love you too."

A sudden warmth burst inside Denver's chest, a warmth that burned the pain of losing Eliza from his heart. "I guess people would go nuts if we kissed."

Tess gave his butt a quick squeeze. "Soon, baby, soon."

Denver laughed. "So I'm your baby now? I've never been called that before."

Nuzzling his neck, Tess squeezed his butt again. "If you thought our night together in December was great, you ain't seen nothing yet."

A finger tapped Denver's shoulder. "Do you mind if I dance with my daughter?" Absalom asked.

Beside him, Oneita offered her hand to Denver. "Which leaves you to me, young man."

* * *

Absalom placed his hands on Tess's waist and steered her away from Denver and Oneita. They both had seen his and Tess's intimate dancing, and it was past time to talk to them about their feelings for each other.

Tess looked up at him. "I know what you and Mama are doing."

"Oh? What might that be, young lady?"

"Your Papa and Mama tones gave you away. You do know I'm eighteen, so I can ignore you now."

Absalom didn't care for Tess's statement. Of everyone in his family, she had left the Amish ways the fastest, turning headstrong and wearing revealing clothes and listening to music he and Oneita didn't approve of. At least she didn't listen to anything that couldn't be played in public, which some of the members of the golf club had told him about.

"You can ignore us all you want," he said. "What we want to know is exactly how serious you and Denver are, and when it happened."

"When y'all went to Kansas last year, the morning after Eliza left Denver. He was a mess, so I helped him through it."

"I can see that. Now, exactly how close are you?"

"We want to date like normal couples and see how it goes. Do you mind?"

"It's a bit strange since he was married to your sister."

"*Was*, Papa. If she doesn't want to make Denver happy, I will."

Absalom pulled away to look into Tess's eyes. "You're my daughter, I don't want you to get hurt. What if Eliza moves back here one day and decides she wants him again?"

"Denver is as sweet as he can be. She'll have a fight on her hands if she tries that."

"It sounds like you love him."

"And if I do?"

Absalom pulled her to him for a hug. "Please don't talk like that to me, Tess. All your mama and I want is for all of our children to be happy." He eased away to look into her eyes again. "Don't you know that?"

Tess blinked once, again, and again, and a tear rolled down her cheek. "I'm sorry, Papa, I know that. It's just … well, it's just this past year has been terrible in so many ways. The first time

I saw Eliza and Denver together, with how they looked at each other, it made me think, 'now that's love, and that's how I want a boy to look at me one day.'"

Absalom kissed her forehead. "I remember you saying that when we were talking to Eliza and Denver on Jon's laptop at his house. I don't blame you for wanting a love like that. Who in their right mind *doesn't* want a love like that?"

"Then you don't mind if we date?"

"Somehow," Absalom said, trying not to grin, "I think it's gone farther than simple dating."

Tess grinned. "Listen to you, always the wise Papa I love so much. We just told each other how we feel, but we want to date and do things out in the open. You know, like I just told you, like normal people."

"I understand, Tess, I understand." The music ended. Absalom released his daughter's waist. "I suppose your mama has given Denver an earful about how he better not hurt you. Go on and dance with him and tell him I said you two can date."

Tess kissed his cheek and hurried to Denver. Oneita went to the food table for tea. Absalom strolled away from the crowd. Except for the circles of light from the lights hanging around the yard, darkness had fallen. At a bench in the deep shadows of an oak, he sat.

Behind him, in tall grass, a cricket chirped, followed by another and another. A warm breeze, possibly the last of the evening, blew from the direction of the ninth green, over by the parking area across the road, bringing the aroma of freshly mown grass. To him, this was the best time of the day, when the world hushed, when the busy day quieted, when he could consider his life with Oneita and his children, including everything he wanted for them.

Guests he didn't know strolled past him on their way to leave, evidenced by vehicle engines starting. The band started the soft notes of another slow song, perfect for young people falling in love to dance by. It was a good thing Ivy was sleeping over at a neighbor's home, with a child her age. If not, she would've been whining about being tired by now.

In the back yard, couples joined: Willow and William, smiling and talking, pausing to kiss. Mark and Leah—what a shock—but maybe she had seen Tess and Denver together and knew she had better bow out before she got hurt. Barely visible in the shadows of a grove of oaks behind the band, Tess raised on tiptoe to kiss Denver, auburn hair catching the light just so. Yes, young people either falling in love or learning about each other, hopefully on their way to falling in love.

Absalom leaned over to place his elbows on his knees and hang his head.

But what about Eliza? Was she happy with her life, whatever it was? The thought made Absalom wipe his eyes and nose. How he loved her. How he loved her.

"Papa?"

Absalom knew that voice. He had heard it when she had started cooing at two-months old, babbling at six-months old, saying "Papa" at ten-months old, and "Mama" at a year old.

He wiped his eyes again. But one night not long after her third birthday, she came to his bed and tugged his hand. "Papa, I'm hot." He lit the kerosene lamp on the nightstand to see watery eyes and swollen eyelids, to hear her stuffy nose and sneezes, to touch her forehead and recoil at the heat within her baby-soft skin. He woke Oneita. They filled their galvanized bathtub with water and lay her in it up to her neck. The water grew warm before she grew cool, shortly before sunrise. She slept. Flat red spots started at her hairline and continued along her forehead, face, and neck. Soon she looked like someone had stuck her with a pitchfork instead of haybale, but thousands of times instead of once. She grew hot again and stayed hot for six more days. The morning her fever broke, she looked around her room, wild-eyed, then slapped her ears and screamed, "Papa! Papa! Papa! I can't hear you! I can't hear you! I can't hear you!"

Absalom choked back a sob and stood to face Eliza behind him, next to the trunk of the huge oak tree. "Eliza …" He couldn't say more because they were hugging each other. "Eliza, I've missed you so much … so much."

She pulled away. "I've missed you too, Papa."

Absalom held her face in his hands. "I haven't seen you in so long. Come out in the light and let me look at you."

"I can't. I don't want anyone to know I'm here."

He lowered his hands. "You're not back for good?"

"I just wanted to see you all, Papa. Is everyone well? Is Mama well? Is Ivy well?"

"She's growing up. She'll go to kindergarten this fall. She asks about you all the time. We tell her you're teaching sign language with Ethan."

Absalom looked behind him. Oneita was facing away, speaking with Willow. He couldn't see Tess and Denver. Maybe they were still hidden in the shadows of the trees. He faced Eliza again, about to ask if she wanted to see Denver. No, not only would her knowing about Tess and Denver break her heart, if she wanted Denver back, it would break Tess's heart.

"Denver's not here."

Standing on her toes, she dropped to her heels. "His pickup is in the parking lot."

Absalom hesitated. What to tell her? What to tell her? "Denver's dating someone. We met her at Lakefest last year."

"Ethan said something about it before I left. He also said Tess has a crush on Denver. Is there anything to that?"

"No, no, that's silly."

"I thought so too."

Absalom took her hands in his. "What's this about you living with that man whose wife is in a coma?"

"I didn't come here to talk about that," Eliza said, her voice hard.

"Ethan sent a photo of his face after you slapped him. He says you've taken that man's son to replace your daughter."

"Ethan doesn't know what he's talking about, Papa."

"Then tell me. I know you, Eliza, but it's hard to not believe what your situation looks like."

"I only came here to see you all because I miss you." Placing her hand on the tree, she stood on her toes again.

"You can get off your toes. Denver left with Leah."

"So, that's her name."

"She's a nice young woman Eliza. As much as I've always thought you and Denver belonged together, don't you dare come here with the intention of ripping his life apart again. He was with us on Christmas Day, when the divorce notice came. He almost fainted, he was so upset. Then he thought your mama and I were his parents and Tess was Willow. I thought he was having a nervous breakdown."

Eliza spun away and then back. Through the leaves of the tree, moonlight dappled her face, illuminating tear-stained cheeks. "I still love him, Papa. I've ruined—I've ruined everything." Her voice broke. She covered her face. Absalom wrapped his arms around her. Her knees buckled but he kept her from falling.

He let her get her cry out. "Eliza, I think it's best if you go home."

She uncovered her face. "I don't have a home, Papa."

"Then go somewhere where Denver isn't. I won't have you breaking his heart again."

"Papa," she whimpered, "what about my heart? I know I was wrong to leave Denver. Doesn't that count for something?"

"He's trying to rebuild his life. I was just sitting on the bench, thinking about how all I wanted was for all of my children to be happy. All of them are but you. I don't know how to make that happen, do you?"

Eliza fisted tears from her eyes. "I know *exactly* how to be happy." That hard voice again, hard as stone. She whirled and left, and Absalom collapsed to the bench.

The last time Eliza acted like this was when she and Oneita had argued on the day Eliza got her paintings for her first art show. She was like a wounded animal, hands signing as if they were claws to scratch out eyes and gouge out chunks of flesh. He had been afraid that day, afraid for Oneita and afraid for their family. Now he was afraid for Denver and Tess.

Car lights flashed on. A motor revved. Tires squalled on pavement.

His daughter drove off into the night, to who knew where, or to what end.

visit

At home after the reception, Denver kicked off his shoes in his room, twisted the top from a bottle of beer, and sat on the sofa with his sock feet on the coffee table. What a night, one he had never expected. Oneita and Absalom had given their blessing for him and Tess to date, and he couldn't wait.

In his room, where he had left his cell phone, it vibrated on the nightstand. Hoping it was Tess, he ran to check the screen. Leah. Wow. She had danced with Mark for every dance after his first dance with Tess, so Denver thought he was in the clear. He swiped the screen. "Hey, Leah. I hope you aren't—"

"Mad, right?"

"Well, yeah."

"I'm not mad. As soon as I saw you and Tess together, I knew I didn't stand a chance. Besides, like the song says, Mark only had eyes for me the rest of the night, and he's a great guy."

Denver dropped to the bed. "I'm sorry if you feel like I was leading you on."

"You were honest from the start. That's better than most guys. I'll see you around. I hope you and Tess are happy, you deserve it."

On the sofa again, Denver flipped TV channels and found nothing. He emptied the beer and threw the bottle away, returned to the living room and went to the fireplace mantel, where his and Eliza's wedding photo sat. Time to clean house.

In the basement, he covered all of Eliza's painting supplies with a tarp and gathered two carboard boxes. Upstairs again, he collected every photo of either him and Eliza or just Eliza and took them to an upstairs bedroom to leave in a dark corner. If he ever got the nerve to see her again, he would ask her if she wanted them, maybe by waving their wedding photo in her face and asking her if she regretted divorcing him yet.

Done with that chore, he took a shower. Beneath the spray of warm water, he yawned again and again. In bed, as the memory of Tess's kisses at the reception made him wish she was with him now, he turned off the nightstand lamp to go to sleep.

But he couldn't.

Never, not even if he lived to be a hundred, would he have thought his life would've taken so many strange and tragic twists in turns, and before he even turned thirty too, much less now at twenty-seven.

He rolled over to face the window. A river of silver, moonlight flowed into the room, moonlight like the night he and Eliza had swam in the lake after he had taken her on the pontoon boat for her first Lakefest fireworks show.

Like the moonlight flooding his room, memory after memory of Eliza flooded his mind. Clamping his eyes shut, he rolled away from the window and its glow of shimmering memories. What would it take to be rid of them once and for all? To be rid of Eliza once and for all?

A cool hand stroked his forehead. Warm lips kissed his cheek. The sheet raised, allowing chilly air from the air conditioner to embrace him. The sheet lowered again. A hand slid across his chest. A dream? Akina? Eliza? Tess? Leah?

"Are you awake, my sweet baby?"

Denver opened his eyes. Propped up on her elbow, Tess lay beside him, moonlight illuminating her auburn hair like the golden halo of an angel.

"What time is it?" he asked, rolling over to face her. "I must've been asleep."

"Two. I wanted to make sure Mama and Papa were asleep before I snuck out of the house."

"Did you drive?"

Tess tapped his nose. "No, you dummy, I walked. Just like I told you I was smart enough to get on the pill before we went to that cabin, I'm smart enough to not start a car engine and wake them."

"We didn't do anything in the cabin."

"You know what I mean."

"It's great they approve of us dating, but they wouldn't approve of you in my bed before we get married."

"Married? Is that a proposal?"

Denver couldn't see the teasing twinkle in her eyes, but he knew it was there. "You know what I mean, Tess the Mess. Wait a minute, how did you get in here?"

"I still have your spare key from when you gave it to me last December, when you asked me to watch the house while you were in D.C."

"Oh, I forgot." Denver raised the sheet. The moonlight penetrating the thin material revealed a bikini. "Pretty sexy there, Tessy. Are you gonna wear that on our honeymoon instead of a nighty?"

"Nope, nope, and nope." Tess kissed his cheek. "Your memory sucks. I once told you how I wanted to swim off your dock in the moonlight."

Denver fingered hair from her eyes. "No, you said you wanted to swim nude in the moonlight."

"And since it's August, we better get to it before the water turns cool." She got out of bed and pulled his hand. "C'mon, old man. I'm only wearing this bikini until we get in the water. I don't want to give any of your neighbors a thrill. Make sure you unplug those LED lights along the path to the dock too. I'd hate to see us on one of those video websites."

Denver got up. "There's enough trees to block their view."

"We can't be too careful. One might have one of those trail cams in a tree to spy on you, like hunters use for deer."

Denver grabbed her for a kiss. "How about we forget swimming and get back in bed?"

"And forget my fantasy? No way." Tess slipped her hand into his. "Let's go."

Under the deck, Denver unplugged the LED lights lining the path to the dock, leaving nothing but moonlight to show them the way. At the end of the dock, Tess looked around. "Lucky us. Like you said, the leaves on the trees block your neighbors view." She turned around. "You get the honor of unwrapping me."

Denver raised his fingers to the knot in the center of her back, untied it slowly, and slipped the straps from her shoulders, which glowed in the moonlight. He moved her hair aside and kissed her neck, nuzzled her ear and worked his way to the curve where her neck joined her shoulder. Leaning her head back, Tess shuddered. "Oh, wow, baby, you really know how to give me chills."

'That's because you inspire me." Denver let her hair fall, kissed down her spine and to the dip in her back.

She lowered her bikini bottom, turned to lower his boxers. "I think we better swim before we forget why we came out here."

Tess dove into the water, sending a splash of glistening spray up from the glassy surface. Denver followed and caught up to her as she swam away, grabbed her foot and pulled her to him. She threw her arms around his neck and kissed him deeply, stopped to look him in the eye. "You really love me?"

Wiping water from his eyes, he nodded. "I do. You really love me too?"

"More than I ever thought possible. All I want is to make you happy and to have a great life together."

"You mentioned kids one time. When do you want to start?"

Tess pushed him way. "Swim to the dock." He did, and she followed. "Hold onto the cleat, baby, we're gonna practice."

Denver did as she said. Pressing smooth, slick skin against smooth, slick skin, she kissed him again. He buried his face into her neck. "I love you, Tess. Love you so, so much."

Afterward, they gathered their clothes and ran back to the house, toweled off and returned to bed. Denver turned the nightstand lamp on, propped himself up on his elbow to finger her damp hair from her face, and gazed into her green eyes. "Do you have any idea how happy you make me?"

The hint of a grin teased her lips. She rolled over on top of him. "I'm clueless, baby. You need to show me again."

Their lovemaking lasted longer this time. Denver stroked her back, rose to kiss her, rose to meet her slow but insistent rhythm until she collapsed onto his chest to whisper, "So, how much do I love you?"

He rubbed slow circles along her back, alternating between the sensual dip at her bottom and the rise of her shoulder blades. "I thought you wanted to know how much I love you?"

She raised up to look him in the eye. "You could roll me over and show me."

"Not tonight," he said, trying not to laugh. "I'm too pooped to show you anything."

"Okay, old man, I'll let you rest." She rolled to his side and snuggled into his shoulder. "I wish I didn't have to go."

"I wish you didn't either."

Saying nothing, Tess ran her fingertips along Denver's chest. With her head on his shoulder, her hair against his cheek, her fingertips running lightly along his skin, her smooth leg draped over his, he was as happy and as content as he had been since he and Eliza had lain like this. No, since he had taken her photos upstairs, he was happier, proven by how he could lay here and not think about her, including while he and Tess had made love.

He rolled over to face her, ran his palm along the rise and fall of her hip. "Leah texted me not long after I came home. She said she hopes you and I are happy."

Tess kissed his cheek. "I may have misjudged her."

"How so?"

"Did you see her and Mark dancing and talking?"

"Yeah, they were smiling non-stop. I hope they're happy too."

The *who-who-whooo* of an owl echoed in the oaks, and Tess smiled, even teeth shining in the lamplight. "Not who, Mr. Owl, Denver and me. We're happier than we've ever been before." She dug her fingers into Denver's ribs. "But I wouldn't mind being happy a third time if he would let me."

Denver grabbed her hands. "Sorry, not ticklish."

"Well, durn, that's no fun." She snuggled into his shoulder again. "Don't let this go to your head, but I knew we would make up."

"How so?"

"I just knew it. I wasn't as mad as I seemed. Well, not as mad as when I broke your guitar."

"Excuse me, Tess, you didn't break my guitar, you turned it into toothpicks."

Tess giggled. "I sure did, didn't I? Was anything salvageable?"

"The neck's okay. I put everything in the case and shoved it under the bed."

"Good. I'm working on another and I can use it."

Denver kissed her—long, warm, and deep. "You call me sweet. You're sweet."

"I don't believe you. You have to prove it."

"I already said I'm too pooped to—"

"Hush. I meant by telling me when you knew you loved me."

"Don't you have a clue? You should."

"Hold that thought," Tess said, hopping up. "Let's share a glass of milk. I'm craving some like crazy." She left and came back, set the glass on the nightstand, and sat up in bed. "Sit up here, old man." She took the glass and drank.

Denver kissed her milk moustache. "Mmm, it's a lot better like that." He drank and gave her the glass. "I'm not sure about you calling me 'old man.' It's not like I'm a hundred."

"You better get used to my teasing, Denny. I can think of worse names than that." Tess drank again. "Oh, I know when you thought you might love me. It was when you saw the headstone I got for Lily."

"Exactly. Between that and how you kept me from going crazy after Eliza left, including that plaster cast of Lily's hands and feet you gave me for Christmas, I knew we had some serious chemistry going on." Denver bumped her shoulder with his. "Your turn. When did you start having feelings for me?"

Drinking milk, Tess lowered the glass and licked her lips. "It sounds a little weird, but the first time I even thought about a guy in that way was when I saw you and Eliza smiling at each other when she came to get her painting for her first art show.

You two were so cute. All I could think was how I wanted a boy to look at me like that one day, and here you are, actually looking at me like that now." She put the glass on the night stand. "Now lie down here and tell me where we're going on our first date."

Denver did as she asked. "What do you like to do besides build guitars and sing? Are you going to keep playing with Mark?"

"I'm gonna stop."

"Not because of me I hope."

"I like building them better than playing and singing. Maybe I'll write a song for our first baby."

"Oh, Tess," Denver said, trying not to cry.

She propped herself up on her elbow, to wipe his cheeks, to kiss him again and again. "You are so sweet. Do you mind if we wait a while before we have kids?"

To clear the emotion from his voice, Denver took a deep breath. "Sorry about that. No, I don't mind. Heck, we haven't even had our first date yet."

Tess smoothed the hair across his forehead. "I don't care as long as I'm with you."

"How about a movie? Have you been to a theatre yet?"

"I'd rather watch something here with you."

"We could go out to eat."

"I don't know. After that place in the mountains, I'm not sure I would like anywhere else."

"How about to the beach for seafood? Virginia's eastern shore is known for that."

"I'd love to see a beach, but Mama and Papa wouldn't like us staying overnight. The only reason they let me go with you to the mountains is because they didn't know we were getting close. Now that they know —" Tess snapped upright in bed, the sheet falling from her chest. "I didn't tell you. I sold a guitar to a guy two months ago. He heard about them from a musician who bought one. The guy builds them too and wants me to tell him how I make my braces."

Denver sat up. "You better cover up. I can't take much of your ... you know."

Tess held the sheet to her neck with one hand while patting his head with the other. "Poor baby. Do I turn you on that much?"

"Dumb question, considering what we've been doing since you got here. You're not gonna tell the guy, are you? Maybe you can get a patent on your design." Denver paused. "What is it? I didn't know you were doing anything special."

Tess dropped the sheet. "Talk about special, huh?"

Denver pulled the sheet to her neck. "Stop that. What're you gonna do about the guy?"

"I called him and talked a while. He's got a huge shop in the Blue Ridge Mountains, not far from Charlottesville. I said I might drive up one day and check his shop out."

"Maybe in the fall." Denver licked his lips. He used to love it when Mom and Dad took him and Willow to the mountains for fresh apples. "For one of our dates, we can check out the leaves and get some apples."

Tess rolled toward the nightstand. "I better go, it's almost four. Mama gets up at five to make breakfast. She's still got *some* Amish in her."

Denver pulled Tess on top of him for a kiss. She sat up just enough so her hair formed a curtain of reddish gold around their faces. "I hear you, old man. I think you want some apples now, and I don't mean those from the mountains."

"No, I want to tell you I love you."

Tess lay on his chest and looked into his eyes. "I love you too." She lowered her head to his shoulder. "And I'll never, ever let you go."

Denver rolled her over, kissed her again, kissed her neck and worked his way to her navel and back up. "Well, well, the future Mrs. Andrews, I think this old man is young again."

homecoming

Driving to Josh's, Eliza glanced in the rear-view mirror. Behind her, Anna and David sat: her on the way home after two months of unsuccessful rehabilitation to help her walk again, him in his car seat, holding her hand.

Beside Eliza, Josh's head turned as he looked out the passenger window. Lining this stretch of road, red maples transformed from green to crimson. Fall was on the way in Ohio, evidenced by a recent first frost, which had coated the front yard in a crystalline white blanket that reflected the rising sun in rainbow hues.

Josh flexed his fingers. "Building that ramp for Anna's wheelchair wore me out."

Eliza glanced his way. His fingers seemed thinner than when she had first met him, his face too. He ate well though, so she saw no need for concern. Work on farms like his, especially since David was too young to help, kept many an Amish man at a lean weight.

She parked in the driveway and popped the latch for the trunk, then got out and took David from his car seat. Josh took

Anna's folding wheelchair from the trunk and helped her into it. "Welcome home, Anna." He kissed her cheek.

David patted her hand. "See your bridge, Mama?"

Anna raised her hands. "What?"

He raised his hands. "Your bridge. Papa made it."

Eliza wanted to kneel and hug him. He had been practicing signs for the last two months, eager to communicate with his mama.

"I see," Anna signed slowly, due to how the stroke had affected her left hand. "Did you help?"

"He did," Josh signed. "Until he hit my finger with a hammer while I held a nail."

"Papa, you said it didn't hurt."

"I'm teasing you, Son."

Like now, Josh and David sometimes forgot to sign while they visited Anna in the long-term care facility. Eliza translated for Anna, who laughed low in her throat.

"Let's get inside," Eliza signed and said. "It's chilly out here." She unlocked the door. David held it open while Josh rolled Anna into the living room. She pointed to the sofa, so Josh helped her onto it.

"Would you like some coffee?" Eliza signed.

"I know I would," Josh signed and said. "That stuff they serve in that facility is decent, but it's nothing like ours." He sat beside Anna and raised his hands. "I'm so happy you're home." The muscles in his throat worked with a hard swallow. Anna palmed his cheek and he fell into her lap, sobbing.

David climbed onto the sofa and hugged them both the best he could, one hand on her shoulder, the other rubbing Josh's back. "It's all right, Papa. It's all right."

Eyes blurring with tears, Eliza hurried to the kitchen. Anna, Josh, and David were her ideal of family, an ideal she once thought she would have with Denver.

Wiping his eyes, Josh came in. "I'm sorry, Eliza. As much as I pray for Anna to get better, I'm still filled with gratitude for how God has allowed her to come home."

Eliza gave him a paper towel and took one for herself. They wiped their eyes, and Eliza threw the paper towels away. "Josh, you're such a good father and husband. Would you mind if I hugged you?"

Josh chuckled. "I'm not sure about how good I am at anything, but you are an amazing woman to come here and help my family." He gave her a quick hug. "I don't mind a hug now and then. I've told Anna about your situation with your husband, and she said to comfort you any way I can."

Eliza fingered more tears from her eyes. "You and Anna remind me of how my husband and I once were. You make me believe I could have that again one day."

"With him or someone else? You never told me how your trip to Virginia went."

"I talked to my papa but not to anyone else. I told you how my sister-in-law was getting married, and I didn't want to intrude. All I really wanted was to see everyone I love again."

Josh filled the coffee maker with water. "How did it feel to see your husband?"

Eliza regretted not telling Josh about sending Denver the divorce papers, but she didn't care to deal with any questions he might ask. "I haven't seen him in a long time, so it was strange."

"Do you think you'll ever go back to him?"

Eliza measured coffee into the maker. "David is getting older now. He'll go to kindergarten next year. He's a smart boy, so he can help around the house by then, can't he?"

Josh pushed the button on the coffeemaker. "It sounds like you're planning to leave next year."

"I can't stay here forever."

"Does that have anything to do with all the paintings you've made? I know how you used to have art shows."

"I want to move back home eventually. Selling my paintings will help me afford a nice home."

Coffee dribbled into the decanter, an aroma Eliza loved because of how she and Denver would drink a second cup on the deck after breakfast on sunny mornings, sometimes regardless of the season. What would it take to return to that time again? One thing that might help was how she had already gotten over her anger at Papa for telling her to leave. One thing that didn't help was how Denver was seeing someone. Yes, she needed to paint and have art shows to get home and break Denver up with whoever he was seeing. To start, she needed to call Jan soon. It was a good thing Jon had said he would stop her from telling anyone about any future art shows. She probably went to Willow's wedding and would've told Denver otherwise.

The coffeemaker gurgled to a stop. Josh filled two cups." Do you want any?"

"Not right now. Do you remember how I wanted to do a family portrait for you?"

"It's a bit cold for that."

"It's just the first week of October. We'll have some nice days off and on until December."

Josh picked up the cups. "That's true."

He left for the living room. She went to her room to look through her paintings, which leaned against the wall by the dresser.

Most were of Anna's flowers at the end of the garden. Several included butterflies and dragonflies. She took her favorite to the bed and sat beside it, to touch the raised paint.

In glistening oil paint instead of water colors, David's blue eyes, with just a hint of gold around the centers, crinkled from a smile that had burned itself into her memory. The sun had dropped behind the trees past the garden, sending shadows along the lawn. David had pointed at two squirrels chasing each other and was telling Eliza how they were wrestling when she knew they had something else in mind. His cowlick stood up. A smudge of dirt from where he had wiped his nose with his fingers stained his upper lip. His small teeth, even like kernels of corn on the cob, were parted as he said, "Look, Mama. Those squirrels are wrestling."

Regardless of committing that moment to memory, including the dirty knees of his pants and the way the sinking sun shaded his brown hair with gold, Eliza had painted it to keep for herself. She might display it during a show, but no amount of money would ever buy it.

She touched the dirty knees, the even teeth, the blue eyes. How she would love to have a son of her own one day, a son who shared both her and Denver's colors.

Closing her eyers, she willed the sadness of the question away. It was time to be strong and call Jan soon, to schedule however many shows it would take to go home again.

Only then would she know her future—a future much more certain than hers had been when she left Denver so long ago.

She put the painting with the rest, closed the door and locked it, and lay on the bed to close her eyes again. Denver appeared within her mind—his smile, his sky-blue eyes, the way he looked at her that made her want to love him—whether they were on the pontoon boat, on the dock, or hiking in Occoneechee State Park. Back before things had gone so wrong between them, her desire for him could hardly be contained, as if it were the smoldering embers of a fire, ready to burst into flame and consume them both.

Imagining his kiss, Eliza touched her lips, and a searing heat filled her, centered below her navel. Unlike the last time she had attempted to make love to him, when she had vomited at the mere thought, which had made her pack and leave that night, could she love him now?

She closed her eyes tighter, imagined his features clearly, imagined him lowering himself onto her, imagined herself arching upward to join him.

She rolled from the bed and fell to her knees in the floor, hoping the pain of the wood against her kneecaps would end the overwhelming urge to vomit.

On the bed again, she sobbed into her pillow. She was sick, she was ruined. Something was twisted deep within the part of her that used to love it when she and Denver turned play into passion.

Done with her cry, she rolled over.

If it were the last thing she ever did on earth, she would end her revulsion at her and Denver's love making, no matter what woman stood in the way.

craftsman

In the passenger seat of Denver's pickup, Tess smirked at him. "What're you smiling about? You've been doing that for the last hour."

Denver cut his eyes her way. "I could be smiling at a lot of things."

"Like what?"

"Like how we didn't watch the movie on our first date. Like how you sneak over to my house every chance you get. Like how I caught the biggest catfish on our second date. Like how you wear the tightest jeans you own while we're working on your latest guitar because you know it drives me crazy. Like how the guy we're going to visit is dying to know your secret to making a guitar sound great. Like how you dance naked at the foot of my bed when I say I'm too tired to fool around again until we do. Like how—"

"Oh, hush. You love it when I dance naked."

"No doubt about it, Tess the Mess. No doubt about it at all."

Tess returned his playful expression. She had been thinking about something for a while, and it was time to mention it.

"Baby, we need to come up with a different pet name for me. I'm kind of getting tired of 'Tess the Mess.'"

"You mean like I'm getting tired of 'old man?' I could always call you 'old woman.'"

"Not if you want me to keep sneaking over to crawl in your bed you won't."

Denver winked. "Then I won't. What name do you have in mind?"

"I don't know, as long as it's sweet."

He pointed. "See that apple stand? Let's get a basket while I think about it."

He parked and they met at the front of his pickup, where he snapped his fingers. "Hey, I can call you Winesap. They're my favorite apples."

"Not very romantic, Mr. Andrews."

"Honeycrisp?"

"Better, but not good enough."

"Golden Delicious?"

"Even better, but still not good enough."

"Auburn delight?"

Tess snorted laughter. "Not bad, but it's too much of a mouthful."

Denver shook his head. "You sure are hard to satisfy."

"Look," she said, almost snorting laughter again, "we both know that's not true." She grabbed his hand. "Buy those apples. You can think about a name while we're on the road."

On the highway again, they each took an apple from the basket between them and crunched through the peeling to release the sweet, tangy flavor of Winesap apples.

To Tess's left, the hazy foothills of the Blue Ridge Mountains caught her attention. "If it weren't for the lake, I wouldn't mind living up here."

Denver swallowed apple. "I could give up a lot of things, but I couldn't give up the lake."

Except for the crunch of apples, they rode on in silence. Here and there, on the quiet two-lane highway, they passed oaks, maples, and hickories, their foliage beginning to turn red, orange, and yellow.

Tess put the apple cores in the floor to throw away letter. Denver kept his eyes on the road.

She loved him so much it hurt. For the longest time she wanted him and Eliza to get back together. That wouldn't happen now if she came back begging.

Denver looked her way. "What're you looking at?"

"I'm looking at my baby."

"Will you change my adult diapers when I'm an old man?"

"As long as I can pop your butt while I'm doing it."

Shaking his head, Denver laughed. "You know, I thought being in love was what I had with Eliza, but she's nothing compared to you."

Tess stopped smiling. "That's not true and you know it. You'll always love her, because she's you're first love like you're my first love."

Denver reached over to palm her cheek. "I didn't mean anything by it, except to say how much I love you."

Tess pressed her hand to his. "I love how you touch me. It makes me feel safe, like we're the only two people in the whole world."

"I'll always make you feel safe, Tess. To me you *are* my whole world."

Tess widened her eyes. "Wow, what a line. If you said it to get lucky tonight, consider it a done deal."

Denver nodded toward the windshield. "See that sign? Fork Union in ten miles. What's the guy's name anyway? You never told me much about him."

"Ezra Jefferson. He's eighty-three and lives on Lake Monticello."

"Jefferson? Mom and Dad took Willow and me to Monticello one time. He's not related to Thomas Jefferson, is he?"

"He didn't say."

"Is he married? Kids? Grandkids?"

"He didn't say."

Denver didn't ask any more questions, so Tess let the conversation end. She wished they couldn't spend the night at a hotel in Charlottesville, visit Monticello, and drive home the next day. On her nightstand at home, her latest book, about Thomas Jefferson and Sally Hemings, including how evidence suggested he fathered her children, intrigued her.

They entered the small town of Fork Union. To her right, several large buildings, one resembling a concrete apartment complex, with more stories and windows than she could easily count, caught her eye. "You've been through here before, Denver. What are all those buildings?"

Denver turned her way. "That's Fork Union Military Academy."

"Military? What kind of military?"

"It's a school for boys who need a little extra discipline before they go to college. When we drove through here on the way to Monticello, Dad threatened to send me there if I ever became a problem. I didn't want to leave the lake, so I never became a problem."

"What kind of problem?"

"The kind teenage boys can get into from peer pressure. I looked it up when we got home. It's structured to help boys learn responsibility. It's Christian-based too."

Facing the passenger window again, Tess caught a glimpse of a cross on a building. "I can see that, sort of like the Amish."

Denver continued down the road and took a left a few minutes later, on Thomas Jefferson Parkway. Tess noted the GPS stuck to the windshield and watched until the voice prompt said to take a right at a roundabout. They did, passed a church to the left, and continued along another two-lane road with trees on both sides.

At a spot with several stores flanking the road, Denver pointed to the right. "Hey, a pizza place and a drug store."

Tess pointed to the left. "A fire department too."

A few minutes later, the GPS said to take left onto a narrow gravel road. Tess glimpsed water through the trees until Denver pulled up to a huge log cabin with an upstairs. To its right stood an equally huge workshop, evidenced by a sign shaped like a guitar over the double-glass doors. Like the cabin, the workshop had an upstairs also.

Denver unbuckled his seatbelt. "Whoa. I didn't know building guitars was this lucrative."

Tess met him at the front of his pickup to poke his side "Look, this little Amish chick didn't go to college. What's 'lucrative' mean?"

Denver poked her back. "It means something that makes a lot of money." He took a few steps toward the shop and stopped. "I can see the lake behind the house. This place is great."

Tess joined him. "A dock with a pontoon boat too."

One of the double doors on the shop opened. A slender man with gray hair and a trimmed beard, who wore jeans and an apron to his knees, waved. "Tess and Denver, right?"

"That's us," Tess said.

"Good deal, y'all come on in."

Tess rubbed her arms. "I should've gotten my jacket out of the pickup."

Ezra held the door open. "Got the perfect remedy for goose bumps inside." Tess and Denver followed him in, where he led them to a cast-iron wood-burning stove with several ladder-back chairs around it. "Have a seat. This here's where some of my friends gather to pick and grin when we get the notion." He went to a counter. "Coffee? Tea? I just bought one of these new-fangled coffee makers that take what they call a pod instead of grinds."

"Coffee sounds great," Denver said.

"What kind of tea do you have?" Tess asked. "My mama likes one with herbs and mint."

Ezra turned a rack that held a number of plastic pods with foil seals. "Tea … tea … tea ..." He took one out. "Got one with rosehips and lemon for the lady pickers and grinners. That be okay?" Tess said it was. Ezra inserted the pod and closed the top. "Y'all take a look around while I tend to this."

Tess motioned Denver to walk with her. Along the walls of the shop, every type of woodworking machine needed to make musical instruments stood in rows: a band saw, planer, table saw, and tables for gluing bodies. From hangers in the ceiling, forms for shaping the curved sides of various sizes of guitars hung. On the far wall, clamps of every size filled a peg board.

Walking a bit stooped over, Ezra joined them with tea and coffee. "Did you notice how the inside space is smaller than the outside?"

Tess took her tea, the mug warming her hands. "Not really."

"I've got a spray room for the final finish on guitars through that door in the far wall. It has a ventilation system for it that carries the fumes outside, but we still wear some nice double-filtered masks so we don't breathe that stuff." He patted one of three belt sanders in the center of the concrete floor, beside three buffing machines. "See those hoses runnin' to the ceiling? They go to a vacuum system to pull out the wood dust. We still wear the masks to keep from breathin it."

Swallowing coffee, Denver lowered his mug. "I see steps in the corner by the window. What's upstairs?"

"I thought I might tempt a fine builder to stay here and work for me one time. He changed his mind at the last minute." Ezra waved them toward another door by the spray room door. "I've got a few toys almost ready. Let's take a look."

Inside the room, Tess counted. "Ten guitars and three mandolins? I didn't know you made those too."

Denver went to a mandolin hanging from the peghead by a wire from the ceiling. "That's some pretty work, Mr. Jefferson."

"Ezra, Denver. We don't stand on formality here."

"How many people work for you?" Tess asked.

"A crew of four. My wife, Bertha, is in town. She makes the crew lunch."

"Do you have any children and grandchildren working for you?" Denver asked.

"I'm 'fraid the good Lord didn't bless us that way. By the time we got it checked on, the doctors said it was my fault and it was too late to worry about." Ezra scratched his bearded chin. "We thought about adoption. I even told Bertha we could try a sperm bank, but she didn't want to go that route. She said as long as we have each other, that's all we need." Ezra led them back to the other room. The coffee maker, a refrigerator, and a table with chairs created a snug corner near the wood heater, where he and his workers must have lunch. He sat. "Rest your bones. Y'all had a long drive."

"About two hours," Denver said. "Not too bad."

One at a time, Ezra eyed them. "Is it me, or do I smell love in the air?"

Tess kissed Denver's cheek. "You've got an accurate nose, Ezra."

"Have you settled on a place to live yet? I've got ten acres on this end of the lake. I'd be glad to sell you a parcel for a nice house on the shore." Ezra paused to grin. "I might even give you a discount if you tell me how you make your guitars sound so fine."

"Isn't the area around the lake a subdivision?" Denver asked. "We saw all the houses on the way in."

"My family owned this land long before those folks started after me to sell. I made a nice profit and built this shop to pursue my hobby. Now I make a nice profit doin' somethin' I love. As you know, Tess, people don't mind payin' for fine craftsmanship."

"I know. My family left the Amish a while ago. My papa builds rocking chairs, foot stools, and outdoor furniture. His customers love his work."

Denver rubbed her shoulder. "The nut didn't fall far from the tree, Ezra. Tess can play and sing too."

Tess shook her head at him. "The word is 'acorn,' not nut, nut."

Ezra chuckled. "I love it when a couple can laugh together. Humor makes for a fine relationship."

The door opened. A woman with shoulder-length gray hair came in with two shopping bags. Khaki work pants and a red flannel shirt fit her medium figure. "I see your miracle guitar builder has arrived, Ez." She gave Tess and Denver a quick wave. "I'm this old man's better half."

"Nice to meet you, Bertha," Tess said. "This shop is amazing."

Bertha set the bags on the counter and took a chair between Tess and Ezra. "Did he charm your secret out of you yet?"

"Not yet."

Ezra glanced at Bertha. "I even offered her a lot on the lake in trade. Heck," he said, facing Tess, "you and your husband can even stay in the apartment upstairs while you get your new house built."

Tess raised her left hand. "We're not married yet."

Denver slid his arm around her shoulders. "We're working on it."

Bertha stood. "I was just about to make a sandwich. Can you stay?"

Denver set his coffee mug on the table. "Thanks, but we need to leave soon. I'd like to get back home before it gets dark and the deer start moving."

"Thanks for the coffee," Tess said as she stood. "It's been great meeting you both."

"Do I get to know your secret before you go?" Ezra asked.

Tess pushed her chair beneath the table. "We know the top can't be too thick, or it won't vibrate properly."

Ezra stroked his beard. "Yeah, no doubt about that. What kind of wood do you use for your tops?"

"I like Adirondack spruce."

"I do too. Some customers want Sitka spruce. Some want Engelmann. Some even want Ezo spruce from Japan, but that stuff's hard to find, and expensive."

"Well," Tess said, "it sounds like we're in the same ball park."

Ezra's white eyebrows raised. "Hmm, I guess you use all the standard tone woods for the backs and sides and braces too, like rosewood and mahogany and spruce."

"They all do everything I want them to do."

"And either ebony or rosewood fingerboards and mahogany necks. Do you custom carve the braces?"

"I know what it is," Denver said. "Tess puts a picture of her in a bikini in every case, and customers just *think* their new guitar sounds better."

Ezra snorted laughter. "I can't be doing anything like that, or they'll stop buyin' from me altogether."

Tess gave Ezra and Bertha a quick hug. They told her to keep in touch and followed her and Denver outside, where they said goodbye.

Minutes later, sleepy from the winding road, Tess yawned. She couldn't wait to get home to be with Denver tonight. Every touch, every kiss, every caress, every laugh, every gasp, every sigh afterward, every quiet conversation—sometimes with Denver setting his alarm clock so they could sleep in each other's arms until she had to leave—each and every one of those things were a sign of how much they loved each other. The only question now was when he would propose.

She yawned again and closed her eyes. Time for a nap.

surprises

As Denver left Fork Union, he glanced at Tess, whose head moved with the motion of the road. He turned the GPS on and chose a route he had never driven before, which would surprise her like she had never been surprised before, as long as she stayed asleep. Then again, good planning should make that possible.

An hour later they entered the outskirts of Richmond, where, due to it being Saturday, the traffic didn't aggravate Denver. An hour later they passed through Williamsburg. He was tempted to wake Tess and tell her how they would have to visit the colonial section one day, including Jamestown. Forty minutes later, as they started across the bridge from Hampton to Norfolk, Tess blinked and closed her eyes. "Mmm, that's what I get for watching that movie last night until three."

Denver grinned at her. He had suggested *Pretty Woman* after they had made love because he knew she would like it, along with hoping she would fall asleep for this drive—and her surprise.

Another forty minutes passed. He backed into a parking spot. "Hey, we're here."

Blinking and yawning, Tess couldn't find the button to release her seatbelt. "Would you please undo this thing for me?" She hung her head, hair hanging over her face.

"Tess?"

"What?"

"Do you trust me?"

"I'm too sleepy to talk. It's your fault for telling me about that movie."

"I didn't make you come over four nights in a row."

"Don't use that against me. It's not like you didn't enjoy it."

"Can you keep your eyes closed? I want to show you something."

"Not a problem if it's your bed. Then I can nap until I don't feel like a zombie."

Denver unclicked her seatbelt. "I'll help you out, be right back." He ran to the passenger door and opened it, took her hand and closed the door. "What do you smell?"

Tess's nostrils flared. "Why don't I smell the leaves in the woods around your house?"

"Try again."

Tess lifted her nose into the air. "I smell water, but it's not like the lake. I hear gulls, but the gulls that come to the lake in the fall sound like that too." She crossed her arms. "Don't laugh at me, you bozo."

Denver held her hand. "You might laugh when you find out where we are." He led her along a sidewalk. "There's a bench here. Sit and raise your feet so I can take your shoes off."

Tess sat and raised her feet. "Is a storm coming? I hear the waves by the dock and feel the wind."

Denver took her shoes off. "We don't usually get storms in October." He leaned over to slide one arm under her legs and the other around her back. "Grab my neck, I'm gonna carry you somewhere."

Eyes still closed, Tess yawned. "I hope it's back to the house and to your bed, and I mean to sleep."

Denver carried her about fifty steps and set her down. "What do you feel?"

Tess scrunched her toes. "The sand by the dock."

Grateful for how his plan had worked to perfection, Denver kissed her. "Open your eyes."

Tess did so. "Is it—we're at—are we really—"

Denver kissed her again. "Yep, we're at the beach. How do you like it?"

Tess ran to where the waves wet the sand with foam. "I love the lake, but this—this is amazing. I've never seen water without a bank on the other side." She whirled to run back to Denver and wrap her arms around his neck. "I don't know how I could love you any more than I do." She stood on tip toe for a kiss and to look into his eyes.

Denver kissed her nose. He could fall into her amazing green eyes forever and be happy. "You might love me more after a fresh seafood supper." He turned and pointed at the hotel behind them. "Then again, you might love me more in the morning, after you wake up in that corner room with the balcony. I got that room so we could watch the sun rise."

Tess pulled away. "You know we can't spend the night. Mama and Papa will have a fit. Besides, I don't have any clothes or bathroom stuff."

"All taken care of. Let's get your shoes and check in. Then I'll tell you how I worked this out." At his pickup, Denver opened the door to the back and took out an overnight bag from behind the seat. "Here's the same bathroom stuff you use at my house. We're only staying one night, so we can wear our jeans again. I brought you a blouse and me a shirt for tonight and for the drive home."

On the way to the hotel lobby, Tess looked up at him. "How did you get one of my blouses?"

"You don't remember wearing one of my white button-up shirts home one night? The sight of you in that and nothing else will always be seared into my memory."

"Oh, *that* night." Tess gave a little shiver. "It gives me the chills just thinking about it."

Denver opened the hotel door. "Me too."

In their room, he set the overnight bag on the bed. Tess opened a door. "No hot tub in the bathroom? Durn, I wanted to make Denver soup." She went to the sliding glass doors and opened the curtains. "Wow, what a view, nothing but sand and water as far as I can see." She closed the curtains and sat by Denver on the bed. "Spill it. What did you tell Mama and Papa so they won't kill me for spending the night with you?"

"You really don't think you could sneak to my house for two months and they not know, do you?"

"Mama caught me one morning when I was late. I told her I went for an early walk. I don't like lying, but I don't like being away from you either. Then she asked me why I was wearing the same clothes as the day before. Then she said whatever I was doing, I better be responsible."

"What did you do then?"

"What do you mean? I didn't admit it. I ate breakfast and went out to the workshop."

"What about that afternoon?"

"I worked until Papa told me to take a nap before I cut my finger off." Tess's mouth fell open. "That's right. If I stay late at your house, I yawn my behind off after lunch."

Denver patted her leg. "You finally got it. When I told them about this trip, they said they didn't like it, but they already knew you were sneaking over to see me. You should've seen them eyeing me like I was some kind of pervert. Then I told them how I wanted to be with you when you saw the ocean for the first time, and your mama looked at your papa and said, "Well, Absalom, I don't care to admit it to Denver, but it isn't like I didn't sneak out at night to see you when I was eighteen."

Tess covered a laugh. "Huh, maybe I get my devious ways from Mama. Then again, I saw some couples kissing when I was Amish. Most people outside the Amish think their strict ways mean they don't do things they shouldn't, and that's just not true for all of them."

Denver stood to open the overnight bag and took out a dark green sweater. He held it up for Tess to see. "I got this for you to wear out to eat."

"Why's the neck so baggy?"

"So I can see one of you bare shoulders with that gorgeous head of hair flowing over it."

Tess held the sweater to her neck. "It'll be interesting without a strapless bra."

Denver stood and took the sweater from her, pulled her hair aside and kissed her neck. "I'm not hungry yet, are you?"

"Oh, yeah," she murmured, tilting her head to one side while pulling his head lower. "I'm hungry for you."

* * *

Satisfied from both the delicious seafood and his and Tess's lovemaking, but rested from going to sleep early, Denver rose when his cell phone alarm beeped and took the present from a zipped pocket in the overnight bag. One more surprise to celebrate his time with Tess, and one to end his disaster with Eliza.

162

He opened the curtains to reveal the sliding glass doors. Beyond the aquamarine swells, the golden hint of a sunrise hinted at a new day.

In jeans, he took Tess the sweater, which would hang low enough to cover her bottom. "Wake up, sunshine. You need to see this."

She rolled over to finger her hair from her eyes, blinked and yawned and rubbed his chest. "Mmm, talk about a great night's sleep."

"Me too. Get up and put this on. We don't want anyone see us naked on the balcony."

Tess did so, but the sight of her legs below the sweater tempted Denver to take her to bed again. Instead, he took her hand and led her to the balcony, where he slipped his hands around her waist and looked over the top of her head at the rising sun.

She leaned back against him. "The sun is nothing compared to how you make me feel, baby."

Denver nuzzled her neck. "The sun shining in your hair looks like a halo."

Tess patted his hands at her stomach. "No angel here, baby."

"Yes, you are. You saved my life when Eliza left and you saved it again when she divorced me." He took the present from his jeans pocket and slipped it onto his pinky. "I'll call you angel on special occasions, like on our honeymoon night and every time our children are born. I'll call you sunshine for every day, because if it weren't for you, all I would know is the dark." He raised his hand and wiggled his pinky. "How about it, angel, will you marry me?"

* * *

The rising sun's glow caught the oval-cut diamond perfectly, creating a prism of light that burst into Tess's eyes. "Denver, I … I …"

He turned her around. "You better not say you don't know what to say. You better say yes."

Sobbing, she buried her face into his chest. She had dreamed of this moment ever since she had seen Denver and Eliza looking at each other, with a love so pure and true, it had made her heart ache to think about it. Now, despite her lingering belief that he and Eliza belonged together, she looked up through tears and nodded. "Yes … yes, I'll marry you."

Denver took her face in his hands, kissed her again and again, tears running down his cheeks like hers. "I love you so much, Tess. I never thought I'd find someone to make me forget Eliza, but I did."

She took his hand and led him to the bed. "Leave the doors open so we can hear the ocean. I want to always remember this morning." She sat and removed her sweater. He took off his jeans and joined her in bed.

He kissed every inch of her, followed with caresses and hesitant touches, his breath hitching in his throat from the intense need he must be feeling like she was feeling. She wanted him now more than ever, wanted his child growing inside her. Slowly, timed with the crash of the waves, they shared each other, until she curled over onto his chest, a wave of flesh and bone and auburn hair that hid them from the world.

She kissed his nose. "You make me so happy."

Denver rolled her to his side and slipped the ring onto her finger. "You make me happy too, angel." He pulled her head to his shoulder and ran his fingers through her hair. She draped her leg over his thigh and rubbed his chest.

This was love—nothing more, nothing less. He was her dream and she was his, and nothing or no one—not even Eliza—would end it.

thanks

At the head of the dining room table, Denver pulled out a chair. "Sit here, Absalom."

"Oh, no," he said, coming over from the living room, where he had been watching football. "You're the head of this household, not me."

Tess brought a huge turkey from the kitchen, the skin golden brown, stuffing bulging from the cavity, and set it on the table. "Come on, Papa, no one can carve a turkey like you can."

From the kitchen, Oneita brought string beans and Ivy brought deviled eggs. "I never ate eggs like these," she said, placing them on the table. "They look yucky."

"You don't have to eat them," Oneita said. "I never made them, but they look delicious."

"It's a Thanksgiving thing in the south," Denver said. He went to the kitchen for the glazed ham, set it in the middle of the table, and sat.

Absalom settled into the chair Denver had left out. Oneita sat beside him, while Ivy did the same opposite her. Tess sat across from Denver. He winked at her and she winked back. They had kept their engagement a secret and planned to share it after the blessing.

"All of this food looks wonderful," Oneita said. "You did a fine job, Tess."

"Thanks to you, Mama. If there's one thing an Amish wife can do for her family, it's cooking."

Ethan came from the living room and sat between Tess and Ivy. "I still don't get football. All those men do is fight like bulls for cows."

"Then why didn't you come to the table when I did?" Absalom asked.

Ethan shrugged. "Well, it *is* kind of entertaining."

Denver surveyed his family. Ethan, who didn't have TV in the sign language school, had never seen a football game, much less a Thanksgiving Day football game. It was great having them here, but a twinge of regret still hovered within the fabric of his family over Eliza's absence. Denver could see it in the downcast eyes of Oneita, Absalom, and Ethan, could hear it in the somber tone of their voices whenever they attempted to lighten the mood, like with Ethan's first experience of football. Even Ivy, who had complained about the deviled eggs, hadn't responded to "doodlebug," or how Tess had made banana pudding for dessert.

"Ivy," Tess said, "would you like to say the blessing?"

"I'm not hungry."

"You said you were hungry when we drove over," Oneita said.

"Hungry or not," Absalom said, "you'll sit and be quiet while the rest of us eat. This is a day for family and giving thanks."

"Tess put her hands together. If no one minds, I'll say the blessing."

Denver waited until everyone bowed their heads before he did. He had considered saying the blessing, but didn't mind

Tess asking Ivy. Still, if he knew the woman he loved, she would do her best to show how thankful she was, not only for her family but for him.

"Dear God, as we gather here to be thankful for our blessings, please let us know how love is at the center of every family. Things sometimes break loved ones apart, but we hope they will return one day, to be welcomed once again with love and forgiveness. Thank You too for the gift of new love, for the gift of new love's future, and for the gift of acceptance from all of those concerned. In Jesus' name we pray, amen."

"Very nice," Oneita said.

Absalom took a carving knife and fork from the table. Denver went around the table to take Tess's hand. As she stood, he faced the raised faces of everyone still sitting. "I want y'all to know how much it means to have you here. I can almost see my mom and dad and Willow sitting where you are."

He paused. Willow was spending Thanksgiving with William's parents in South Hill, but a phone call would fill her in.

Oneita clapped her hands. "I know what's going on."

"Hush, Mama," Tess said.

Denver took the ring from his pants pocket and put it on Tess's finger. She held it up for everyone to see. "Guess who's getting married?"

Ethan stood to hug her. "Congratulations." He shook Denver's hand. "You realize I'll move back here and make your life miserable if you hurt my sister, right?"

Denver released his hand. "That's something you don't have to worry about, future brother-in-law."

Absalom hugged them both, wrapping his huge arms around their shoulders at once. "I've prayed for nothing but happiness since—well, we know what I was about to say—but this is fine news. You two are perfect for each other."

Oneita rounded the table and threw her arms around them too, but one at the time. "You make me so happy." She returned to her seat. "Have you set a date? And I mean for having grandchildren too. We didn't leave the Amish and move all the way here from Ohio for nothing, you know."

Beside her again, Absalom patted her hand. "I think we should stop reminding ourselves about Eliza."

"It's not fair, I miss her," Ivy said. She faced Denver. "Mama and Papa told me how Eliza left because of Lily, but she didn't have to divorce you. You should go see her and talk to her. She might love you and want to marry you again." Ivy crossed her arms. "It's not fair."

Tess knelt beside her. "Eliza's been gone a long time and isn't coming back. Don't you think she would have by now if she loved Denver?"

"Maybe she would if you—"

"That's enough," Absalom said. "You should be happy for Denver and Tess."

"Papa's right," Ethan said. "It's time for Denver to be happy again, and if Tess makes him happy, we should be happy." He faced Tess. "I'm glad for you and Denver. It doesn't take a genius to see how much you care about each other."

"I agree," Oneita said.

Absalom carved the turkey while Denver carved the ham. Ivy, now in kindergarten, should get over her mood soon, but her questions mirrored the same ones he sometimes thought: Did Eliza still love him? Should he see her and talk to her? Would she marry him again if it were possible?

He placed ham on Tess's plate.

Crazy thoughts, ones he should never think again. He and Tess would get married, have a family, and live happily for the rest of their lives.

"Mmm, great turkey," Ethan said.

"The ham too," Absalom said.

Oneita forked green beans. "Denver, you say you sauteed these in olive oil and garlic and added lemon juice and thyme?"

"The lemon juice comes after, with some chopped parsley."

"They're delicious. I'll have to try them myself."

Ivy took a deviled egg from the platter and nibbled, eyes rolling. "You can make these too, Mama." She went to Denver, arms out for a hug. "I'm sorry. I just miss Eliza."

Denver kissed her cheek. As much as he hated to admit it, especially after asking Tess to marry him, he missed Eliza too. Maybe, like Ivy had suggested, he should drive to Ohio and see her, if for no other reason than to settle things between them.

Ivy returned to her seat. Denver returned to his meal. Then again, his anger at how she had left and divorced him, without a single word of goodbye or explanation, still made him furious when he thought about it.

No, Eliza was his past while Tess was his future. Time to forget her and move on with his life.

* * *

Between bites of food, Tess glanced at Denver. Ivy might have a good idea. Before she and Denver set a date, he should talk to Eliza. If any feelings remained—feelings that would affect their future—they should sort them out now instead of later. The last thing Tess wanted was for Eliza to come home and want Denver back. She might be estranged from her family, but if that happened, the rift might never be repaired.

In the kitchen after supper, she and Mama wrapped leftovers, while Ivy and the men watched football. Mama put a container in the refrigerator and returned to the counter. "You didn't answer about a date. Do you and Denver have one in mind?"

"We haven't talked about it. Spring would be nice."

"Will you invite Eliza?"

Tess ripped wrap from the roll. "I'm kind of getting over being mad at her. It would be nice if we all could make up, but I'm not sure how Denver feels about it."

Mama took the piece of wrap from Tess and covered another container. "Do you think he still loves her?"

The question made Tess drop the carton of wrap. There were times when Denver stared out the sliding glass doors at the lake, when she wondered if he were thinking about Eliza. A love like theirs was hard to forget—and he never would—but if it lingered to the point of genuine regret, including if the desire to rekindle it hid within his subconscious, it would be better to know now than later, an entirely different thing than simply sorting feelings out.

Mama picked up the wrap. "I see worry in those green eyes of yours, Tess. I love you and Denver. I love Eliza too, despite everything she's done, but I can't help having the feeling that there's more to her living with that man and his son than it seems."

"I know what you mean," Tess said, taking the wrap. "As much as she loved—loves—whatever—Denver, she wouldn't have feelings for another man so soon."

Mama put another container in the refrigerator. "All I know is things need to be settled before you set a date." She palmed Tess's cheek. "If you thought they were still in love, what would you do? I see how happy you and Denver are. It would break your heart, and that's the last thing I want for you."

"I ..."

"Yes?"

Tess appreciated Mama's candor. All she wanted was for her children to be happy, and that meant telling the truth. "I've thought about that too. For the longest time I wanted them to get together again. If that happens, yes, it'll break my heart."

Mama kissed her cheek. "You know you're stronger than Eliza, don't you? Growing up deaf affected her. Your Papa and I regret how we didn't take her to a doctor all those years ago, when she had the measles, but we believed God would heal her. I realize deaf people are the same as hearing people, but Eliza's experience made her vulnerable because she couldn't understand the world and the people around her, especially because we were Amish." Mama paused. "What I'm asking is this—if you lose Denver, will you be all right?"

"I would, but I'm not sure how I would handle it." Tess took another container to the refrigerator and returned to the counter. "We know Amish people who make all kinds of mistakes. Why do people who think they know the Amish, like those who read Amish novels, think we're perfect because we follow whatever ordnung we follow?"

"You're right," Mama said. "Amish people have gone to jail for theft. Amish men have been arrested for hurting their wives. Amish people have been caught taking money from church collections. For the most part they live much more honest lives than other people, but they're capable of dishonesty as well. Why do you ask?"

Tess dropped the wrap in a drawer. "Because I don't know what I would do if I lost Denver." Blinking tears, she turned away.

Mama's hand on her shoulder turned her around. "You really love him, don't you?"

Tess swallowed. "He's my heart, Mama. If I lost him, I would have to take a part of his heart with me to keep from giving up, and that's impossible."

"Wipe your eyes." Mama gave Tess a paper towel. "I've seen how Denver looks at you, so he'll never leave you." She took the wet paper towel from Tess and dropped it in the trash container. "Let's go see what football is about. I've never seen it either."

Mama sat in a chair near Absalom. Ivy was lying in the floor with a magazine. Tess sat on the sofa, between Denver and Ethan.

"I saw Leah in the grocery," she said to Denver. "She said her and Mark are engaged."

Denver's eyes widened. "Really? Only four months after they met?"

"It turns out she can sing, so they have that in common."

"Huh, I didn't know that."

Tess leaned close to Denver's ear. "It's not like you were interested in her voice, you know."

He rubbed her leg. "Hush, I'm glad they're happy."

"She's learning to play the bass. Mark asked if I could help out at some dates until she gets better. I said I would."

"Glad to hear it. I haven't seen y'all play together yet, and I'd like to. Any idea when?"

"Maybe in—"

"C'mon," Ethan said, "I can't hear the football."

Tess leaned near Denver's ear again. "I'll tell you when the cheerleaders are gone."

Mama faced Tess, her eyes narrowing. "Aren't you coming home with us?"

"I'll be there soon. Turn back around and watch the football." Tess got up and winked at Denver. "I think I'll get a jacket and walk to the dock. Wanna come?"

Ivy hopped up. "I wanna go."

"We're leaving in a minute," Absalom said. "I need to get up early to start on another order of furniture."

Ethan got up. "We might as well go. All that food has made me sleepy." He hugged Tess. "I'm happy for you and Denver. Let me know the date."

Mama and Papa got up too. "Come along, Ivy." He grinned at Denver and Tess. "Now you can stay inside instead of going to the dock."

At the front door, they all donned jackets and said their goodbyes. Tess led Denver to the sofa. "I love them, but I wanted to talk to you in private."

Denver put his arm around her shoulders. "Durn, I thought you wanted some snuggle time."

"No, I want to make sure you don't mind one of the dates Mark is planning. He's been hired to play for a wedding in Nags Head, on the Outer Banks of North Carolina. It's a big wedding destination."

"That's a five-hour drive. Will you stay overnight?"

"We'll leave the day before and come back the day after. Do you want to go?"

"We already pushed our luck when we spent the night in Virginia Beach. You saw how your mama wanted you to leave with them."

"That's true." Tess turned the TV off. "That means we better get our snuggle time in now."

more thanks

In her room, Eliza threw the food-stained apron in the clothes hamper, kicked off her shoes, and fell back on her bed. What a day. Between rising early to bathe and dress Anna, cooking turkey and all the side dishes for Thanksgiving, along with washing pots and pans afterward, she needed a solid eight hours of sleep to recuperate.

Wiggling her toes in her sock feet, she missed the feel of the sand beside Denver's dock. Helping other people was fine, but lying by the lake had its positive points.

She crossed her ankles. So, Denver was dating some woman who thought she was a better match for him than her. Fine. Wonderful. Amazing. Eliza uncrossed her ankles. When Anna grew strong enough to care for herself, with Josh's help, Jan would set up enough art shows to earn the money to move back to Clarksville.

Eliza sat up, took her phone from the nightstand, and called Jan. "My goodness," Jan said. "To what do I owe a call from my favorite Amish artist?"

Eliza ignored Jan's fake confusion. "Jon said you wanted to know if I want to have any more art shows. I am, but under certain conditions."

"Would those conditions have anything to do with a certain ex-husband of yours?"

"They do. You keep our business to yourself, is that understood?"

"Business is business. I assume my usual commission applies?"

"That goes without saying, Jan. Do we have a deal?"

"When would you like your first show?"

"Three. I've been painting for three months."

"Really?" Jan asked, the silky tone of income in her voice. "Then we'll have *three* deals, starting when?"

"The second Saturday in December. I'll send twenty paintings tomorrow so you can frame and advertise them."

"I look forward to seeing them." Jan paused. "A little bird told me Denver's seeing someone."

Eliza chewed her lower lip. "Denver can do whatever he wants."

"Of course he can. Look, Eliza, let's cut to the chase. Despite what happened between you and Denver, I'm on both your sides. It took me a while to see it, but you two were made for each other, and still are. Why don't you let me tell him about your December show and see if he comes? It's never too late for true love, and that's what you two have."

Eliza considered Jan's request. If she and Denver were to have a chance at making up, they needed to talk, and they could only talk if he wanted to. "Tell him and no one else. If he comes we'll talk. If not we won't."

"Will do. I'll text you when the paintings arrive."

Eliza ended the call. Time to tell Josh and Anna her plans, but after David went to bed. If he thought she was leaving soon, regardless of her telling him she wasn't, the sadness in his blue eyes would be hard to live with.

Shoes on again, Eliza went to the living room. Josh and Anna were on the sofa, David between them. As Eliza sat in the chair across from them, he looked up from the book in his lap. "I'm showing Mama and Papa the signs for the animals in my book, 'Liza."

Grateful for how he took her advice to call her 'Liza instead of "mama" since Anna was home, Eliza nodded. "How many have you taught them?" she signed and said.

Anna raised her hands. "All of them in this book. He says he has two more." Her left-hand fingers curved slowly during the signs.

Josh raised his hands. "I haven't told you, Eliza, but I just told Anna and David. I spoke to my bishop and explained how my anger made me leave our order. He understood and said to pretend my leaving had never happened."

"What about the heating and air conditioning and your truck?"

"He said I can keep everything until the weather breaks. He's letting me keep the truck to take Anna to rehabilitation. I appreciate him making those allowances."

David yawned, and Eliza stood. "Are you ready for bed?"

He kissed and hugged Josh and Anna and raised his hands. "Goodnight, Mama. Goodnight, Papa."

Anna palmed his cheek and kissed his forehead. "Goodnight, I love you."

In the bathroom, after David brushed his teeth and washed his face, he let Eliza put his pajamas on him. "We'll have to get you a bath in the morning," she said. "I was too busy today."

He padded across the hall to his room and climbed in bed. Eliza tucked him in and kissed his cheek. She had no idea a little boy could be so sweet. Whether at bedtime or in the morning, he did whatever she asked without question. Aching to tell him how much she loved him, she fingered his hair away from his forehead. He was her son in every way but name only. As much as her heart had broken to leave Denver, the idea of leaving David made her cry in the night, muffling her sobs with her pillow.

David raised his arms for a hug. Baby-soft hair against her cheek. Aroma of soap on his skin. Hint of mint on his breath from brushing his teeth.

David released her. "Mama?"

Eliza had told him he could call her that when they were alone, just their secret and no one else's. "What is it, you monkey?"

"Why can't Mama walk?"

His question surprised Eliza. Josh should've talked to him about Anna's problems, but in a way in which David could understand them while giving him hope.

"What's wrong with her hand and mouth too?"

"She can't walk because her leg muscles are weak from sleeping so long."

"Will she get better?"

"She's still going to the place where they exercise her legs, remember?"

"Why is it taking so long?"

"Because she slept so long."

"What about her hand and mouth? Her signs look funny. She can't smile like she used to."

Eliza patted his stomach. "She's still your mama, right?"

"I was just wondering."

"It's okay to wonder. Just remember to keep her in your prayers. Are you ready to say them?"

David put his hands together and closed his eyes. "Dear God, thank you for Mama and Papa and 'Liza. Please help mama get better so she can walk and smile and sign like she used to. Please help Papa not be sad. I see him crying sometimes, and I know it's 'cause he wishes Mama would get better. I see Mama making a face like she hurts, so help her too. I don't like it when people hurt, like Meemaw hurt. Bless Mama and Papa and 'Liza and all the people in the world, amen."

Eliza hugged him again. How she would love to have a son exactly like this sweet boy one day. David rubbed her back. "Are you okay? I feel tears on my cheek."

Eliza sat up and wiped her eyes. "I can't get anything by you, can I, you monkey?"

David bared his teeth and scratched under his arms. "Eee, eee, eee. I'm a *real* monkey, Mama."

She tousled his hair. "And you made me smile, you *real* monkey."

He touched her cheek. "But what's wrong?"

Indecision tugged at Eliza's heart. Tell him about her life before she came here or not? She knelt by his bed. "I was married before I came here. My husband and I loved each other very, very much, but something made us very, very sad. That's why I came here."

"What made you sad?"

Tears threatened again. "Oh, this and that."

"How can that make you sad?"

"Sometimes things happen that grownups can't explain."

"Are you happy here?"

"What a silly question to ask. Maybe you *are* a real monkey." Eliza pulled the blanket to his chin. As she stood, David grabbed her hand.

"Do you think Mama and Papa will have me a brother or a sister?"

"You asked me that one time before." Eliza sat on the bed. "Which would you like?"

"A sister, if she was nice like you."

"Ahh, nice like me. What if she were a monkey like you? Would you share your banana pudding?"

"I like nanner puddin'."

"I do too." Eliza kissed his forehead. "Goodnight."

In the living room, she returned to her chair and raised her hands. "I called the woman who used to handle my art shows. We're scheduling one for December."

Josh and Anna looked at each other. Anna raised her hands. "Will you be gone long?"

"I'll leave on a Friday and come back on a Sunday. Josh can tend to things while I'm gone."

"It sounds like you plan to leave us," Josh signed and said.

"I can't stay forever."

"I understand, but it sounds like you want to leave sooner than we need you too."

Anna raised her hands. "She has a life besides us, Josh." She faced Eliza. "Please stay as long as you can. I enjoy our time together, and David does too. Please? It would mean so much to us."

Anna's crooked signs and lopsided lips threatened Eliza with tears again. "I'll stay as long as you need me." She stood. "Josh, can you bring Anna into the bathroom so I can help her wash?"

"I guess I should start doing that." He picked Anna's frail body up and lowered her into the wheelchair, grimacing as if he were in pain. Standing, he placed his hand to his lower back. "I'm getting to be an old man, I suppose. Stooped and thin like one too."

"You've been working too hard trying to plow the garden," Anna signed.

"That's because I let the weeds take it and the ground has been frozen all week." Josh pushed the wheelchair down the hall.

Eliza stacked David's books on a table in the corner, where he kept the rest of them and some of the carved animals Josh had made for him. He had said he wanted a sister. Wouldn't it be a miracle if that happened? Well, stranger things had happened, like Josh returning to the Amish after he blamed them for Anna's accident.

In the kitchen, Eliza ate a small bowl of banana pudding and followed it with ice cold milk. Denver used to love the combination, especially when they shared a bowl with banana flavored kisses afterward.

Shaking her head, she rinsed the bowl and glass, turned off the lights, and went to her room. No, any miracles she might hope for between her and Denver were gone, exactly like the miracle of Anna and Josh having a sister for David.

lie

Denver stepped back to admire the Christmas tree in front of the fireplace. He and Tess had just finished decorating it and he was relieved, not only for how no memories of Eliza had ruined it for him, but for how Tess hadn't mentioned her. Beside him, she slipped her arm around his waist. "Our first tree together."

He kissed her cheek. "I guess we should set a date so we'll be married for our next tree. Your parents have asked enough in the last two weeks."

"Have you told anyone?"

"I told Willow. After our dancing at her reception, she had a hint. She hates what happened between Eliza and me, but she wants me to be happy."

"I told Mark when I called to let him know I can help with that music in Nags Head."

Denver adjusted a ball on the tree. "When is that?"

"The first of May."

"I thought couples who wanted to get married at the beach wanted it to be summer."

"Love is love." Tess stood on tiptoe and kissed him. "I need to get home soon. Wanna head to the bedroom first?"

"Good grief, woman. If I didn't know any better, I'd say you wanted kids now instead of later."

"Aww," Tess said, pouting, "are you tired of me already?"

"Not at all. I need to put away all the decoration boxes and get to bed myself. After all, we know who's been keeping me up late at night, don't we?"

Tess popped his behind. "Keep complaining, old man, and I'll accuse you of being an old man." She left for the hall.

Denver followed to help her with her coat and kiss her again. "I love you, sunshine."

"I love you too. See you tomorrow."

As the door closed behind Tess, Denver went to the stack of boxes by the tree. He could always watch some TV and put this stuff away tomorrow. In his room, his phone rang with Jan's violin music. Sitting on his bed, he swiped the screen. "How's my ex? Are you missing me during the holidays?"

"I could always come over and take you away from Tess like she took you away from Eliza. You two dancing at Willow's reception left nothing to the imagination."

"Not gonna happen and you know it."

"Is it serious or is it lust? She's gorgeous, you cradle robber."

"It's the real deal, Jan, as real as it gets. I asked her to marry me and she said yes."

"Wow, color me surprised. Have you told Eliza?"

"No. Let her rot in Ohio for all I care."

"Denver Andrews, that's cruel. That girl still loves you and you know it."

Denver glared at the screen. Jan was always one for drama. "Regardless of how Eliza divorced me and broke my heart, why are you calling?"

"I'm not sure how it'll affect you, so I'll just say it. Eliza's painting again, and she's having a show this Saturday. Would you like to come over and say hi?"

A knot filled Denver's throat. Despite how Eliza had hurt him, he had wanted to see her for months, if for no other reason than to ask why she had divorced him without any explanation at all. Then again, who knew what might happen if he saw her? He could easily see himself having a panic attack from how he had reacted to those divorce papers on Christmas Day, of all days. "What time is the show?"

"Two in the afternoon. She sent me twenty paintings. I've been advertising in all the art magazines and expect a huge crowd."

"Did she say what made her start painting again?"

"No and I didn't ask. All I care about are my commissions."

Vintage Jan, loving her commissions. Denver rolled his eyes. "I'll either make it or I won't. I expect you to keep this conversation to yourself."

"Poor baby," Jan said, using her most *non*-sympathetic tone. "Are you afraid Tess will find out?"

Denver worked his jaw. As much as he admired Jan for various things, she should've figured out by now why their relationship had been doomed from the start, and her lack of relating to his feelings was one of them. "Just do like I ask. If I come, it's because Eliza owes me an explanation for the divorce."

"I can see that. It's bad to hang onto someone while they fall in love with someone else. Does that sound familiar?"

"Too familiar. Thanks for calling."

Denver ended the call, drew the phone back to his shoulder, and dropped it on the bed instead of throwing it.

Go to the art show or not? Since tomorrow was Saturday, he needed to—

He called Tess. "Hey, angel. Didn't you say you were working on that new guitar tomorrow, like Mark's but with electronics?"

"I'd like to get it done before the Nags Head show, why?"

"We haven't talked about wedding rings. I was thinking about driving to some jewelry stores in Raleigh tomorrow and checking some out."

"Will you buy them too?"

"Sure, why not. Do you care what they look like?"

"I'm fine with a plain gold band. You know me, country girl that I am."

"Cool. I have your size from when I bought your engagement ring."

"Okay, see you when you get back. I love you."

"Love you too, goodnight."

Denver fell back on the bed, guilt gnawing at him because of the first lie—and hopefully the last—he would ever tell Tess.

* * *

At twelve the next day, a cold rain splattered Denver's face as he ran to his pickup. Drive to the show. Get there early. Watch for Eliza. See how she affected him. If she didn't, follow her in and pull her aside to some private area and have it out, then get the wedding rings.

At the turn onto highway 15, he gave a signal to go south. Did he really want to see the woman who had crushed his heart, not to mention his soul? No, but he needed closure, and this was as good a time as any.

Leaving Oxford, North Carolina to merge onto the interstate, he squeezed the steering wheel with both hands. Turn around at the next exit—definitely.

185

The next exit passed. Turn around at the next one. That one passed too. He loosened his grip on the steering wheel. Just go and get it over with.

He started to turn the radio on but jerked his hand back at the thought of some old love song, like *Unchained Melody*, making him cry over Eliza.

Durham passed. Exit after exit passed. His knee bounced by itself. He willed it to stop and slapped it when it didn't.

At the museum parking lot, he parked on the back row and checked the time on the dashboard. 1:15. He must've broken the speed limit getting here, not that he knew why.

Cars entered and parked—expensive makes and models with wax jobs beading the rain. Well-dressed men and women entered the museum's double-glass doors, black umbrellas over their heads.

Denver raised a pair of birdwatching binoculars he had put in the truck last night. Had Eliza bought a new car? None of these looked like hers. He checked the time: 1:45. A silver Toyota Camry entered the lot. He dropped the binoculars. That might be her. He snatched the binoculars from the floor and brought them to his eyes. The Camry parked in a visitor spot near the doors. A black umbrella opened. Long, slender legs extended from the open car door—legs he had once loved to run his fingertips along. Hands shaking, he dropped the binoculars again and picked them up in time to see her tall, slim figure in a black, knee-length dress enter the double doors, dark hair to the middle of her back.

He flung the pickup door open and ran to the tailgate, hyperventilating as if he had just paddled his canoe non-stop from the dock to Clarksville and back.

He grabbed the tailgate and leaned over, the urge to vomit thick in his throat. God help him. God help him. There was no way he would could see her for an extended amount of time, much less talk to her.

The cold rain wetting his hair and streaming down his face reminded him to get in the pickup before he was soaked.

Time to get the heck back to Clarksville and to Tess.

At home again, he ran through the rain and to his room to change clothes. Warm and dry again, he went to the kitchen to make coffee, and the front door clicked open. "Hey, baby."

Denver looked down the hall, where Tess was hanging her jacket on the coat rack beside his. She came to the kitchen and stopped to rub his head. "Did you forget your umbrella? I want to see our rings?"

"How did you know I was here?"

"I didn't. I was going to town and saw you turn into your road. Did you find us something nice?"

Denver's mouth opened but nothing came out. He had hated lying to start with. Time to tell the truth. "I hope you won't be mad, but I went to Raleigh because Jan called last night and told me Eliza was having an art show today."

Tess blinked once, twice, and once again. "You lied about going there to get the rings? How do I know you aren't lying when you say you want to marry me? For all I know you want my stupid sister back."

"I went to confront her about the divorce. Don't you think I deserve an explanation?"

"It's been a year, you want an explanation now?" Tess's nostrils flared. "You still love her, admit it."

Denver leaned against the kitchen counter. Did he still love Eliza? What a dumb question. How could he love someone—anyone—who made him feel like he was going to either pass out or throw up when he saw them? He held his arms out. "Can I hold you? Please let me hold you."

"Sex isn't getting you out of this, dammit."

"Don't curse, Tess. That's not you and you know it."

"Then don't treat me like Ivy. You can't hug me and think I'll be all better. You lied to *me*, the person you claim you want to marry. Out with it. You still love her, don't you?"

Denver ran his fingers through his damp hair. Along with questioning his feelings for Eliza, if he were honest—and he needed to be honest—part of him was curious about seeing her. Truth be told she looked great, and despite his physical reaction at seeing her, another part—the part that remembered each of their romantic times together—wanted to run to her and hold her and tell how much he missed her and could they please start over again.

"I love you and no one else, Tess. When we're apart, all I can think about is seeing you again. Yes, I lied. Yes, I'm scum. Yes, I sometimes wonder how my life would be different if Eliza and I hadn't lost Lily." He reached out to finger a lock of Tess's hair from her temple. "You're my angel, Tess, and I don't deserve you. I can't change what happened between Eliza and me any more than I can change how much I love you. Please forgive me, okay? I don't know what I would do if I lost you too."

Tess's perfect lips quirked to one side to form a perfect smirk. "Well, at least Mark took that brunette bimbo Leah away from you, so I don't have to worry about you running back to her."

Denver took her face in his hands. "Do you forgive me?"

Tess pulled his shirt up and ran her fingers through his chest hair. "That depends on how sincere you are, Mr. Liar."

Denver unbuttoned her blouse, revealing the lace of her bra at the beginning of her ample cleavage. "Oh, I'm just oozing sincerity, sunshine." He opened the refrigerator for a container of whipped cream. "And if you get undressed, I'll prove it by having you for dessert right here in the kitchen."

* * *

Tess grabbed the cold can of whipped cream and put it back in the refrigerator. "I don't feel like getting sticky."

Denver stuck out his tongue. "We'll pretend you're a bowl of milk and I'm a cat. It worked before."

Tess took his hand and led him to the sofa. "I like the sound of that, but without the whipped cream. You sit here while I lie beneath the Christmas tree. Then we can unwrap each other like we're presents." She plugged the lights in and lay on her side beneath the tree, propping her head in her hand and licking her lips. "How do you like your present, baby?"

"Well …"

She finished the buttons on her shirt and opened it, revealing the dip at her waist, the rise of her hip, and her navel. "You do appreciate my hourglass by now, right?"

"You kill me."

"I've tried" —Tess giggled— "as we well know."

"I remember. I thought I needed a chiropractor."

Denver took off his shirt and unbuttoned and unzipped his jeans to reveal the waistband of his navy-blue boxers. He lay on the sofa like she lay under the tree. "How do like *your* present, sunshine?"

"Raise your knee like mine and give me a sexy pout."

Trying—and failing—to not laugh, Denver pursed his lips. "How's dish?"

Snorting laughter, Tess rolled onto her back and held her stomach with one hand while slapping the floor with the other. Denver buttoned his jeans, took her in his arms, and carried her giggling self to his bed.

They undressed each other frantically, throwing their clothes in the floor. To love like this was the miracle of all miracles, except for the miracle of the day when their child would grow within her.

Kissing, holding, touching, sharing—each passed all too quickly, leaving them panting in each other's arms, their sweat-slickened bodies still pressed together.

Tess rolled off him to her side and pulled the sheet over them. He rolled over against her back and rested his hand on her stomach. A minute passed, maybe more, maybe less. His breath grew even against her shoulder with the rhythm of sleep.

Despite their peaceful moment, his lie about the rings reminded her of how he might never be free of Eliza.

Tess pulled his hand between her breasts. No, she would make sure he got over Eliza—if not with love, then with children as soon as possible. As many as he wanted. Two, four, six, whatever. What a family they would have—a house filled with love, filled with gatherings at every holiday, especially at Thanksgiving and Christmas.

She closed her eyes and saw Denver in that place between dreams and sleep, saw his smile, his blue eyes crinkling with the purest love she had ever seen.

She snapped her eyes open, eased Denver's hand away so she wouldn't wake him, and ran to the guestroom bathroom, where she closed the door and covered her mouth with a towel to muffle her coughing sobs.

Like she had told herself so many times before, the purest love she had ever seen was when she saw him looking at Eliza for the first time.

What if she came back? What if she wanted him again? Even worse, what if he wanted her again?

Tess finished crying, wiped her face, and faced the mirror. Red eyes and cheeks. Nose still running. Auburn hair framing her face and covering her shoulders, both still damp with sweat from making love to Denver.

Regardless of her questions, no matter if the worst happened, she would never give Denver up. One way or another, like she had told Mama, she would take part of his heart with her, because he would always have part of hers with him.

portrait

At the end of the garden, where Eliza and David had painted last summer, Anna's flowers budded and bloomed. In the yard near the chicken coop, hens scratched and pecked in the greening grass. The oaks, maples, and hickories bordering the yard were sprouting tiny leaves, giving the trees the appearance of green ghosts with dark limbs barely visible.

Eliza left the sink and the window over it and placed the last breakfast dish in the cabinet. The long winter was finally releasing its frigid grip on the land, and she could paint the portrait of her family.

She poured more coffee and sipped while enjoying the view once more.

After Thanksgiving, David hadn't mentioned brothers or sisters again, perhaps taking to heart Eliza's explanation of how Anna's illness would prevent that. Josh continued to do more for her: bathing and dressing her, brushing her hair and putting her to bed, exercising her legs between rehabilitation visits, which kept her muscles from atrophying too much. He never failed to be gentle and caring, taking his time, showing love and patience, all of which made Eliza miss Denver even more.

Christmas had come and gone with presents but no tree, as the Amish didn't lavishly decorate for the holiday like the English. Instead, Anna had Josh tack red and green bows over the doorways and gave Eliza the recipes for favorite family treats, like pork tenderloin, potato rolls, sweet potato pancakes, turkey pot pie, and applesauce cake, but David still insisted on "nanner puddin'."

Then January and February had come and gone, including hard freezes and deep snows, ending any thoughts of family portraits outside, followed by March winds and April rains.

During the passing months inside, David, Anna, and Josh had learned enough signs to easily converse. David had grown also, and Eliza had taken him into town for new clothes twice.

Finished with the last sip of coffee, she rinsed the cup, left it in the sink, and went to the living room. Anna and David, looking at one of his new animal books while sitting on the sofa, raised their heads as Eliza sat in the chair across from them and raised her hands. "Who's ready to let me paint their family portrait?"

David shot his hand into the air. "Me! I am!"

Anna raised her hands. "I don't need him to sign to know he agrees."

"Are you sure?" Eliza signed to David. "You'll have to sit still for a long time."

"What if I have to go to the bathroom?"

"We'll take breaks for that."

"Good. When can we start?"

"Now, if you'll help me with my things."

David hopped off the sofa. "I'll tell—"

Josh came in the front door, from where he had been on the porch with a farm magazine. "I love a screened door for letting in the fresh air. I also love it for hearing plans about our family portrait."

At the end of the garden, as Josh stood beside Anna in her wheelchair, with David in her lap, Eliza started to add the various colors of flesh-toned oil paints to the palette but stopped. Shaking her head, she set the pallet aside and raised her hands. "I'm sorry, you all don't need to be out here yet. I need to do the background before I can paint you."

"That's all right," Josh signed. "I suppose you were as excited to start our portrait as we were and forgot. David, hop down from your mama's lap so I can take her inside."

"I'd rather stay out for now," Anna signed. "You can take David fishing if you'd like."

"Yeah, Papa, let's go fishing." David ran to the barn behind the chicken coop, where Josh kept their fishing tackle."

Chuckling softly, Josh raised his hands. "I was going to finish my magazine, but I better take that boy fishing." He left for the barn.

Eliza waited until they were walking down the road before facing Anna. "You have a wonderful family."

Anna raised her hands. "When you leave, will you go back to your family?"

"I hope so."

"What about your husband?"

"I don't know yet."

A warm breeze fluttered Anna's dark hair. Fingering it from her eyes, she raised her head toward the blue sky. "I sometimes think about going to Heaven. I hate being a burden to Josh and David."

Eliza knelt beside her. "Don't say that. You and Josh give me the hope to believe in being with my husband again. He's so patient with David and gentle with you, he makes me think anything's possible."

Anna shared the slightest of smiles, somewhat lopsided because of how the left side of her mouth refused to rise. "I was once afraid Josh might fall in love with you." She looked away and back. "I know better. If I went to Heaven, I have the feeling he would too, as much as he loves me."

"He does that," Eliza signed. "He's as devoted a husband and father as I have ever known."

Anna touched Eliza's cheek, just a whisper of fingertips against her skin. "You're so beautiful, but your outer beauty is nothing compared to your inner beauty. Josh never said why you divorced your husband, but if he did something he shouldn't have, I'm sure you could forgive him. After all, you've been so kind, living here and helping us when few people would do that." The breeze stirred again, and Anna closed her eyes. "Sometimes I think God touches us to show us how to forgive." She opened her eyes. "If Josh had fallen in love with you, I could forgive him because I know you and I know him. Is your husband in love with another woman?"

Eliza paused at Anna's line of questioning, one she had never expected. "I was told he was seeing someone. I don't know her, so I don't know if I could forgive her or not. He's a wonderful man and person. If it doesn't work out between us, it would be wrong to not want him to be happy, even if he were happy with someone else."

Anna softly smiled again. "Love is strange."

"How so?"

"I'm sure you've noticed how Josh isn't physically attractive, but he's capable of more love than I ever thought possible. When love is involved, the heart is what matters. What matters too is its willingness to understand how happiness is more than a beating muscle within our chests, especially if it's big enough to understand what a person needs to live a life filled with love.

Josh needs me and I need him. I think you need your husband and he needs you. That other woman might know him as well as you do, so she might need him like you do too." Anna's lips pursed as if she were fighting a grin. "Not that I would ever expect anyone to share someone they love. It would take an extraordinary person to do that."

Eliza stood. "When I met my husband, he was dating someone. I played a trick on her and laughed until my stomach ached."

"You do seem the type—tall and strong and proud." Anna fluttered her hand as if shooing a fly. "Don't pay any attention to me. I'm just a romantic woman who wants everyone to be as happy as Josh and I are."

Eliza pulled her chair to Anna's side. After a moment, Anna took her hand and released it. "I wish I could speak so I could hold your hand while I sign. Josh told me he asked if you would adopt David."

"That was before you woke up from the coma. He was afraid you would leave him."

"He worries me."

"How so?"

He doesn't eat like he used to. I think it's because he's worried about me."

Eliza rubbed the back of Anna's hand. "I would be worried about you if I were him too. He's as dedicated to you and David as anyone I've known." Eliza smiled. "Except for my papa."

A gust of wind rustled the flowers, split them asunder as if it were the tongue of a dog licking them. Anna's hair flew around her face. "I love when the wind blows like that. It's like God is blowing me a kiss." She fingered the stray strands, black and glossy in the sunlight, behind her ears. "God understands us better then we understand ourselves. He knows we're not perfect and accepts us anyway. He knows our earthly needs and wants and forgives us when we make choices that people don't understand. Love is like that. Like when I married Josh, I'm sure people wondered, 'Why is she marrying that ugly man? Even if she's deaf, she could find someone better.'"

Eliza tilted her head to one side. "I don't understand what you mean."

"I mean he was the one perfect man for me in all the world. Some people probably judged me for my choice, but how can anyone judge love?"

"I agree," Eliza signed. "Anyone who judges a person's love for someone else has no business doing that. It's like when my husband and I fell in love. Except for Papa, I wasn't close to my family. No, that's not right. I remember Tess watching me paint and smiling to let me know she liked what I was doing. Along with Papa, she's one of the reasons I kept painting. Anyway, when I fell in love with my husband, my family was learning sign language so they could communicate with me. I had always dreamed of them loving me, and then I found out they did all along without me knowing it. Then, when my husband said he loved me, I had to choose between him and them because I was Amish, and I didn't want them to shun me."

Anna raised her hands. "Then how did you marry him?"

"They left the Amish and moved to where my husband lives to be close to me. That's how much they wanted me to be happy."

The memory of her family's love, along with everything she had lost, including her daughter and Denver, made her turn away so Anna couldn't see her cry. Try as she might to stop her sobs, her shoulders shook with them.

A gentle hand rubbed her back—a gentle hand like Mama's, when Eliza was sick with the measles—a gentle hand like Papa's, when he hugged her on the day she lost her hearing—a gentle hand like Ethan's, when he pulled her to him at her daughter's funeral—a gentle hand like Ivy's, when she held Eliza's hand there too—a gentle hand like Tess's, when she palmed Eliza's cheek while kissing her other cheek to congratulate her for marrying Denver—a gentle hand like—

Denver.

Her entire world began and ended with his love, whenever he held her face and looked into her eyes with his own, a shade of blue so deep and pure, it was like swimming into the depths of his soul.

Anna tugged her shoulder. Eliza turned around. "I'm all right."

Anna palmed Eliza's cheek and rubbed a gentle circle near her temple. "We're like sisters, you and I. We have hearts that know where they belong and where they're going. It's just a matter of finding out what it takes to get there. The thing is whether we take both forks in the road or one."

Eliza covered Anna's hand with her own. Yes, they were sisters, bound together with love for the men in their lives. Although Anna had taken the fork that had led her to Josh and David, she had taken the fork that had led to her accident. Her words about Heaven meant she had taken that fork without regret, because she had experienced love and all it had to offer.

Anna pulled Eliza close for a hug.

But what fork of love would lead her to Denver and to all he had to offer? Were there more choices along the way? More than one fork, two, or even three?

Only time would tell.

fear

Denver threw away the take-out containers from his and Tess's supper and returned to her on the sofa, where she held a glass of ice tea. "That new brewery by the lake downtown makes a great burger," he said, sitting beside her.

She put the glass on a coaster on the coffee table. "Let's walk down to the dock. I love the lake in spring, when all the trees are budding new leaves."

On the dock, they sat on the wooden bench. Tess leaned her head on his shoulder. "I'll miss you this weekend."

Denver put his arm around her. "It's too bad that wedding is so far away. You could drive back right after you and Mark and Leah finish playing."

An osprey's call, almost like the squeak of a rusty door hinge, drew their attention to the sky, where a pair of them circled in the dimming light. "They remind me of us," Tess said. "We circled each other after Eliza left, trying to deny the love hiding beneath the water of all the mess she left behind, until we finally found each other."

Denver kissed her hair. "You're quite the poetic angel, sunshine."

"Am I poetic enough for us to set a date for the wedding?"

"I'm ready anytime you are."

Tess turned to face him. "You're gonna hate me for this, but I want you to go to Ohio and talk to Eliza before we set a date. You can go Saturday, while I'm at Nags Head."

Denver didn't like Tess's idea. After his reaction at seeing Eliza in Raleigh, the last thing he wanted was to see her again, let alone talk to her.

"What will talking to Eliza accomplish?" he asked. "She made up her mind when she divorced me."

"Don't you need closure after the divor— Wait a minute, you went to see her when you lied about buying our wedding rings and never said how that went."

"That's because you forgave me and we made up."

"Well, what happened?"

Denver didn't want to lie, but he didn't want Tess to know how seeing Eliza had affected him. If she knew, she might think he was still in love with her and cancel their engagement.

"I turned around in the museum parking lot and came home."

"Good," Tess said, giving him a quick kiss. "That means you're not still in love with her, and you can go talk to her while I'm gone." She got up to sit in Denver's lap, facing him. "Kiss me, baby. The twilight's turning me on."

* * *

After Tess left, Denver packed an overnight bag. Tomorrow was Friday, and she was leaving for Nags Head in the morning. He might as well get up and drive to Ohio, rent a room at the hotel in the nearest town, and see Eliza Saturday and get it over with. Regardless of how she had affected him in Raleigh, he deserved an explanation for the divorce, and the sooner the better.

* * *

The ten-hour drive passed reasonably well, but as the miles rolled by, Denver caught himself squeezing the steering wheel over and over again. He checked into a room, went out for a bite to eat, bought a six-pack of beer, and returned to the room to drink three while watching TV. Not used to drinking so much, he went to bed with a headache pounding in his temples and fear in his gut, which bordered on nausea because of what might happen when he saw Eliza. He woke to the buzz hotel alarm clock, rubbed bleary eyes, and fell back onto the pillow. The heck with this. Pack, check out of the room, and drive back to Clarksville as fast as the road would carry him.

In his pickup, he stopped at the hotel parking lot exit. Flip the turn signal to the right or to the left, where who knew what might happen? He flipped it to the left. What was the worst that could happen? Considering how he had reacted in Raleigh, including how the guy Eliza was living with might be around, *anything* might happen.

As he traveled along the two-lane road, the sun rose over the rolling hills, a possible positive sign. On the gravel road, where the house Eliza had once lived in was located, he slowed to look for her car. Nearing a grove of oaks, he saw her silver Camry at a house up ahead and stopped behind a tree to roll the window down for some fresh air, as he needed all he could get to keep from passing out.

Voices came from behind the house. Denver sat up as tall in the seat as possible. At the end of the plowed rows of a garden, just past the red, blue, and purple blooms of a mass of wildflowers, Eliza was hugging a thin man with dark hair.

Denver cranked the pickup and whipped the wheel around for a U-turn. He hit the accelerator. The rear tires spun. Gravel rattled beneath the fenders. He looked in the rear-view mirror and back to the road—just in time to swerve around a huge dairy truck and come face to face with the rear of an Amish buggy. He jerked the wheel to the right. The pickup went down an embankment and rolled over and over. Pain speared into his head. Shards of glass flew into his face. The metallic flavor of blood filled his mouth. Grass and dirt clouded his vision. The pickup landed upside-down, to leave him hanging from the seat belt. The black pants legs of the Amish man ran toward him, then faded to gray.

This must be death, where people in white shrouds hovered around a person, shouting behind white masks and cutting the soul from their body.

Better to die and get it over with. Die and give up on love like when Eliza had left him that first time so long ago. Die and give up on being a great husband and a dad like his own dad had been.

Tess—and Eliza—would be better off without him.

* * *

Hazy light penetrated his eyelids. The insistent *beep-beep-beep* of a heart monitor toned nearby.

Not dead. Not dead.

A door swished open. Footsteps came close and went away, followed by the door thumping closed.

The smell of a hospital, sour and medicinal, told the story. He had wrecked his pickup and was hurt, evidenced by the pain in his head and neck from not hitting anything, which would've exploded the air bag. Instead, as the pickup had rolled over and over, he had been tossed around inside it to hit his head on the driver-side glass while wrenching his neck.

He touched the compression collar below his chin, then fingered the bump above his left ear. No bandage so no cut. Opening his eyes, he raised his hands. The tops of them were scratched and red. His toes wiggled on command, so he wasn't paralyzed.

Sand … someone had poured the driest sand in the world into his mouth, leaving it there to mummify his shriveled tongue. He ran it inside his lower lip and found a cut, which is why he had tasted blood during the crash.

He looked around the room. One bed. A window. An LED TV on the wall. A private room with a view instead of an emergency room or an intensive care unit. A vase filled with wildflowers on the window sill.

No, no, not that.

Find the call button. Jab it over and over until his fingertip stung. "Nurse," he croaked. "Nurse."

A man in white pants and a white shirt came in. "Yes, sir, how are you feeling?"

"How long have I been here?"

"Since yesterday afternoon, so your chart says. I just started my shift."

Denver pointed at the flowers. "Who brought those?"

"A woman brought them late last night. The night shift nurse said she held your hand and said how much she loved you."

The news satisfied Denver. Tess must've come and had even brought flowers. Thank goodness. There was no way could he handle seeing Eliza. He asked the nurse what he knew about his accident. He studied the heart monitor screen before facing Denver. "Your pickup is totaled, so the police said. All your belongings are in the cabinet in the corner."

"Can you get my phone for me?"

"Sorry, the screen is shattered."

"How long do I have to stay here?"

"You have a slight concussion and strained neck muscles. Your doctor wants to keep you for observation another twenty-four hours."

Denver rubbed his eyes. Another twenty-four hours—long enough for Eliza to show up. She must've heard the crash but didn't know it was him.

Someone knocked on the door. The nurse went out, leaving it partially open. "He's awake. I'm sure he'll be happy to see you, but keep his excitement to a minimum." The nurse left and Eliza came in.

Grabbing the call button, Denver jabbed it while jerking upright. "Nurse!" he croaked, as loud as his parched throat would allow.

"Denver, please. I saw the crash. I stayed all night. I need to explain—"

"Nurse! Nurse!"

The nurse came in. "Ma'am, what's—"

Denver shot a finger toward Eliza. "Get her out of here—now!"

The nurse stepped between Denver and Eliza. "I told you not to excite him—out."

"But—"

"Don't make me call securi—"

The door opened. Tess grabbed Eliza's arm and jerked her around. "What are you doing here? You almost killed him once with that stupid divorce—are you trying to kill him again by making him crash his pickup?"

"It was an acci—"

"Get her out!" Denver yelled.

The nurse opened the door. "Out now, unless you want security to escort you out."

Eliza stopped in the doorway and turned, tears shining on her cheeks. "I ... I never meant for any of this to happen."

"Whether you meant it to happen or not," Tess said, raising her left hand in front of Eliza's face, "this happened."

"You're engaged?" Eliza asked, her chin trembling. "I thought he was dating someone else."

"That's all over. We're engaged and getting married and you can't stop it. You're with that guy whose wife had the accident. Just go and let Denver be happy."

"I … I hope …" With a huge sob, Eliza ran out the door.

The nurse faced Tess. "It isn't any of my business, but how can two women be in love with the same man?" He waved the question away. "Never mind, I don't want to know. I'll leave you to your fiancé."

Tess went to Denver. "Are you okay? Eliza called Papa and he called me. I drove straight through from Nags Head."

"You've got to be worn out."

"Pretty much, but I had to know what happened. Eliza told Papa you were in an accident but you weren't hurt too bad."

"The nurse said I've got a slight concussion and I need to stay another night for observation. Can you get me some water? I'm about to thirst to death."

Tess looked around the room. "Oh, there's a pitcher and some cups on a table behind the flow—" She filled a cup and gave it to him. "I guess Eliza brought the flowers."

"I thought you did."

Tess took the flowers from the vase and dropped them into a trash container by the bed. "Are you allergic? Maybe she wanted you to sneeze yourself to death."

Ignoring the question, Denver swallowed the cold water. "Oh, wow, that's great." He took another swallow. "I guess you want to know what happened with the accident."

"Not if you'd rather rest." Tess pulled over a chair from a corner. "Let me sit before I fall from that drive. I wonder what Eliza thinks of our engagement."

"She looked shocked," Denver said. "I wonder who told her I was dating someone."

"From that time I called Ethan, not long after she left. I didn't name Leah, but I thought Eliza would come to her senses about everything if Ethan told her she was going to lose you for good."

"The nurse said she stayed last night and kept saying she loves me. I never would've believed it otherwise."

"It's too late now. Besides, she might say that from seeing you lying in a hospital bed."

Denver sat up a bit more and drank water. "I hope I didn't scare your family too much."

"They were glad you weren't seriously hurt. I told them I'd let them know what happened, especially whatever Eliza had to do with it since she called them." Tess refilled the cup. Denver drank again.

"When I found her car," he said, "I stopped on the road to crack the window for some fresh air. I was nervous about not talking to her for so long and needed to get my head on straight."

"I'm sure," Tess said.

Denver hesitated. Time to tell the truth. "I lied about not seeing Eliza in Raleigh. I saw her just long enough to hyperventilate and almost throw up. Yesterday, at the house where her car was parked, I saw her hugging that guy she's living with. To say I panicked is an understatement. I took off spinning gravel, almost hit a huge dairy truck and rear-ended a buggy, and rolled my pickup down an embankment. What a day, huh?"

Tess stood to kiss him. "I'm glad you're alive to tell me about it." She frowned. "If Eliza is in some kind of weird relationship with a man whose wife is in a coma, why would she say she loves you?"

Drinking water, Denver lowered the cup. "It doesn't matter now."

Tess yawned. "This chair doesn't feel like a good place for a nap."

"I drove up yesterday morning and stayed in a hotel in town. You might as well do the same and get some sleep."

"Good idea." Yawning again, Tess stood. "Did your pickup do better or worse than you did?"

"Totaled, so the police told the nurse."

"If you rolled over like you said, I'm not surprised." She yawned again. "Now we can put buying you a pickup on the agenda, along with setting a wedding date. I don't see any reason to wait much longer after this mess, do you?"

Denver raised his arms for a hug. Tess held him as best she could, teasing him with her soft hair in his face and the hint of perfume on her neck. He popped her bottom. "I've got to get out of here and get this thing off my neck. You know what happens after that, right?"

Tess stood, a sexy pout pursing her lips. "No doubt about it, baby. Let me find that hotel room before I pass out. See you soon."

choice

On the way to Josh's house, Eliza parked on the side of road. If not, she might have an accident from crying so hard. How could her own sister turn against her? More than anyone, she knew how much Denver meant to her. No doubt Ethan had spread those lies about Josh to everyone between Clarksville and Ohio.

Eliza wiped her face and continued down the road. She had enough money for a down payment on a house in the same subdivision where Denver and her family lived. There she would do whatever she could to make Denver see how Tess was nothing but an immature eighteen-year-old with no clue as to what real love was. Still, knowing Denver, he had probably been attracted to Tess's voluptuous body, meaning they were having sex, not only in his house, but in the bed she and Denver had once shared.

She parked in Josh's driveway and went inside. Although she had promised to paint his family's portrait, that would have to wait. Denver had to come first—nothing else mattered. At least the portrait was done, except for adding Josh, Anna, and David.

She passed through the empty living room and kitchen and went to the hall. Voices came from Josh and Anna's room, behind the closed door. Eliza knocked. Josh came out, closing the door behind him. "How's your husband?"

"He's not hurt seriously."

"Did he say why he was here and why he left like he did?"

"I didn't get a chance to ask him." Eliza didn't care to complicate the conversation by bringing Tess into it. "He was unconscious and woke today. I couldn't talk to him because a doctor was with him. One of the nurses said he has a mild concussion, and he's staying another night. I assume he'll rent a car and drive home tomorrow."

Josh leaned close. "David's with Anna. I need to talk to you where he can't hear."

Eliza followed him to the kitchen, where he faced her. "Anna's had a minor stroke. David hasn't noticed it, but her mouth and hand are worse." Clenching his teeth, Josh eased into a chair at the table. "I realize you had your art shows so you could earn the money to go back home, but I need you to stay to help with Anna. My back is worse than ever. I can't help her into her wheelchair, much less bathe and dress her."

"Can't you hire someone to help? Agencies have people who do that kind of thing."

"I mentioned it to Anna. She doesn't want a stranger seeing her without clothes." Josh rubbed his forehead. "I have a feeling she won't be with us much longer. I hope you'll stay to help David get through it. I won't be in any shape to comfort him, if you know what I mean."

Eliza gave him a quick hug. Her problems were nothing compared to Josh and David's. Denver and Tess could have sex all they wanted, wherever they wanted. They wouldn't get married unless Mama and Papa forced them too. Like the

English sometimes said: why marry the cow when you can get the milk for free.

"I'll stay as long as you need me, Josh. Anna and I have become close. She's like an older sister I can look up to."

"Thank you, Eliza. I don't have the words to say how much you mean to me and my family. We would be lost without you."

"I would be lost without you all too. You gave me a peaceful place to live when I needed it. You gave me the experience of loving David as if he were my own son. You showed me how two people can love each other as deeply as you and Anna love each other. You two have given me the faith to believe in love again." She took a basket from the top of the refrigerator and went to the back door. "Do you need me to gather the eggs?"

Grimacing again, Josh got up. "Please. I don't think I could make it out to the coop without falling on my face."

In the chicken coop, Eliza reached under a hen's warm bottom and took out an egg, but it collapsed within her grip before she could put it in the basket. In a shaft of sunlight streaming through a gap at the top of the door, she studied the shell. Papa said hens needed calcium to avoid these thin-shelled eggs. Maybe Josh didn't know about that.

Eliza fingered the bits of broken shell in her palm, mixed with the golden yolk. How fragile a thing, like her relationships with everyone she loved, ready to be crushed with the slightest word or action.

It was wrong to think of Denver and Tess's engagement as anything less than love. Both were as entwined with each other as they were entwined with her.

Anna—wonderful, sweet, loyal, loving, Anna—a woman who had not only given Eliza the faith to believe in love again, but the woman who had shown how important a sister could be.

Denver.

Why had he come here, and what could've made him drive away, spinning tires and throwing gravel, only to roll down an embankment?

The mix of broken shell and yolk slid between her fingers and fell to the dirt at Eliza's feet.

No. No. *No!*

She had been setting up the easel to paint more of the wildflowers that had bloomed. Josh was with her, holding a jar of paint brushes, and he had mentioned wanting to pick wildflowers for Anna's room. The gesture had touched Eliza's heart, resulting in her hugging him, and Denver had seen it all.

Sobbing, she collapsed to the dirt floor. No wonder he had driven away like he had, including how he didn't want her in his room at the hospital.

Eliza wiped her eyes and raised her head.

But did his actions mean he hated her or loved her? She didn't know, but she knew how to find out.

Contact a realtor in Clarksville to find a new home, preferably within walking distance of the homes of everyone she loved. Sooner or later, one way or another, she would make sure they all supported and cared for each other again, before pain and heartache and confusion crushed them all, like the bits fragile egg still clinging to her palm.

home

Lying on the sofa at home, Denver wiggled his toes in Tess's lap. "I'm glad my doctor let me get rid of that collar around my neck. A week of it was all I could handle."

"Me too, but you still need to take it easy." Tess ran a fingernail along the sole of his foot.

"Sorry, sunshine. I already told you I'm not ticklish."

She raised his feet, turned sideways on the sofa, and lowered them to her lap again. "I'm glad Mama and Papa don't mind me staying here to do stuff around the house until you're not so sore."

"Right, and you're letting them think you're sleeping in the guest room."

"I think that's for Ivy's sake."

"What did they say about Eliza and the accident and why I was there?"

"Why didn't you ask me when I got back from getting my clothes and telling them?"

"Because I was tired from that freaking ten-hour ride in your cramped little car. Besides, I knew you'd tell me eventually."

"They understood why I wanted you to talk to her."

Denver had figured as much. As far as the accident, to avoid any complications concerning Eliza, he and Tess had decided to tell Absalom and Oneita how he had crashed on the way to see her and had never talked to her. It wasn't like Eliza would come here and tell them the truth.

Tess eased his feet to the sofa and stood. "Ready for lunch?"

Denver stood too. "I better move around and loosen up. The soreness is a lot better."

"That's because of those massages I've been giving you. If you feel better, it's time I got one too, along with something else."

Eyeing the fit of her jeans, Denver followed her to the kitchen. "It's a miracle, sunshine, your jeans have healed me!"

She turned around. "Stop yelling. You're supposed to wave your hands in the air when you say 'it's a miracle.' At the refrigerator, she gave him two containers. "Roast beef or chicken?"

"Both—with a side of you."

"When we start doing that again, maybe we should go ahead and get pregnant."

At the counter, Denver opened the container of sliced chicken. "Not cool. Your mama and papa would have a fit."

"I'm teasing." Tess brought mayo from the frig and a loaf of bread from the breadbox. "How long do you want to wait after we're married?"

"I don't know. I'd like to have some time by ourselves instead of going straight to diapers and 3 a.m. feedings."

Tess opened the container of roast beef. "I want at least two kids. A boy with blue eyes and brown hair like you, and a girl with hair like mine and blue eyes too, would be perfect."

Denver laughed. "It's too bad we can't put our order in."

They made sandwiches and poured iced tea and returned to the sofa, where they placed everything on the coffee table.

Outside the sliding glass doors, the midday sun shimmered on the lake. The oaks, maples, and hickories bordering the lot were filling with leaves. A pontoon boat hummed by, with a family taking a ride.

Denver sipped coffee. Almost June. Almost a year without Eliza. Almost a year without seeing her slender figure and long, black hair moving around the house as if she were in slow motion, like the ghosts they had become when they had lost Lily.

How could they find each other again, not in love but as friends and family? He hated all this confusion, hated what it had done to everyone concerned. Like with the years of misunderstanding between Eliza and Oneita, stemming from when Oneita had slapped Eliza as a child at the well to make her get water there instead of at the river, it took next to nothing to break the fragile bonds of love within a family.

Tess bumped her shoulder with his. "Baby for your thoughts."

"'Baby?' What happened to 'penny?'"

"Can I help it if I can't wait to have your baby?"

"It'll be pretty cool when we do. I assume you'll breast feed."

"Uh-huh, the typical man, looking down instead of into my eyes."

"It's not my fault I got used to your hourglass." He looked down again. "With sand in all the right places."

"Yes, I'll breast feed. I'll also use a pump so you can help. Just the thought of you feeding our baby makes me so happy."

Taking a bite of sandwich, Denver chuckled.

Tess poked his side. "What are you laughing at?"

Denver sipped tea to wash the sandwich down. "I think I'll like watching you feed our baby more than you'll like watching me feed our baby."

She slapped his knee. "Behave. We'll teach our kids to play the guitar and sing too, right?"

"That's *your* job. My talent for singing and playing the guitar is no better than my ability to breast feed."

"How's your talent with a hammer and nails?"

"Decent, why?"

"Did you forget how I want a guitar shop? I've got to keep you honest by making you earn your way into my bed every night."

About to take a bite of sandwich, Denver stopped. "What did you do to earn your way into my bed when you walked over to sneak into it all those times?"

"It's not my fault Mama and Papa bought a house within walking distance of yours."

Denver finished his meal and went to the sliding glass doors. He missed the days when he, Willow, Mom, and Dad rolled the propane grill from under the deck and cooked and ate and swam until the sun set behind them. Homemade ice cream usually followed. They always ate their fill, whether peach, strawberry, banana, chocolate, or vanilla, with Willow teasing him about getting a brain-freeze when he ate too fast.

Saying nothing, Tess joined him to lean her head against his shoulder. He kissed her hair, loving the softness of it against his lips, the aroma of sunshine and fresh air from a walk she had taken earlier, and faced the doors again.

He and Eliza had invited her family over for a similar cookout a few times after they were married, including when she was not quite nine-months pregnant. Even Absalom and

Ethan took turns feeling Lily kick or shove against the taught skin of her stomach beneath the elastic of her maternity pants.

What a beauty she had been when she was born, with porcelain skin, black brows and lashes, and a headful of black hair like Eliza's.

As tears threatened, Denver buried his face into Tess's hair. Yes, this family needed to reunite again, if for no other reason than to discover the love that had made them a family to begin with.

* * *

Tess turned to look up into Denver's eyes. "Are you okay? You're quiet like you sometimes get when you stand here and watch the lake."

"Just thinking."

Tess said nothing. The only thing he could be thinking about was Eliza. She faced the lake and took his hands to join them at her stomach, leaning back against him.

He was such a sweet man—loving and fun, kind and gentle—strong enough to handle the combined tragedy of losing his daughter and his wife. Still, like the day he had found out Eliza was divorcing him, he was as fragile as she had been when Lily died. What a nightmare no one had foreseen: Eliza staying in a tent at the cemetery, holding that small mound of red dirt, saying over and over how she would never leave her daughter, all while refusing to let Denver comfort her. Then a doctor had written a prescription for something to make her sleep, and Denver had taken her to a mental facility.

Yes, this man with his arms around her was thinking of his past life and how it would've turned out differently if Lily had lived, giving him and Eliza all the love they could ever need or want.

Tess raised his hands and kissed them, placed one palm against her cheek and held it there, lowered his other hand to her stomach. How would it feel to have their baby growing inside her, to have his hand there to feel a kick or a push, to have him smile and tell her how much he loved her?

Yes, she had been teasing him about getting pregnant before they were married, but the idea pleased her. Still, although she pressed his hand to her stomach a bit firmer at the thought, she couldn't do that. They would get married soon and start their family. All of their loved ones would gather for a cookout like those they had before things went so wrong between him and Eliza.

But what about Eliza? If she still loved him, did she want him back? For the longest time, everyone acquainted with them—from their combined family to Akina and Jan—believed in their love like Tess did, never questioning it, always inspired by it. As terrible as the tragedy of Lily's death had been, the ending of Eliza and Denver's life together was no less tragic. To have a love like theirs and lose it—Tess couldn't imagine it, nor could she imagine losing him either. Whatever happened, no matter who loved who, she would find a way to a create a happy ending for the three of them.

She turned in Denver's arms and stood on tiptoe to kiss him, kiss the corners of his mouth, kiss his upper and lower lip, press her hands into the small of his back. He responded with equal touch and taste, waiting—like they sometimes did—to let their need build to an overwhelming crescendo before they undressed and shared each other.

Hugging him as tight as she could, Tess imagined crawling inside his chest. If she could do that, if she could gather his ribs around her as a cage of protection, could use his heart as a pillow, could use his lungs as a blanket, she could love him without the overwhelming fear of Eliza returning to take him away.

Without a word, he led her to his bed. Undressed, they lay on their sides beneath the sheet, his fingers in her hair, hers in his, while they looked into each other's eyes. Tears threatened. Tess banished them. No, they weren't remembering each other for when Eliza returned; they were photographing each other, using their eyes as cameras, their souls as film. She touched the corner of an eye, where the beginnings of crow's feet sometimes showed his worry; touched his mouth, where she loved to tease with nibbling kisses; touched the cleft in his chin, where she loved to focus when he said *I love you, angel.*

His fingers left her hair. He touched between her eyebrows, where her knot of worry sometimes showed; touched the tip of her nose, where he kissed as lightly as a butterfly's wingbeat; touched each corner of her mouth, where her lips curved upward slightly, even when she wasn't smiling.

He rolled her over and hovered above her, resting himself on his elbows while running his fingertips through her hair. "I love your eyes, especially those tiny flecks of gold around the centers."

"I love yours too, especially the flecks of green around the centers. It's like we're the same and never knew it."

His lips grazed the tip of her nose, lingered on the corners of her mouth, lowered to her chin and to her throat. She threaded her fingers into his hair and guided him lower, where he kissed her stomach and paused at her navel.

Tess raised her head to watch him. He sat up and ran his fingertips along her thighs. "Every time I try to think of the words to describe you, all I can come up with are, Marylin Monroe, eat your heart out." He stroked her thighs again, down her calves and back up, then kissed every line his fingertips had traced.

Tess sat up and pulled him to her. "Slowly, baby, oh, so slowly."

"I don't think I can."

"Pretend I'm the lake. Pretend you're paddling along while thinking of me. Pretend the paddle dips into the water so slowly it hardly leaves a wake."

Shifting above her, Denver closed his eyes and so did Tess. "Oh, yes … oh, yes. I'm your lake, Denver. I'm water and love and you're sunshine and blue sky. Love me … love me so slowly."

He raised up, and she opened her eyes to look into his. How could she ever let him go?

Still sharing their exquisitely slow rhythm, he kissed the tip of her nose again. "You are so unbelievably amazing, angel. I could die right now and be happy."

"No, baby. We've got our whole lives ahead of us."

Face tensing, he closed his eyes as his body tightened over and over again. Seconds later, Tess did the same, reveling in how they could share each other so perfectly.

Through the window and along a bedroom wall, the sun left the shadows of tree limbs. A bass boat roared somewhere on the lake. The air conditioner fluttered the curtains.

Denver rolled over and Tess followed, wrapping an arm around his waist and snuggling the back of his neck. He reached back to trace the curve of her hip.

They lay like this all afternoon. As the sun set and the room darkened, Tess napped and woke to the sound of Denver mumbling in his sleep. Who was he dreaming of? Just now, after their most amazing time together to date, he should be dreaming of her. Then again, how many amazing times had he and Eliza spent in this bed while doing the same things?

Tess shrugged. She didn't mind that as much as she minded the thought of never making love to Denver again, or never having his children, or never having all the things married couples shared.

No matter. Whatever she had to do, she and Denver would have all that.

Regardless of Eliza or not.

smiles

At the far end of the garden, near Anna's flowers, Eliza chose the smallest brush from a jar, dabbed the tip into dark-brown oil paint, and finished Josh's right eye on the canvas.

"That looks just like Papa, 'Liza." David crawled from Anna's lap and came close to peer at the painting. "What about Mama and me?"

Josh came over to tousle David's hair. "Give her time, Son. A painting like that takes a lot of patience to make."

In her wheelchair, Anna slowly raised her hands. "Your papa's right, sweetheart."

Eliza noted how the fingers on Anna's left hand were even more curled, including how the left side of her mouth drooped lower than before. If she had suffered another stroke, Josh hadn't mentioned it.

"Are you through for today?" Josh asked, rubbing his shoulder. "I'm stiff from standing here so long."

"I'm tired," Anna said.

"I'm not," David said. He whirled around to face Eliza. "I know, let's go fishing."

Eliza dropped the paint brush into a jar of solvent. "I've got to clean up right now. Maybe later."

Josh picked up the jar of clean bushes. "I'll take these to the house and come back for Anna." Turning toward the house, he stumbled and fell, spilling the brushes in the grass. David rushed over to grab his arm. "Let me help, Papa."

Josh worked his way to one knee and then to his feet. "I guess I'm just clumsy, Son."

"You're tired from planting the garden the last two days," Anna signed.

Josh brushed grass from his pants. "I was in a hurry because I was late planting."

David put the spilled brushes in the jar. "I'll take them, Papa."

"And I'll roll Anna in," Eliza said. "You two go on. I'll come back for everything else later."

In the living room, Eliza lifted Anna to the sofa beside Josh. The poor woman's body felt like a bag of bones. David got one of his books and climbed up between them.

At the end of the garden again. Eliza admired the painting, which she considered to be one of her best. Yes, Anna was thin, and the doctors had given up on her rehab months ago, but Eliza planned to paint her lovely features from memory, with high cheekbones, full lips, and a stunning smile, along with shining hair, black and thick, streaming down her shoulders. Although Josh had returned to the Amish, he had told Eliza how he wanted this portrait to be of his family in their natural state, as if the accident had never happened and they weren't wearing Amish clothes. "Make us all smile whether we grow too tired to smile or not," he had said. "Make us smile as if we're in Heaven, with no more sorrows, no more pain, and surrounded by the love of God."

She had done so with Josh, giving him a smile that turned his plain features into handsome ones, although rugged from his slightly crooked nose. The next time she would add Anna and David, blending the family into the wildflowers behind them, adding a white background of clouds with a blue sky peeking through.

Eliza took the painting from the easel and lay it flat on the grass. She started to fold the easel to carry inside, but the phone in her pocket vibrated. The screen showed the name of the real estate agent she was working with. "Hello, Kathy. Any luck?"

"I found exactly what you're looking for, Mrs. Andrews."

"Please, call me Eliza."

"All right, Eliza it is. The home is in the area you requested and on the lake. It's on the small side—three bedrooms and two full baths—but it has a large kitchen and dining room and family room."

"What about a basement or garage? I need one or the other to store my painting supplies."

"No basement, I'm afraid. It does have an attached garage. The lot has plenty of room to build a large garage, or even an art studio. Doesn't that sound wonderful?"

"It does."

"I'll send some pictures. If you like it, we can make an appointment so you can see it. Oh, the house is only a few years old, so all the plumbing and the heating and air conditioning is like new—the kitchen appliances and the washer and dryer too. It's really a great find, and at a good price."

Eliza pumped her fist. It was about time something positive happened. "It sounds great, Kathy. Send the photos. If I like it, I'll send a deposit and come down to see it. If I *really* like it, we'll tell the buyer to put a Sold sign in the yard."

"If so, when would you like to move in? I can recommend an attorney for the closing and get the ball rolling. That way you can come whenever you're ready."

"I'm not sure." Eliza paused. She would stay with Josh and Anna and David at least through the winter. He would have to make arrangements for help after that. His Amish friends would surely lend a hand. "That's a good idea," she told Kathy. "We never know when plans will change."

Eliza ended the call. The photos came and the house was just as Kathy had described it. A text sealed deal, and Eliza pumped her fist again, excited to soon own her own home.

David ran out to help her with the rest of her supplies. "I'm sorry, Mama, I forgot to help."

With his solemn tone, Eliza's positive mood turned sour. As great as moving into her new home would be, moving into it without David would take a long time to get over.

They got everything inside and put away. Eliza checked the time and went to the living room to find David, who was on the sofa between Josh and Anna again. "I think I know a sweet young man who wants to go fishing. Does anyone here know someone like that?"

David pulled Josh's hand around his shoulders and snuggled against Anna's side. "Not now, 'Liza. Mama and Papa need me."

"You can go if you want to," Josh said.

"No, Papa," David said, shaking his head. "I have to stay right here."

Anna raised her hands. "You're such a sweet boy. If I didn't know any better, I'd say your papa and I were in Heaven with an angel."

In tears, Eliza hurried to her room and closed the door. How could she leave this wonderful family, especially David? Her knees buckled, and she dropped to the bed. David was almost five. If her and Denver's daughter had lived, she would be two and a half, running around behind them wherever they went, talking, wanting hugs, wanting kisses.

Eliza palmed the tears from her eyes, pressing so hard her cheekbones ached. What would it take to end the pain of losing her daughter? Being with Denver again? Having children? Knowing she could make love to him to get pregnant?

Something needed to happen to make all those things possible, including a time when she could visit the cemetery without crying her eyes out.

Maybe soon. Maybe later. But it *had* to happen.

ultimatum

In Clarksville, Tess climbed from her car and met Denver on the sidewalk in front of his barber shop. They hadn't strolled the town in a while. With it being the first of August, she wanted to do it in the morning, before it got hot like when they had walked the streets during Lakefest last year. She slipped her hand in his. "Where would you like to shop first, handsome?"

"I don't know, gorgeous. This was your idea."

Tess pulled him along. "Let's see what catches our eye."

They passed the furniture store. Denver had plenty of furniture for when she would move in after they got married, so she saw no need to go in. A consignment shop was next. It wasn't open yet, but Tess had enjoyed browsing there before. Across the street, the brick structure and tall steeple of a church caught the midmorning sun just so. Further along, they passed two real estate agencies and the pizza place. Mark had mentioned playing there before she had stopped helping him with gigs. At the walk-in mall near the center of town, Denver reminded her how he had bought her first guitar there. After passing another real estate place, butter pecan ice cream tempted her at a shop that had great hot dogs and barbecue sandwiches, but they had talked about walking the other side of the street first, then returning to this end of town to eat at the new brewery. At the next street, Denver mentioned visiting the thrift shop to the right for used books. She said she had bought several more about Thomas Jefferson and Sally Hemings, along with three novels about the Outer Banks of North Carolina, saying all of those would keep her reading for at least a year. They crossed the street at the end of town, where the business bridge started across the lake. As they walked away from the bridge, the sun warmed their backs. Nearing an antique and knickknack and candle shop, she caught the scent of cinnamon as a customer opened the door. They crossed a side street and passed more storefronts. Denver paused at one to say how his dad used to ride his bike there as a kid, to buy either a balsa wood glider or a rubber band-driven plane. At home again, he would fly them until they broke, or once, in the case of the glider, until an updraft carried it out of sight in the sky. At Tess's car, they walked back to the end of town and to the brewery, where they ordered burgers, fries, ice tea with lemon for her, and a glass of beer for him. Outside, with a great view of the lake, including the business bridge to the right and the railroad bridge to the left, they sat to enjoy their meal.

Although Tess had loved living in the country in Ohio, the small-town charm of Clarksville had grown on her. People were friendly. The stores, including the clothing store where she loved to shop, had anything she wanted, and the chamber of commerce held several events during the year for citizens and visitors alike. Yes, Clarksville was a fine place, especially to raise her and Denver's children.

Beside her, he patted her hand. "You've been quiet for most of our walk. Is something on your mind?"

"We've let June pass without setting a wedding date."

"Ah, you're ready to make an honest woman out of yourself instead of sneaking to my house every other night and climbing into my bed."

"You never complained before."

"I'm not complaining now. We're just lucky you live within walking distance."

"If you wanted, you could even sneak into my bed if Mama and Papa and Ivy ever go somewhere overnight."

Denver clinked his beer glass to her tea glass. "I'll remember that. What about a date?"

"How big a wedding should we have? The two hotels on this end of the lake can hold plenty of people."

One side of Denver's mouth quirked with a half-grin. "I doubt your Amish friends will drive their buggies all the way here from Ohio for a wedding."

Tess dipped a fry in ketchup. "Well, there's Akina and Jan and Jon and his family."

"And Leah and Mark. Did I tell you she called the other day? They got married last week, right after the Nags Head gig."

"Romance is in the air, baby." Tess swallowed the fry. "Do you want a big wedding or not? All I care about inviting is close friends and family."

"That means Willow and William and your family. Where would you like the wedding?"

"I like your backyard. We can have a cookout for the reception. I'll make sure everyone knows casual dress—like *lake country* casual dress—is required."

Denver's eyes widened. "If you mean you don't need an expensive wedding dress, you realize you're the world's perfect woman, don't you?"

"Only when I'm with you, baby, only when I'm with you." Tess finished her burger and dawdled over the fries. "How about a honeymoon? Should we stay home and keep wearing out your bed, or should we try out another one somewhere else?"

Denver drank the last of his beer. "Virginia has lots of choices. We both like the mountains and the beach and the lake."

Tess waggled a finger at him. "Don't you even think about taking me to the same cabin in the park where you took Eliza."

"It's the only honeymoon cabin. It's not like we haven't been sleeping in the same bed where she and I slept."

"That doesn't bother me. I'd rather have our honeymoon at someplace different and out of the way like— I know, one of my novels is about Ocracoke Island. That's not too far. It's out of the way too."

"Great idea," Denver said. "All we have to do is set a date and check with your folks and Willow. Then we can reserve a place on Ocracoke and we're good to go."

* * *

Back at his house, Tess leaned over in the car to kiss him. "I'll go talk to Mama and Papa about a date."

"How about next Saturday? I can reserve a place on Ocracoke now and call Willow."

Tess rubbed his chest. "Mmm, you can't wait to be my husband any more than I can wait to be your wife, can you?"

Denver tapped her nose with a fingertip. "You got it, sunshine. Come back after you talk to your folks and we'll practice for the honeymoon." He kissed her and waved as she drove away. Never in his wildest dreams would he have believed another woman—let alone the woman who used to be his sister-in-law—could make him every bit as happy as Eliza had.

He took the laptop from his bedroom and brought it to the dining room table. Time to find a romantic hotel room on Ocracoke.

Scrolling through several pages of rooms, Denver stopped. Why stay at a hotel when a waterfront cottage would be perfect? He scrolled through those choices: some on Silver Lake Harbor with a picturesque setting of boats of all kinds tied to docks of all sizes, some on canals with screened porches and decks and hammocks.

He stopped scrolling at the photo of a gorgeous, two-story home—on the Pamlico Sound at that. A dock with a kayak? Rocking Adirondack chairs on a massive deck? A propane grill listed in the amenities? A jacuzzi large enough for two? A hot tub? A double hammock hanging from the deck, where huge timbers elevated the house off the sand in case of hurricanes?

As he was about to read the list of amenities again, the name of the house jumped off the monitor at him.

Second Chance.

If that wasn't a sign that he and Tess belonged together instead of him and Eliza, nothing was.

Denver bookmarked the page and looked at his watch? Tess should've been here by now. It should only take a few minutes to check a wedding date with her folks. Well, he could call Willow and get that out of the way.

The front door clicked open. Tess's footsteps padded down the hall. Denver held the laptop up. "Look what I—" He set the laptop down.

"I knew this would happen," Tess said, wiping tears. "I just knew it."

Denver went to her. "What's wrong?" He couldn't imagine Absalom or Oneita objecting to their marriage, so what—

Tess led him to the sofa. "I'm so afraid you'll hate me when I tell you this."

"Tell me what? Did something happen at your house?"

She nodded. "Eliza happened."

"What do you mean? She's in Ohio."

"She hasn't been in Ohio since the middle of June. She bought a house the next road down from your road."

Denver jumped from the sofa. "I don't care where she lives," he said, waving his arms, "I don't have to see her. In fact, she can go straight to he—"

"Stop it!" Tess screamed. "No matter what she's done, she's still my sister!"

"You're defending her after everything she put me through? What the hell is wrong with you?"

Tess stood. She took him in her arms, resting her head on his chest. "I'm the woman who loves you enough to let you go."

Her shoulders shook as she cried, and all Denver could do was hold her. This had to be a mistake. Eliza couldn't just show up and snap her fingers and demand that Tess give him up.

She let go of him, went to the kitchen for a paper towel, and came back, wiping her eyes. On the sofa again, she looked up at him, eyes red, chin trembling. Whatever she needed to say, Denver needed to calm her down first. Then they could fix whatever was happening. He palmed her cheek, kissed her forehead. "I'm sorry for blowing up. Tell me what it is so we can deal with it."

"That's just it, I can't tell you. Eliza has to tell you. I will say this—everything we thought she was doing with that man in Ohio is wrong."

"She divorced me, Tess. That's all I need to know."

She stood and went to the sliding glass doors. She didn't turn to face him. "You need to give her another chance," she said, her voice barely a whisper. "There are things you don't know.

Things about me too. If you knew them, you might not want to marry me."

Denver started to go to her but didn't. What could she have done except— "If you and Mark slept together, I don't care."

She shook her head. Her auburn ponytail slowly brushed her back and shoulders. "I told you the truth when I said we weren't dating, so it's nothing like that."

"Then what—?"

She came back to the sofa. "I told Eliza and she'll tell you." She took his hand and placed his palm to her cheek. "But you'll hate me when I tell you what I'll do if you don't give her another chance."

Denver was tempted to jerk his hand from her cheek. At least she hadn't said to give Eliza a *Second Chance*, like the name of the house in Ocracoke. It was his and Tess's sign that they belonged together, no matter what she or Eliza thoug— He took his hand from her cheek. "What do you mean? What will you do if I don't give her another chance?"

"This is the part you'll hate me for."

"Then don't say—"

"I won't marry you."

Denver got up from the sofa. "Look, I don't know how she's brainwashed you, but—"

"She hasn't brainwashed anybody. She told everybody the truth and apologized. She even told Ethan before she left."

"Then why hasn't he called me or you?"

"She wanted to tell Mama and Papa and me herself."

Denver rubbed his eyes. So this was why Tess didn't come back right away. He sat beside her. "I love you, okay?"

"But are you *in love* with me? And think before you answer."

"I don't have to think. Every minute we've spent together is amazing because *you're* amazing. I'm as in love with you as I ever was with Eliza."

Tess pointed toward the sliding glass doors. "I've seen you standing there looking at the lake more times than I can count. Be honest, how many of those times were you thinking about Eliza and how much you love her?"

Denver looked away. If anyone knew how to jab the needle of truth into him, Tess did. "Okay, fine. Part of me is still in love with Eliza. I've thought about my accident off and on and that might be why it happened."

Tess shook her head. "I knew it."

"No, Tess, part of me hates her too. If we were to ever talk, I'm scared of what I'll say. You saw how I reacted when I got those damn divorce papers. I almost passed out."

"Please don't curse," Tess said, touching his arm. "Like you say cursing isn't me, it's not you either."

"Whatever." Denver rubbed his eyes again. Why all of this now, right when his life was getting on track from losing Eliza? He lowered his hand. "What do I have to do? The sooner I can get it over with, the sooner we can get married."

"I want her to come here for a month."

"You're insane." Denver closed his eyes for a second. "I'm sorry, I didn't mean that. A month is easy. I just won't have anything to do with her."

A knot formed between Tess's eyebrows. She rubbed it, squinting, and lowered her hand. "That's not giving her a chance and you know it. You have to at least be civil. Talk. Eat together. Walk somewhere. Go out on the pontoon boat. Paddle the canoe."

"What are we supposed to talk about, how she hurt me more than anyone has ever hurt me? Hell, she hurt me more than when my parents or Lily died, and I thought those times were all the hurt I could stand."

"What about when you saw Lily for the first time in the coff—"

"Don't you dare. If you say that I hate you."

Tess took his hand; he jerked it away. "Fine, I'll spend a month with her. I'll even be civil, but that's it. Then you better spend a damn month making up for what you're putting me through."

Tess's chin trembled again. "Please—" Her voice broke. "Please hold me."

"Why should I?"

"Because I'll marry you if you don't want Eliza after you spend a month with her. Because I want to spend a week with you in Ocracoke before you spend a month with Eliza. Because I love you more than I ever thought a person could love someone. Aren't those good reasons?"

Denver wanted to take her in his arms—*ached* to take her in his arms—but not yet. "What's this about going to Ocracoke?"

"Did you find a place to stay?"

"I did."

"Is it nice?"

"It would be nicer if we were spending our honeymoon there."

"Can't we pretend we are? I don't want to think about anything but us while we're there."

"Did you talk about this to your folks? They might not want—"

"I'll talk to them, but I'm old enough to do what I want."

Denver thought he knew the answer to this, but he might not. "Did you plan all this with Eliza?"

"She doesn't like it any more than you do. I talked to her outside, after she told us everything at Papa's house."

"What do you mean she doesn't like it?"

"That's for her to tell. Will you do like I ask?"

"If it means us getting married, I don't have a choice."

Tess slid close and lay her head on his shoulder. "I wouldn't do this if I didn't love you so much. Do you believe me?"

Denver took her into his arms, stroked her back, nuzzled her hair. Eliza could stay with him a month, six months, a year, or a million years. That wouldn't make him change his mind about Tess. He eased her away to look into her amazing green eyes. The gold flecks in the center tugged at his heart. She was his sunshine, his angel, and she always would be those things. "I'll never let you go, Tess, no matter what. Our week away will be so great, you'll forget all this nonsense."

Tess nodded, gave him a slight smile and kissed him, opened her mouth and shared her sweet taste.

They undressed and made love on the sofa, lay there until the sun set and the lake turned from blueish-gray to gray to orange on the far bank as it reflected the dying light. He showed her the house on Pamlico Sound. She said she loved it. He made the reservation. She smiled and hugged his neck. He called in an order of crab dip from the restaurant. She picked it up. He lay a blanket on the dock and plugged in the LED lights. She brought a bottle of wine and two glasses down. They ate and talked, serenaded by the chirp of crickets, the wash of the waves against the bank, the *who-whoooo* of an owl. The ozone aroma of the lake surrounded them like a gray blanket, soft and barely there.

How he loved her. How he loved her. How he loved her.

Ocracoke

Driving south along N.C. Highway 12, Denver pointed. "Wow, the Cape Hatteras Lighthouse. Let's come back and climb it one day."

"That looks like a lot of steps." Tess reached over from the passenger seat to rub his leg. "If I have my way, you'll be too tired from doing other things."

Denver patted her hand. "You've been having your way with me every night since you told me about Eliza."

Tess smacked his leg. "Hush. We promised to forget about all that."

They passed the lighthouse to their left and continued into Buxton. Tess pointed to the right. "Buxton Village Books. I bet they have some great novels about the area."

"Didn't you say you have enough to last a year?" Denver asked.

"I brought the one about Ocracoke. It's about two eighteen-year-old sisters who live there during World War II. They're twins, but they're nothing alike."

Denver slowed for a car leaving a post office. "How are they different?"

"One's blonde and one's dark," Tess said. "The dark one's serious and the blonde one thinks about boys. I'd say they're like Eliza and me, but we're serious when we need to be and romantic when we need to be."

"What happened to not talking about her?" Denver asked, cutting his eyes toward Tess.

She glanced at him. "She's my sister. We need to figure out how to deal with each other if you take her back."

"Ain't happening, Tess. Not in a million years. Let's not bring her up anymore."

They left Buxton. To their right, the Pamlico Sound stretched in an endless sight of sparkling water. Denver loved his lake, but for size, the Pamlico had it beat.

In Frisco, they passed the Native American Museum, something interesting for the trip back home. By the time they reached Hatteras, they had passed all kinds of shops and places to eat. Hatteras even had a campground and the Teach's Lair Marina, more places to consider for future visits.

About a half mile further, Tess leaned forward in her seat. "Are all those lines of cars waiting for the ferry to Ocracoke?"

Denver slowed to a stop in one of the lines. "Patience, sunshine, patience."

"Patience my behind." Tess snorted laughter. "You didn't want to be patient when we finally slept together after your accident." She unbuckled her seat belt and slid over to run her hand under his shirt. "I wonder if anyone will notice if I—" She whispered in his ear.

"You better not, sunshine. Someone might report us for indecent exposure." Denver removed his seatbelt too. "We might as well sit back and wait." Minutes passed. More cars filled the lines behind them. "What interests you about Thomas Jefferson and Sally Hemings to buy more books about them?"

"I sympathize with her. Jefferson took her to France when she was only fourteen. She got pregnant there at sixteen."

Denver didn't know that. "Whoa. I can't even begin to imagine that."

Tess turned in the seat to face him. "Me neither, especially the part about being a slave. France had ended slavery. She was free there, but she told Jefferson she would come back to Monticello for certain privileges for herself and if he freed any children they had. That's one woman who knew how to make a deal, and I mean from a position of weakness like being a slave."

"It sounds like you admire her."

"Definitely. In one of the books I read, her son Madison said she became Jefferson's concubine in France. Imagine how strong she had to be to give up any chance of freedom there for herself so her children could have a chance at freedom at home."

The muffled roar of an engine came from toward the sound, and a ferry swung their way.

Denver faced Tess. "That's strong all right. Do any of the books you've read say if she and Jefferson were more than just slave and owner?"

"Nothing specific." Tess ran her foot along Denver's leg. "You know me, the romantic. When Jefferson died, she moved in with two of her children in Charlottesville. She took some of his personal belongings, so maybe they meant more to each other than just concubine and owner."

The ferry pulled up to the lines of cars. Denver clicked his seatbelt. "What woman these days would want that kind of relationship?"

"I guess it depends on the woman," Tess said, clicking her seatbelt too. "When I have kids, I want the man to be my husband and all that goes with it. There's no way I could live like that."

The lines of cars moved forward. Following a man's directions, Denver parked behind a car near the middle of the ferry. As it left the other cars behind for the next ferry, people climbed from their vehicles. He and Tess got out too, to thread through the vehicles to stand at the front of the ferry, near a length of orange netting that hung across the opening where everyone would drive off.

Tess leaned against him. He wrapped his arms around her. The aroma of salt air revived him from his wait for the ferry, whose engine rumbled beneath the deck. He nuzzled Tess's neck, bare from a ponytail, and tasted the combination of salt from her skin and the coconut of some new kind of sunscreen she was trying. If life got any better than this, he wouldn't be able to stand it. He kissed her ear. "I love you, angel. I'll spend the rest of my life proving it to you."

She took one of his hands and kissed its palm. "I love you too, baby. I know it whether you prove it or not."

The bow of the ferry broke through the smooth water of the sound, similar to the rolling rush of waves at Virginia Beach. The hot July sun seared down, creating a runnel of sweat that left a trail from Denver's underarms to his sides. The warmth between him and Tess grew, but he didn't let her go because he would *never* let her go. She leaned back against him even more, their bare legs in shorts weaving together like they had woven together time and time again, whenever they made love and after, as they lay within each other's arms.

Regardless of any plan she had for Eliza and him, she was the love of his life now, and nothing—or no one, or any apology or story by Eliza—would change that. Still, if everyone could find their way to friendship again, including Eliza's family, that would be a positive. After all, he had thought about that recently, and it would be the best way to resolve all the problems between him and Eliza and all the tragedy surrounding Lily's death.

At the end of Hatteras, the ferry turned west into the wind. The sound went from smooth to choppy, scattering spray upward from the bow. A single gull flew to the right, white breast feathers parting in the wind. It turned its head toward the ferry, to focus its yellow eye on Denver as if to ask if he was sure of what and who he wanted. Another gull joined it, then another, and the trio of white banked toward the strip of sand and marsh in the distance, which marked Ocracoke Island.

Denver nuzzled Tess's neck again. Whatever this week brought—no matter what they did or where they went—he would make sure she knew how much he loved her and how much he wanted to spend the rest of his life with her.

cemetery

Tess placed the last of the breakfast dishes in the strainer. Beside her, Denver dried a coffee mug and put it away. He moved behind her and slipped his hands around her waist. She had been wearing a bikini top since they had arrived in the house called *Second Chance*, so his hands felt deliciously inviting as they warmed her stomach. She backed up against him. "We just did that last night, you know."

He ran a fingertip in a circle around her navel. "Is it my fault we can't get enough of each other?"

She reached back to thread her fingers into his hair. "You got that right, baby." Pulling him down to her neck, she leaned her head over. "Do you see anything you'd like to kiss?"

"I love your new earrings." He kissed her ear lobe. "Gold hoops turn me on."

She shimmied her shoulders, which shook the bikini top side-to-side. "How about these?"

He popped her bottom. "And this, Marylin."

Tess turned within his arms. "As much as I'd like to spend some more time in bed, we need to see some sites today."

"I guess you're right," Denver said, taking his hands from around her waist. "We've already spent three days eating out and fooling around every chance we get. What's on your agenda?"

"Let's visit the cemetery. My novel says four British seamen were buried there after they washed up on the beach, when a German U-boat sank their ship. I thought it was fiction until I looked it up."

Tess helped Denver dry the dishes and put them away. In the bedroom, she put an Outer Banks T-shirt on over her bikini top, slipped on sandals, and turned around. "Do I look beachy or what?"

Denver pulled on a pair of floral shorts, a shirt that matched Tess's, and added sandals. "Me too. Can we walk to the cemetery?"

"We sure can, let's go."

On the road leading from the house and the Pamlico Sound, Tess admired how the live oak limbs shaded her and Denver. Shaped by the prevailing winds, they tended to reach one way, like arms reaching for a lover.

As they walked, he entwined his fingers into hers, smiling at her. If the worst happened, if he and Eliza got back together—No, that wasn't the worst that could happen. The worst that could happen was if her plan to deal with it failed. It shouldn't though. All of her plans, except for falling in love with Denver, had worked out so far. What would he think of her when Eliza told him everything her little sister had done? It was hard to tell, but knowing Denver, he would understand.

Tess pulled her hand free from Denver's and jumped on his back. "Give me a ride, cowboy!" She wrapped her arms around his neck and her legs around his waist. "Git along there and show me what you got."

Denver trotted down the road, whinnying and snorting, until he stopped, breathing hard. "All right, cowgirl, this horse needs a break."

Tess patted his chest. "I can't wear you out. I want you to have plenty of energy for tonight."

"Like we—" Denver paused for a breath. "Like we haven't done that enough. Three times a day is kind of overdoing it, don't you think?"

Tess took his hand and pulled him along. "Hush, or I'll make it four."

A few minutes later, they passed the Ocracoke Cemetery, filled with lichen-etched headstones of all shapes and sizes, including several small ones for children. Tess said nothing. She didn't want to remind Denver of Lily's death.

She led him along the far side of the cemetery, beneath more of those reaching live oak limbs, and stopped at a white fence. Inside it, white pebbles covered the ground around four headstones.

Denver pointed at a large plaque. "'In memory of the HMT Bedfordshire and its crew. Destroyed by torpedo from German submarine U-558 in May 1942.' Wow, those men coming here to help us is amazing."

Tess moved closer to the plaque. "I read on the internet how the Bedfordshire was an armed trawler. We weren't ready for World War II, so the British refitted trawlers with guns and came here to patrol for U-boats. Imagine these men leaving their families to do that."

Denver put his arm around her shoulders. "I hate to bring Eliza up, but before we got pregnant, part of the reason I wanted kids was because of how your folks love all of you. They remind me of how Mom and Dad loved Willow and me. All of that made me want a family."

Tess looked up at him. "You know your mom and dad still love you. I'm sure they're taking care of Lily and having a ball."

Denver looked away. A breeze swirled sand at their feet, rustling the leaves of the live oak trees at the same time. He looked back. "That's what I believe. If not, I would've gone insane when she died."

"Like Eliza did," Tess said. "I felt so bad for her, stuck in that mental facility all alone. Then, when she came home and did nothing but sit in the rocking chair or on the dock, it was even worse."

"It was a terrible time," Denver said. "We were like two different people, strangers really."

"Did she blame herself?"

"She never said so during our appointments with the psychiatrist."

"What did she say?"

"Just that she would get over it eventually."

"Did y'all talk about having more kids?"

"I never brought it up and neither did she. I guess we were doomed from the start."

Tess held him and lay her head on his chest. After everything he and Eliza had been through, they deserved all the happiness in the world. If she could make that happen, she would.

She pressed herself into him, wishing she could become part of him, like when DNA miraculously merged to create a baby within the womb. He was her life and always would be, regardless of what might happen between him and Eliza.

"All right," Denver said, patting her back. "It's time we perked up. What do you want to do now?"

"Let's get your pickup and drive to the bookstore here. I can never have enough books."

"Cool, we can grab some lunch while we're out. You know I gotta build up my energy for tonight."

Tess popped his behind. "And for the rest of the week too."

After a quick walk to the house, they climbed into the pickup. Tess gave him directions to the bookstore. "Oh, wow," he said, getting out, "I like this place already. I like the name too, Books to be Red."

Tess met him at the front of the pickup. "It's like an old farmhouse. I love the porch and the blue railings."

Inside, they browsed shelves and turned pages. Tess took a book from a shelf and waved Denver over. "See this one? It's one of the Outer Banks novels I have. It's about a Spanish guy who left his daughter in Spain because he couldn't handle his wife's death."

Denver touched the cover. "What about the horses?"

"It takes place in 1521. The guy and his horse are on a ship, and— Hey, I better not tell you in case you read it." Tess held the back toward Denver so he could read it. "It sounds great, huh?"

"Another story about family, like those British men in the cemetery who left theirs."

Tess nodded. "Umm-hmm, like family is important to us."

Denver took another book from beside the first one and turned the back cover to him. "This one is by the same author. It's set in Nags Head."

"I've got that one too," Tess said. "It sounds sad, but I hope the main character has a happy ending."

Denver's eyes tracked as he read. "Whoa, he gets kidnapped after his wife dies? How does he get a happy ending out of that?"

"I haven't read it yet, but I definitely like happy endings." Tess didn't say what hovered on the tip of her tongue: *Like I hope you, me, and Eliza have a happy ending.*

Two more customers came in. She took the book from Denver and put it back. "Let's find a burger place for lunch. I need a change from seafood."

Denver returned to the main road and took a left. "There's a place advertised this way as a pub. They should have burgers." Minutes later he parked outside the pub, where the wood exterior, including the porch, steps, and railings, were weathered a dark gray.

Inside, a greeter seated them at a booth and took their orders of sweet tea with lemon. Chairs and tables filled the aisle beside the booths. Beer logos and photos of the area lined the walls. Not far from their booth, a British flag hung overhead. A waiter returned with the tea, took orders of burgers and fries, and left.

Denver sipped tea. "This is nice place. It's got lots of character."

"It dure is," Tess said. "I'm glad we came."

"You mean to Ocracoke, right?"

"Absolutely." Tess sipped tea. She didn't want to bring this subject up, but if Denver and Eliza didn't get back together, it would be nice to think of the future. After more tea, she patted his hand. "We talked about having kids. How many would you like for real?"

"Two for sure. If more come along, that would be cool too."

"What about names? I think we both agree how Lily is too special to use again."

Denver smiled softly. "You having her headstone made was the nicest thing anyone has ever done for me."

"Even though I hoped you would think Eliza did it?"

"I doubt that's the only reason, angel. Was it?"

Tess took his hand in hers. "I had the feeling I was falling in love with you even then, so the answer is no."

Denver leaned over the table to kiss her. "Now, names for kids. How about Thomas for a boy, after Thomas Jefferson?"

Rolling her eyes, Tess shook her head. "I want to name my first son Denver. If I have another one, maybe Thomas will work for him."

"What if you have a girl? Sally?"

"I admire her, but I'd rather have something else. What's your mom's name?"

"Beth. Dad's name was Alan."

"Then it's Beth Lily Andrews for a girl and Denver Alan Andrews for a boy. What do you think?"

Denver's forehead wrinkled. "Denver Alan?"

Footsteps neared. The waiter set their meals and a bottle of ketchup on the table, asked if they needed anything else, and left when Denver and Tess said no.

She dipped a fry in ketchup. "Saved by lunch, huh? What's wrong with Denver Alan?"

"I don't know," Denver said, pouring ketchup over his fries. "You know how you hear a name and you don't like it right away? I guess that's it."

Tess sipped tea. "I'll think of something else before then."

As they ate, she couldn't help but wonder if she would ever get the chance to consider another name, much less her and Denver getting married. Yes, she wanted both more than anything, but he and Eliza deserved a chance at love again. If not, it would be hard to believe in love, even though love sat across the table eating a burger with ketchup on the corner of his mouth.

Tess reached over the table to finger the ketchup away and lick it from her fingertip. "You know I wouldn't do that for just anyone, right?"

Denver finished chewing and swallowed. "I love you, sunshine. You'll have the rest of your life to wipe ketchup off my mouth anytime you want."

"That's right, along with teaching our kids how to swim and fish and drive the pontoon boat."

"And paddle the canoe and hike," Denver said, nodding.

Emotion filled Tess's throat. Like salt from the ocean spray, tears burned her eyes. She stood. "I'll be right back. The lady's room is calling."

She hurried down the aisle, her sandals slapping the wood floor. In a stall, she sat and unrolled toilet paper, balled it up and held it to her mouth to muffle her sobs.

She and Denver didn't have a chance at a life together, or with children, or with teaching them everything they were just talking about, not after Eliza explained everything to him.

Done crying, Tess wiped her eyes while looking in the mirror over the sink. "What a mess you are, girl. You're in love with a man who's in love with two women and you hope we all have a happy ending?" She threw the toilet paper in the trash and re-applied mascara. "Well, it's possible, but a lot has to happen. The first is getting Denver back home to my sister." She dropped the mascara in her purse. "And making sure they don't kill each other before they realize they still love each other."

confrontation

Denver pulled into his driveway and took Tess's suitcases to her car. She got out, unlocked the trunk, and closed it after he put them in. He took his suitcases to the front door, started to unlock it, but didn't when she didn't join him. As he turned to see her at her car door, he waved her toward him. "You're not leaving me like that," he said. "Get in here so we can plan our wedding." He took the suitcases to his room, and she followed him in.

"We need to get this over with," she said, dropping to the bed with no hint of happiness on her face.

He sat beside her, not sure what she meant. "The first Saturday after Eliza leaves, we'll get married. Then we'll go right back to Ocracoke for another week."

Tess leaned against his shoulder. "Do you have any idea how much I love you?"

The sadness in her voice crushed Denver. "Where's my sunshine, sunshine? Everything's gonna work out."

Tess lay on the bed. "Lie down here and hold me."

Denver did, loving the way her head rested on his shoulder, the luxurious feel of her silky hair against his cheek, the way her body molded against his, the way she rolled over to lay her leg across both of his.

He kissed her forehead. "You're really gonna make me and Eliza spend a month together?"

"Yes."

"What will you do all that time?"

"Build guitars and read. I might drive up to see Ezra. Maybe I'll visit Monticello while I'm there." Tess propped herself up on her elbow to look into his eyes. "You have to stay away from Mama and Papa and me. You can go for groceries, that's it. Don't buy any beer or wine. Eliza told me how you were drinking too much before she left, and it worried her." Tess lay back down. A minute passed, then another. She fingered a button on his shirt and giggled. "We really went at it in Ocracoke, didn't we?"

Denver laughed. "Uh-huh. In bed. On the sofa. In the hot tub. In the jacuzzi. In the shower. On the deck at night."

"Don't forget the hammock, baby. That rocking motion was amazing, except for all those X marks on your back and butt when we got up."

"They were on your knees too."

"Uh-huh. We looked like someone had been playing tic-tac-toe on us, and the only letter they knew how to make was an X."

Denver propped himself up on his elbow and looked into her amazing green eyes. "You're my ocean, angel. I could drown in you and be completely happy." He moved her hair aside and kissed her ear lobe. "Want to?"

Tess heaved a huge sigh and got up. "I better go. Eliza is—" The doorbell rang. "That's her now. I called her at our last bathroom stop and told her when we would get here."

Denver got up too and took her into his arms. "A month will pass in no time. Then we'll get married and have the rest of our lives together."

Tess raised on tiptoe, kissed him, and left. He followed her to the beginning of the hall, where he stopped. She opened the door. With two suitcases, Eliza came in and set them down. "Please don't make us do this, Tess."

Tess went to the door and turned to face Eliza. "You said you'd give him a chance. I expect you to do exactly that." She looked around Eliza and pointed at Denver. "And I expect you to do the same for my sister." She held out her hand toward Eliza. Eliza took something from her purse and gave it to Tess, who closed the door behind her.

Denver crossed his arms. No sensation of throwing up filled his throat, which was something, but a seething anger, fueled by a hot wave of adrenalin, filled his chest. "You know where the guest room is. You used it enough for a year and a half."

Eliza put her suitcases away and came back. "You might wonder what I gave Tess."

Denver went to the sliding glass doors to face the lake. He clenched his fists. "Whatever."

"It was the key to my house. She wants to be alone because she knows she'll be upset for a while, and she doesn't want to be around Mama and Papa and Ivy."

"Oh, I can damn well understand that." Denver wanted to punch the sliding glass doors, but ending up with a broken hand wouldn't do him any good. He whirled around. "Do you have any idea how much you hurt me, any idea at all?"

Eliza sank onto the sofa. Her black hair was longer than Denver remembered, hanging over her shoulders and shining with the sunlight reflecting off the lake. She wore a gray dress with short sleeves. The hem fell just below her knees, accenting her slender legs. She and Tess were so different. Tess took after Oneita, full figured and on the short side, but with Absalom's thick head of red hair. Eliza took after Absalom, tall and stately, classy even, but with Oneita's black hair and brows, and eyes like two simmering lumps of burning coal.

She crossed her legs. The hem of the dress slid upward, revealing her thighs. She tugged it to her knees and held it there with crossed hands. "Tess told me what happened at Christmas. I didn't know—"

"Right, you didn't know I would get *your* divorce notice on Christmas, the day that's meant for families to share their love for each other instead of their hate."

A quick downward look of those dark eyes. "I don't hate you. I—"

Denver jabbed a finger at her, cutting her off. "Don't you *dare* say you love me." He didn't care if he looked like a snarling dog or not, she needed to know what she had done to him. "People who love someone don't do what you did to me."

"I was going to say I'm sorry." A single tear rolled down her cheek, leaving a wet trail from eye to chin, where it hung until it dripped to the gray dress, making a spot near the high-cut collar that spread like a thundercloud. She blinked, blinked again, blinked again, as if she were a woman who came here without the any intention of crying and hated it that she had. The muscles in her neck worked with a hard swallow, again, and again. She stood and turned to walk down the hall to the door, flats slapping the hardwood, and closed the door behind her. Her car engine started and faded away down the road.

Denver fell to the chair by the fireplace. Like before, she had run out on him again, when things were getting too near the truth.

Still, there was something about her, something about how she had held her composure until she had said she was sorry.

Yes, no doubt she *was* sorry now, but sorry was only a word, while actions meant more than any words ever spoken.

He went to the refrigerator and jerked the door open for a beer. Two bottles and one can waited. He closed the door. No, to rely on alcohol to ease his anger wouldn't help. The only thing that would help was letting Eliza know exactly how angry he was, regardless of where it led.

He snatched his phone from his pocket, dialed three numbers, and stopped at the sound of a car engine getting closer. Returning to the chair, he put the phone in his pocket. In front of the house, a car door slammed. Eliza came in with a wooden case, similar to the one downstairs, which held her oil paints. She took it to the basement and made three more trips, taking an easel, a covered painting, and more painting supplies. Each time her hair flew about her face and shoulders, like a crow on the wing within a storm, the gray dress a swirling cloud around her.

After closing the basement door, she returned to the sofa and crossed her legs again. Beads of sweat glistened on her brow. Her nostril flared with heavy exhales. Her chest rose and fell, rose and fell. When it slowed, she licked her lips. "I understand I hurt you. I never meant for any of this to happen … for us to lose Lily … for us to lose each other."

Denver tilted his head to one side. "Do you know about the headstone Tess had made?"

"Tess told me about it. She said she wanted you to think I did it so you would come to Ohio and see me. She's … she's … I don't have the words to describe how wonderful a sister she is … how wonderful a woman she is. I don't doubt her love for you and I don't doubt your love for her. That's why I don't like this any better than you do. After what I put you through, you deserve to be happy. If Tess can do that, I want her to."

Eliza's admission made Denver look away. Maybe she didn't love him after all, and this month would end with him and Tess getting married. She had to know he and Tess were lovers, had to know how intimate they had been, had to know he had done everything with her that he had done with Eliza, yet she didn't seem the least bit jealous.

He faced her again. This would hurt, but Eliza deserved it. "Loving Tess is the best thing to ever happen to me. She's everything I ever wanted in a woman, a lover, a wife. We'll be happier than I could ever have been with you." He stood, knees driving him out of the chair, a scream building in his throat.

"I loved you, Eliza! You ripped my heart out, you ripped my soul apart! All that and part of me still loves you but part me despises the day I ever met you." He fell to the chair again, exhausted from the outpouring of confusion and emotion coursing through his body, leaving him to barely whisper those last words.

She blinked again and again, an ancient owl with huge, dark eyes, cheek feathers wet with tears. "All ..." She swallowed. "All I can say is I'm sorry." She stood. "I'm tired." She started toward the guestroom but stopped on the way. "Did Tess tell you I didn't do any of those things in Ohio that it seemed I did?"

"She did."

"I'm going to tell you everything, but not all at once. It's going to take time to make you understand why I left and why I stayed, and why I slapped Ethan and why David called me mama. I was too confused to understand those things at the time, and I only realized that when Josh and Anna—" Eliza looked away, like a lost child, then back. "Do you know I've been here over a month?"

"Tess told me."

"I've been seeing my psychiatrist. She's helping me understand a lot of things about myself and why I couldn't make love to you. I just wish I could've understood those things before they made me leave you."

As the guest room door softly closed, Denver leaned over to prop his elbows on his knees and hold his head in his hands. More words had just passed between he and Eliza than in the year and a half they had spent together after Lily died. Good or bad, he didn't know, but either way, both frightened him, not only for how he might forgive Eliza, but for how his forgiveness might cause him to lose Tess.

At the refrigerator, he took out a bottle of beer, wrenched the top off, and downed the cold, bitter liquid in one long pull.

Eliza might deserve forgiveness, but not at the cost of losing Tess.

He returned to the chair with another beer. The long drive from Ocracoke had left him with gritty eyes, while the intense confrontation with Eliza had left him emotionally exhausted. Between swallows of beer, his eyes closed and opened, closed and opened.

On the lake, beyond the dock as the sun set, the water reflected the dying light, a soft pink instead of its normal orange, to red, to ochre.

He closed his eyes. The light shifted and darkened, visible through the thin layer of skin protecting him from seeing how his world was collapsing around him. The refrigerator hummed. A car passed the house, tires crunching bits of gravel. The light darkened further, even to blackness. Thunder rumbled long and low and ended. A gust of wind swished in the trees and stopped. Rain pattered against the sliding glass doors. Eyes still closed, Denver finished the beer and left the bottle between his legs. He would get up and throw it away and go to bed in a minute. Right now he wanted to sit and listen to the rain and dream of Tess making love to him, which would give them their first child, maybe a boy to love and tickle and take fishing and show how to paddle a canoe.

With a fingertip, he swiped a tear from the corner of one eye. The rain pattered harder. No wind. No thunder. No Tess to hold him through the long lonely night and tell him how everything would be all right.

What an idiot he was to be in love with two women—and two sisters at that. Before this mess was over, he might need a psychiatrist himself.

Yawning, he settled back in the chair, wishing Tess would come and run her fingers through his hair and tell him it was time for bed, time for them to share each other, time for them to sink into each other's souls as only they could.

Goodnight, angel. I love you.

Josh

Up from bed, Eliza dressed in old lake clothes: jeans, a T-shirt, and sandals. It felt great to be home, but it felt terrible to be an enemy in her home. She found Denver asleep in the same chair in the living room, a beer bottle between his legs. At least he had slept after their confrontation last night. To have him tell her he despised the day they met had hurt, but she deserved it.

He softly snored. His brown hair hung across his forehead. His lips twitched, possible from a dream of kissing Tess. His usually clean-shaven face bristled with a day-old shadow, including the cleft in his chin.

An old habit returning, she reached out to finger the hair from his forehead. No, not now, possibly never. He belonged to Tess and she belonged to him. Despite everything she had done to keep him single over the past year, which Denver should know soon, they were in love or they wouldn't be engaged.

As Eliza's fingertips touched Denver's hair, she pulled them away and went to the kitchen to make breakfast. While eggs boiled, bacon sizzled, and coffee dribbled into the carafe, she went to check on Denver. He was gone, leaving the beer bottle. She threw it in the trash and plated the food, poured coffee and took everything to the table. He came from his room and took one of the plates and one of the mugs to the kitchen, where he dumped the plate in the trash and poured the coffee into the sink. With a bottle of water from the refrigerator and an apple from the counter, he went outside. Minutes later, the scrape of the aluminum hull of the canoe came from the gravel path to the dock. Eliza went to the sliding glass doors. He slid the canoe into the water, climbed in and paddled away. It was only then that she realized it was raining. His blue T-shirt turned dark with it. His hair soon lay flat to his head. He faded away into the gray curtain of water, a ghost of her past.

She picked at her food, washed the dishes, and went to the sliding glass doors, but the gray curtain refused to part. Standing there waiting, she refused to cry. She deserved his anger, deserved every bit of it. The destruction of their lives demanded it, but she longed to hold him, longed to tell him how much she loved him.

Tess.

Eliza could hardly believe the lengths her sister had gone through to keep him single, things he needed to know, things she was afraid to tell him. Regardless, he would understand, because Tess had done those things with love in her heart.

In Eliza's back pocket, her phone vibrated. The screen showed Tess's number. "How's it going, big sister?" she asked. "Have you two killed each other yet?"

"I made him breakfast. He threw it in the trash and went out in his canoe."

"In the rain?"

"Yes."

"He told me he would try—that's not trying. Anything else?"

"He said he despised the day he met me."

"Mmm, not good. Still, he's got to get his anger out before he can start to talk to you about things."

"I suppose, but I hope it happens sooner than later."

"Me too. Holler if you need me."

Eliza ended the call and went to the sliding glass doors again. The rain was slowing, the gray curtain lifting. The silver bow of the canoe, along with Denver's blue shirt, black with water, and his brown hair hanging in his eyes, appeared. Her ghost, hers alone. The sun broke through the clouds. Take a chance? He could only push her away like he already was pushing her away, so what did it matter?

Towel in hand, Eliza arrived at the water's edge as he pulled the canoe onto the bank. When he turned to face her, she toweled his hair and face. Like a statue he stood there, and she couldn't help but smile at how he resembled David: a little blue-eyed boy with a mop of brown hair, wet after a bath.

The clouds closed, cutting off the sun. Rain pattered on the lake again. They stood there, both with runnels of water streaming down their faces. Eliza wasn't wearing a bra, and she grew acutely aware of how the thin shirt was accentuating her modest breasts, clinging to them, revealing peaks and valleys.

Denver's eyes lowered and returned to hers. He palmed her cheek, ran his thumb over her lips. Yes, she wanted him, but with love instead of lust, and his reaction to seeing her like this—water wetting her long black hair, soaking her shirt as if she wore no shirt, beading upon her cheeks and lips—was lust. She stepped away. "You love Tess. This can't happen until you decide if you want me or not."

Closed eyes, a shake of his head. He opened his eyes. "You two have me so messed up, I can hardly think."

Eliza palmed his cheek. "You're in love with two women. Despite that, when we were together, I knew you didn't have much control when it came to sex. We both know how attractive Tess is. I'm sure your control lacked with her too."

"If you're saying I'm weak, it's true. I told you how I didn't date in high school or college except for Jan." Denver ran a finger between her breasts. "Part of me hates you. You broke my heart to where I didn't want to love again. Then Tess came along and I fell in love with her."

"Do you want me? We can if it's for love."

The rain fell harder. It splattered the leaves on the trees, making them dance up and down. It struck the lake, adding the pattering sound that once serenaded them as they made love on a long ago night on the pontoon boat.

"I want you but it's wrong," Denver said. "We have too many things to work out, things I don't want to work out because I love Tess and want to marry her. She'll never hurt me like you did. I know that like I know it's raining. I know that like I know I want to take you to the bed where she and I made love and imagine you're her instead of you so you'll know everything I did with her."

Nearly in tears, Eliza ran to the house. Despite the ache in her heart, she deserved it. Even if she and Denver were together again, he would always love Tess, even to the point of wanting her physically.

In the bathroom, she undressed and toweled off. Heavy footsteps thudded to the door. "I need me some towels from the closet in there. I don't have any."

She opened the door to give him the towels. He grabbed her hand and pulled her to him, pressing their naked bodies together. "Is this what you want?" she asked, looking directly into his eyes. "To take me when it isn't because you love me?"

He tried to kiss her; she turned her head. He lowered his face to her chest; she pushed him away. He carried her to the guest room bed; she got up as soon as he put her down. "I still love you, but not enough to let you force me."

Denver left. She wrapped a blanket around herself and followed him to his bed. He fell into it and buried his face into his pillow and sobbed. She covered him with a sheet, rubbed his heaving back, fingered his wet hair. What had she done to this wonderful man?

Without looking up from the pillow, he pushed her away. "Go, just leave."

"Denver?"

"Why can't you just leave?"

"Please stop crying."

He rolled over and wiped his eyes. "You have no idea how much I've done that since you left."

"I've cried my share too. Did Tess tell you about something she did, something you might not like?"

"All she said was you'd tell me." Denver sat up to lean his back against the headboard. "It won't make any difference how I feel about her, so go ahead."

Eliza tightened the blanket around her breasts. "Let's get dressed first. Even though I said that about forcing me, it wouldn't take much for me to do the same to you. That's one of the things I've been working on with my psychiatrist. She helped me see how I couldn't make love to you because I was afraid I would get pregnant and lose the baby again."

"You didn't lose the baby." Denver looked away and back. "She just died and we don't know why."

"Lily, remember? Because Tess told me about the headstone."

"Right, and how she did that to make me think you did it so I would go see you."

"She's an amazing sister," Eliza said, standing. "Let's get dressed and make coffee. Then we'll talk."

On the sofa, both wearing dry jeans and T-shirts, both barefoot, both with mugs of steaming coffee, they faced each other. Sips passed, then more. Eliza lowered her mug. "Promise you won't get angry with Tess for what she did."

"I would forgive her anything. Tell me whatever it is and get it over with."

Crossing a leg beneath her, Eliza faced him. "She told me about you dating Leah. Didn't you wonder how Tess showed up every time you and Leah were alone?"

"Yeah, I did. She even found Leah and me on the pontoon boat when we went out to see the Lakefest fireworks."

Eliza couldn't help grinning. "She told me about the red flag she put on the pontoon boat. She saw you and Leah talking at Lakefest and thought you might take her out to watch the fireworks. She didn't want you two to make any fireworks of your own."

"What about after? She didn't—" Denver's mouth fell open. "Did she tell Jan about me and Leah?"

"Jan was already here for Lakefest. When Tess found you and Leah on the pontoon boat, she called Jan to tell her about Leah. Jan said she would stop by and check on you after the fireworks."

"Huh, so those two ganged up on me. What about Tess coming over when Leah and I were …"

Eliza patted the sofa. "Go ahead and say it—when you and Leah were getting naked right where we're sitting, and Tess showed up at the sliding glass doors to interrupt you."

Denver's cheeks reddened. "Yeah, I'm just a weak man."

"Tess knew that too." Eliza stood. "Let me show you how she spied on you." At the sliding glass doors, she pointed to a large oak at the edge of the lot. "Look at that tree and tell me what you see."

"It's just a tree."

"Uh-huh, a tree with two of those cameras on it that hunters use to watch deer. There's another one on a pine in the front yard. Anytime someone came over, Tess got an alarm on her phone."

"Sheesh, I had no idea," Denver said.

"Exactly," Eliza said. "Do you know why she did all those things?"

"Because she didn't like Leah."

"She didn't, but the main reason was to keep you from marrying someone who wouldn't give you up. She also knew you wouldn't marry anyone you didn't love, so you wouldn't divorce someone to be with me either. Like I said while ago, she's an amazing sister. Even though I hurt you, she believed in love because of how she saw us looking at each other when we went to my house for the paintings for my first art show." Eliza sipped coffee. "So, are you mad at her?"

"Not at all. She did it because she loves me."

"Not really. She did it because she loves *us*."

"Which makes me love her even more."

Eliza went back to the sofa for their coffee mugs, left them in the kitchen sink, and returned to Denver. "Let's go to the basement. I want to show you something."

At the bottom of the steps, she flipped the light switch. The rows of overhead fixtures flickered on, illuminating both old and new art supplies to the left of the sliding glass doors, like the same sliding glass doors upstairs.

Denver went to them and opened the curtains. The rain had stopped. Rays of sunshine peeked through the parting clouds and turned the lake from almost black to gray.

He returned to Eliza's side, where she pointed at a partially covered easel. "This is Josh. I'm painting a portrait of his family for them."

A low growl came from Denver's throat. "Great. The guy you moved in with."

"How much do you know about his family?"

"His wife's in a coma. You moved in with him and his son. He calls you mama." Denver's jaw muscles tightened. "What the hell is all that about?"

"It's about how I wanted to be a mother," Eliza said. "My psychiatrist helped me see how losing Lily affected me to the point of using Josh's son as a replacement for her."

"What about Josh? Did you use him as a replacement for me?"

"I felt sorry for him. He loves his wife and son but needed someone to stay with David so he could stay with Anna."

"Anna's his wife and David's his son?"

"That's them. He's a wonderful father and husband." Eliza touched the raised oil paint of Josh's nose. "I was kind to him in his portrait. He's thin and not handsome. Anna loves him regardless." Eliza leaned against Denver's shoulder. "They remind me of us."

Denver moved away. "They remind me of Tess and me." He stomped up the stairs and slammed the door.

Eliza went to the sliding glass doors. The clouds closed, blocking the sun. Rain drizzled again, then became a downpour. She lowered her head, letting her tears wet the concrete at her feet.

Having gotten her cry out, she returned to the easel. It was time to add Anna so she could tell Denver her story.

Anna

In the basement at the easel, Eliza admired the finished painting of Anna. Although it had taken a week, the time was worth it. The serenely beautiful woman carried the aura of love and acceptance about her—the first for her family, the second for her deafness—captured in the hint of a confidant smile and in the light reflecting in her crystalline blue eyes.

Eliza placed the last dirty brush in solvent and removed the shirt Denver had given her to paint in so long ago. She held it to her nose. Despite washing it every day and drying it on the deck railing, it still held his unique aroma, a mix of fresh air and his aftershave. Yes, she was imagining it, but it was as real to her as the hope of them being together again.

His footsteps thumped overhead. They hadn't suffered any more setbacks or fights—no threats of sex either—wanted or unwanted. They ate together, spoke rarely, and signed here and there. Still, she sometimes caught him watching her, intensity in his blue eyes as if he were trying to dissect her heart and soul to understand what she wanted from him. When those times occurred, she ignored him for the most part. Once though, when she smiled at him, his face reddened like an embarrassed Amish boy watching a group of Amish girls walking by.

His boyish expression had thrilled her. It was one of the first things that had caught her eye when he was teaching her sign language in Ohio. She loved to tease him then, crossing her legs as she sat in her desk, waiting for his eyes to dart to her bare ankles.

The solvent loosened the paint, which clouded the jar. She put them in another jar of solvent, soaked them for a few minutes, and wiped them clean with a rag. The palette, scraped clean with a putty knife, then wiped down, waited until tomorrow, when she would start David's portrait.

At the laundry sink, Eliza washed and dried her hands. About to go upstairs, she noticed an oily stain on her white blouse from cleaning the brushes. She took it off and left it on the washer for later. If it didn't come out, she would use it for a rag.

Upstairs, she found Denver placing two steaks in a plate. She joined him at the counter and raised her hands. "On the grill I hope."

Occupied with seasoning the steaks, he didn't see her. She poked his arm. He raised his head, widened his eyes, and she signed, "On the grill?"

He raised his hands. "You're wearing a ponytail and I can see your hearing aids. Why are you signing?"

"Why not?"

His eyes darted down and back. "I'm glad you're wearing a bra. You know what happened when you didn't."

"It wasn't that, it was the rain."

His cheeks reddened. "I'm sorry about how I acted."

"I know." Eliza untied her ponytail and combed her hair out with her fingers; it flowed around her shoulders and down her back, a waterfall of black silk that Denver once loved to hold in his hands. He licked his lips. Yes, she loved teasing him, and it felt wonderful to do it again.

He raised his hands. "You're a very bad woman."

Eliza shared the hint of a smile. "I try." She hurried to the guest room to bury her face into the pillow and giggle. Fun, teasing, and suggestive smiles—all the things that had helped them fall in love to start with.

She rolled over. While those things thrilled her soul, they would destroy Tess. Then again, her sister had demanded this month, knowing what might happen, saying how they all deserved a happy ending. Whatever that might be, Eliza had no idea.

She put on a clean blouse and went to the kitchen. "Can I help?"

"You can wash and oil two potatoes for the microwave."

Eliza did so, leaving them on a plate. "Anything else?"

"Would you like a glass of red wine while the steaks cook? I bought a bottle at the grocery when I went for the steaks."

At the counter beside him, Eliza touched his arm. "Are you drinking as much as you did when I left?"

"Why, because of the beer bottle I left in the chair the other day?"

"Because I knew how much you drank back then and it worried me."

"You never said anything about it. People who care about each other tell them when they're worried." Denver paused for a deep breath. "I tried to sleep with you in the tent at the cemetery because I was worried. I got advice from a psychiatrist to put something in your food to make you sleep so I could get you some help because I was worried. I drank because I was worried about our marriage. I stopped when you left and Tess came into my life. That's just one of the reasons I love her." The muscles in his jaw tightened. "And I won't stop loving her, Eliza. All I want is to marry her and start a family."

Eliza went to the guest room, hardly believing what she was about to do. She took a key from her purse and came back to put it on the counter. "That's a key to my house. Like Tess snuck here at night to see you, you can do the same with her."

"She wouldn't let me."

Eliza leaned her head against his. "Like she loves us both, I love you both. If she's willing to let us be together, I'm willing to let you and her be together."

Facing her, Denver grabbed her shoulders. "Do you know what you're saying?"

"I can't deny you that happiness, Denver, not after I denied you our happiness." Eliza touched his brow with her fingertips. "Look at you, that boyish face, so handsome and so cute, blue eyes like the sky. I loved your face almost from the first time I saw you."

Denver's grip relaxed. His lips formed the hint of a smile. "You had just taken your first shower in the stall behind the sign language school. When I opened the door, you fell into my arms. Your hair was wet and shining, down to your waist. Your eyes—I had never seen eyes so dark. When I caught your profile, I wondered about your strong nose and defined lips and high cheekbones. You reminded me of a Greek statue."

Eliza placed his palm to her cheek. "You're the man I fell in love with in Ohio, and I'm a stupid woman to put that at risk. I hate myself for what I did to you. If you give me the chance to make up for it, I'll spend the rest of my life loving you any way I can, even if that means sharing you with Tess."

Denver jerked away from her. "That's crazy, Eliza."

"No crazier than my family leaving the Amish to be with me here. The Amish are people like anyone else. They live and love and make mistakes. Sometimes, like with my family, they leave the Amish. Sometimes they even go back. When Anna had her accident, Josh left the Amish because he blamed them for her losing her hearing because of the mumps. Then, when she woke up from her coma, he was so grateful to God that he joined the Amish again." Eliza stopped talking. Denver said nothing. She took the potatoes from the cabinet. "Let's cook. I want to show you something after supper."

* * *

Full from the juicy steak, Eliza took Denver to the basement. She turned the lights on and went to the easel. "This is Anna. I was kind to her like I was to Josh. She had lost a lot of weight, so I filled in her cheeks."

Denver came closer. "Long black hair and dark eyes—she reminds me of you."

"She's stronger than me. She never complained about being deaf. The accident left her with a stroke, and she never complained about that. It also left her unable to walk, and she stook that in stride also. She's an amazing woman."

"She must be to do all that. You know me, I complain when I get a cold."

"Aww, poor baby," Eliza said, tousling his hair.

Denver grabbed her hand. "Stop teasing. I remember how you wanted breakfast in bed whenever you had a cold." He let her hand go. "She woke up? Is that why you left them?"

"I stayed for a while to help bathe and dress her. I think Josh was too embarrassed to do it."

"What about now?"

"I'll get to that after I paint David's portrait." Eliza went to the sliding glass doors. "Let's go to the dock. The sun is setting, and I'd like to watch the lake turn colors."

At the dock, they sat on the wooden bench. Night after night, Denver drank here, even to the point of throwing up and passing out. Eliza was grateful to Tess for helping him stop that.

She turned to look over her shoulder. Filtering through the trees, the golden rays of the sun illuminated the woods as if they were on fire. She faced the lake, where the gray water transformed into a shimmering crimson pool as the sun set further, like lava in the crater of a volcano.

Taking a chance, she slipped her fingers into Denver's and lay her head on his shoulder. How many times had they done this before Lily had left them? More than she could count.

He raised her hand. As his lips brushed it, he let it go and leaned over to hold his head in his hands. "I can't do this. Every time I think about you that way, I see Tess."

Eliza rubbed his back. "I understand. That's why I said—"

"I can't be with both of you. How can I do that?"

"How do you know until you try?"

Denver sat up. "It goes against everything I know. A marriage is about two people and two people only. Doing what you're saying is as wrong as wrong gets."

"Would you do the same for me?"

"Hell no. It was bad enough when I thought you were sleeping with Josh." "Wait a minute," Denver said, turning on the bench to face her. "Why did you slap Ethan if you weren't sleeping with Josh? He sent Absalom a photo of his cheek and I saw the marks."

"I was upset because he believed the worst about me, and only because David called me mama. Josh and Anna understood why, and my own brother couldn't. He knew about Anna's accident and everything her family was going through, but he could only think I had moved in with Josh to replace you and to replace Lily." Eliza looked into Denver's eyes for a hint of understanding. "Do you believe me?"

He looked away. "Tess said you explained everything to your family. I guess that includes Ethan."

"I saw him before I left Ohio. I apologized for slapping him and he apologized for thinking the worst. He said he should've known better because of how much I loved you before we lost Lily." Eliza turned Denver's face toward her. "Please say you believe me. It's the truth, every word."

"Don't look at me like that. When you look at me like that I see Tess, and I want—"

"Then pretend I'm her. I've missed you more than I can say, and I'm ready to make love to you like we used to."

How do you know that from talking to your psychiatrist? That doesn't mean anything."

"Remember the night I left, when we kissed and I ran to the bathroom to get sick?"

"I remember."

"That was a reaction to my fear of getting pregnant and thinking I would lose the baby like I lost Lily. If we kiss and I don't have that reaction, the rest will be"—Eliza kissed the tip of his nose— "like a miracle." She hovered over his mouth, his breath warming her lips, the tingling sensation of need prickling throughout her body. "I want you, Denver. I want you worse than I ever have. That's tells me my fear is gone. That tells me I want your baby. That tells me we can have everything we had before we lost our sweet Lily."

Denver pulled away from her and stood. "I can't. When I think about all that, I think about Tess. She's my heart, Eliza, and she always will be. I don't know how I can change that, and I don't want to try."

She reached out for his hand and pulled him back to the bench. "Just one kiss. The rest will come like it always did."

As she stared into his eyes, the LED lights around the edge of the dock came on, illuminating the gray boards with yellow light, chasing away the darkness settling upon the water.

He did nothing, simply returned her stare as if it were an invisible wall separating them, one he could keep there with the sheer force of his will.

Eliza stood, unbuttoned her blouse, took off her jeans, and sat astride him to wrap her arms around his neck. Again, he did nothing, until he raised his fingertips to her back and traced warm lines from her neck to her shoulder blades, to where her back curved to her bottom. All three combined to release the heat of anticipation deep within her, a heat she hadn't enjoyed in— Could it have really been almost three years?

She pressed against him. Yes, it had been that long, or she wouldn't be doing this, almost melting into him.

The kiss started softly and grew hard, almost violent, mouths open, tongues entwining, until Denver turned his face away. "Get up. I told you I can't do this."

Eliza kissed his ear. "You can if you try," she whispered. "I know you want me like I want you. You know I can tell."

"I can't help that and you know it. Get up."

Eliza did so, got dressed, and sat again. "I'm willing to wait. Until then, go sneak into Tess's bed tonight if you want to. The key to my house is still on the counter."

She got up and left for the house. To think of him with Tess that way bothered her more than she was willing to say, but like life, happiness had a way of sorting itself out. Whatever he did, she would deal with it, because she wanted a happy ending to their story as much as Tess did.

* * *

Still on the bench, Denver didn't watch Eliza go inside. If he did, he would follow her and—

What kind of game was she and Tess playing, talking about happy endings when no happy ending would ever happen with their situation?

Darkness deepened around him, almost to the point of consuming the LED lights. Or maybe he was going insane. Or maybe Lily was covering each light with her tiny hands, showing him the way toward the darkness that Eliza and Tess were trying to envelop him in.

Moonlight gleamed in the trees across the lake, sending shards of brilliance to reflect off the water, million and millions of diamonds, or stars, or the souls of loved ones in Heaven.

He raised his head to see the stars, but the moon bursting over the trees dimmed them into faint pinpoints in the sky. Impossible, as impossible as anything he had ever heard of, happy endings were for romance novels, movies, and TV, not real life, but he could have an hour of happiness with Tess tonight, even if he never had it again.

In the house, no light shone under Eliza's door. He opened it and went inside. Her hearing aids lay on the nightstand. Her hair was spread upon the pillow. Her bare back faced him, revealed by a sheet only to her waist, revealed even more by the moonlight pouring through the window. He knelt by her, ran his fingers above her skin, touched the tip of his nose to her hair, breathed in fresh air and starlight. What he wouldn't give to undress and pull her blanket of hair over him and do nothing but sleep.

He closed the door. In his room, the LED alarm clock read 8:30, a little more than an hour after sunset in mid-September. Eliza had always gone to bed early unless they planned something, like binging on Jane Austen movies. Denver grinned, not that he would ever admit to any men how he loved *Sense and Sensibility* and *Pride and Prejudice*. Well, maybe that was where he got his romantic tendencies from. Then again, *Pretty Woman* and *The Notebook* could've contributed too. What a wuss he was, a wuss who was in love with two of the most amazing women he had ever known.

He set the alarm for 1 a.m. And he would visit one of them tonight, like she used to visit him.

Still in his shorts and T-shirt, he went to bed. Regardless of dozing off, he managed to cut the alarm off at 12:45, took the key from the counter, and started down the road to Eliza's house, moonlight showing him the way. At the end of his road, he turned, walked to the next road, and turned again, looking for Tess's car. At the next to the last house, where the road circled back, he stopped at the driveway where Tess's car sat. No lights shone in the single-story, vinyl-sides house, but the moon glimmered on the lake through the woods behind it.

At the front door, on a porch similar to his, Denver inserted the key. The knob turned. The door creaked. He stopped. The entire walk, visions of Tess in bed had hurried his pace. Now, when those visions were about to come true, all he could imagine was Eliza in bed, where he had just left.

He closed the door and locked it, sat on the steps and leaned back on his elbows.

Anyone who could read his mind might think his attraction to both women was about sex. Yes, that was a fair part of it, but it was more than that—*much* more than that. Tess was vivacious and fun and sharp-witted. She never let him get away with anything. Truth be told, he loved how she stood up to him.

Eliza though, with those black eyes of hers, could pierce his soul with a single glance, as if she knew all his secrets and faults and loved him in spite of them—or even *because* of them— because they made him the unique person he was.

Yes, Eliza and Tess were made from the same mold, but each was engraved with their unique selves too, selves he wasn't sure he could live without.

Denver got up and walked home. What a mess, one he didn't know how to fix. Since Eliza and Tess claimed they could create a happy ending for everyone, he would be better off to leave it up to them, as insane as it seemed.

David

At the grocery store, Denver put a carton of eggs in the cart. Eliza loved french toast, and he hadn't made it in the three weeks they had been together. He added milk, some veggies for salad, a loaf of bread, and a few canned goods to stock the cabinets.

On the way home, he tapped the steering wheel in time with the music on the radio. The night he went to see Tess a week ago—once he got in bed and thought about it—he had decided that no matter what happened between him and Eliza, he would marry Tess. She was the love of his life now, and nothing would change that.

At home, he parked and got out with the grocery bags, closed the pickup door and looked around. The first week in October. Leaves hinting at their fall colors. The herbal smell of them on the breeze, heightened by a brief rain. His and Eliza's wedding—had it really been almost five years ago? Shaking his head at the shock of where the time had gone, he went inside.

He started down the hall and stopped. A keen, undulating wail, as if an animal were moaning in pain, came from somewhere in the house. He dropped the bags and rain toward the sound. Sitting on his bed, Eliza was rocking back and forth, her arms wrapped around her middle. The sight of her—hair shifting back and forth over her face, tears running down her cheeks, her face contorted in misery—broke Denver's heart. Yes, he was going to marry Tess, but how could he ignore Eliza's pain and what was causing it?

He sat beside her to rub her back. "Hey, what's wrong? It can't be that bad."

She stopped rocking and unwrapped her arms from around her middle. The plaster cast of Lily's hand and footprints fell to her lap. "I— I was looking for our wedding pictures, and—" Sobbing again with that keen wail, she leaned against Denver.

He set the cast aside before it fell to the floor and took Eliza in his arms. "Shh, it's all right, it's all right."

Her head shook against his shoulder. "It'll never be all right." Wailing again, she wrapped her arms around his neck. "Oh, God, what have I done? I've— I've ruined everything." She raised her head, eyes bloodshot, nose running. "I'm so stupid. I had everything I ever wanted right here and I threw it all away."

Denver fingered the wet hair from her cheeks. "C'mon now, everyone you love has forgiven you. They understand what happened and why you left."

The muscles in Eliza's neck tightened with a hard swallow. "Do you forgive me? I can't imagine how you felt when you got those divorce papers at Christmas."

"I forgive you. Losing Lily devastated both of us, and we didn't know how to handle it."

Eliza looked into his eyes. "You really forgive me?"

"I have to, Eliza. If I didn't, I would be treating you worse than you did when you left me."

She took the cast from beside her and traced Lily's hand and footprints with her fingertips. "I don't remember this."

"I didn't know about it until your family gave it to me on that same Christmas. After Lily died, Tess asked a nurse if she could have the cast made."

"Why didn't she give to us then?"

"She didn't say. It's not like we were in any shape to accept it." Denver took the cast and returned it to the dresser. "You said you were looking for our wedding photos?"

"I was stupid to do that too. I bet you threw them away when you got those divorce papers."

"They're in a box upstairs." He rubbed her back again. "Are you okay now?"

"I am since you forgave me." Leaning against him, she kissed his cheek and rubbed his chest, then kissed his cheek again, lingering this time. "I've missed you so much."

Her breath warmed his lips. The last time he had wanted to kiss her, it was from anger instead of love. This time it was from that same love as long ago, when she had first kissed him on the dock on the night he had brought her here, to stay until her first art show. Her lips were inches away. All he had to do was kiss them, undress her, caress every inch of her slender body and—

He jumped from the bed. "I'm sorry, Eliza. I don't want to hurt you, but I still want to marry Tess."

She reached for his hand. "Love me, Denver. Please love me like you used to."

He took a step backwards. "I can't do that."

"Don't you want to? It's been so long and I miss you."

Denver's cheeks flared with heat. "That's not fair. I comforted you because I care. Now you want to take advantage of me."

"You're right." She stood, took some tissues from a box on his dresser, and wiped her eyes. "It's time I get used to the idea of you marrying my sister."

Denver followed her to the kitchen. Good. Great. Finish this week and let Tess know they could plan their wedding.

He went down the hall for the grocery bags—no broken eggs, thank goodness—and put everything away. Eliza threw the bags in the trash. "I finished the painting last night. Can I show it to you?"

"Sure. I like learning about Josh and his family."

Downstairs, Eliza turned the overhead lights on and went to the easel. "This young man is David. See his brown hair and blue eyes? He reminds me of you."

Denver stepped closer. "He's looks like a handful, with that grin."

"He loves to fish. I've been teaching him to paint too. He loves books and the outdoors and digging worms."

"Yeah? He sounds like me when I was a kid."

Eliza touched the raised oil paint of David's cowlick. "He's as sweet as you too. While Anna was in a coma, he asked if he could call me mama. I think he wanted to because he missed her so much. That's how Ethan heard him that day."

Someone tapped on the sliding glass doors. Tess and—to Denver's shock—David stood there, so he opened the doors. "Hey, you two," she said. "Is it okay if David and I fish from the dock?"

Denver faced Eliza. It was all he could do to keep his mouth from falling open. She went to the doors. "Do you have bait?"

"Hey, 'Liza," David said. "We got some worms from the store."

"Oh, you did, did you?" Eliza asked, patting his shoulder. "Are they as big as those in the chicken manure pile back home?"

"They're kinda skinny."

Tess tugged his hand. "C'mon here and let those two get back to whatever they were doing. The fishing poles are on the pontoon boat." Hand in hand, Tess and David walked along the gravel path and out onto the dock.

Denver tapped Eliza's shoulder. "Do I get to know what's going on?"

She turned around. "On the sofa with a box of tissues. I'm sure I'll need them again."

Upstairs, Denver brought the tissues to the sofa and sat beside Eliza. She took the box and put it between them. "From what I've told you about Josh and Anna, you know they love each other, right?"

Denver nodded. "I get that."

"Well, you might need to know a little more, because her story is similar to mine. Although they returned to the Amish, they didn't wear the traditional clothes for their portrait and I didn't ask why. One reason, I think, is because of Anna's physical problems. I didn't see the need to dress her in a dress and pin her hair for a bonnet, and Josh never mentioned it. Anyway, they're as devoted to each other as any couple I've ever known." Eliza took a tissue from the box. "When she woke from the coma, Josh told me she had suffered a stroke from her brain injury. The left side of her mouth drooped and she couldn't move her left hand like normal. Josh said one of her doctors was afraid she might have a worse stroke and die."

"That's terrible," Denver said. "How does Josh deal with knowing she might die at any time?"

"Well, about a week before I moved here, I found them both dead in bed."

"How did that happen? Was Josh so upset he committed suicide?"

"That's what I thought at first. I had seen him sneaking a drink of something from a brown bottle. I caught it on his breath a couple of times and it was strong alcohol. He was taking sleeping pills too, so I thought he might've done both until I saw how he and Anna were holding each other." Eliza wiped her eyes. "Their bed wasn't large. So Anna would have more room, Josh slept on the sofa after she came home. He was wearing his clothes when I found them, holding each other's hands. It's almost as if they made a promise to die together because they were suffering so much."

Denver sat back on the sofa. "I can't imagine knowing my wife could die at any time. That's suffering."

Eliza wiped her eyes again. "I hated telling David, but he handled it like the sweet boy he is. He cried and hugged them and told me they didn't hurt any more, like his meemaw."

"His grandmother?"

"Josh's mother. She had health issues and used a wheelchair. She died while I was there. Josh and Anna had no other relatives."

"Are you adopting David?" Denver asked.

"Not long after Anna was in the accident, he asked me about it. At the time I thought it was because he thought she would never wake from the coma. Then, after their autopsy, his attorney told me how Josh had the same cancer his father died from. I noticed him getting thinner. He would complain of having a sore back, but he said it was from working. In his will, he left me everything and said he and Anna wanted me to adopt David."

Eliza left the sofa for the sliding glass doors. Denver went to join her. Tess and David were sitting on the end of the dock, their feet in the water, fishing poles in their hands, red and white corks bobbing on the lake.

"I realize I was using David to replace Lily," Eliza said, "but I love him now as if he were my own child." She faced Denver.

"Maybe it's a good thing you're marrying Tess. If you weren't, I would want you to adopt that sweet little boy too, and you might not want to do that. Still, he needs a father, and I know you'll be a wonderful father to any children you and Tess have."

The regret in Eliza's somber voice made Denver close his eyes. He could see himself adopting David if they got married again, but he and Tess would have their own family.

Eliza lay her head on his shoulder. "Could you adopt him anyway? Tess said she doesn't mind."

Denver opened his eyes. "I'll have to think about it. It's not something to do on the spur of the moment."

Slipping her arm around his waist, Eliza pressed against him. "You are such a miracle, Denver. No matter what, I'll always love you."

"Do you think you'll find someone else?"

"David and I will be fine."

Denver hated to think of her and David alone—her without a loving husband, him without a father. Of all the paths his life had taken, never—not in a million years—would he have believed his path would've taken him to this moment.

Eliza opened the sliding glass doors. At the deck rail, she cupped her hands around her mouth. "I don't see anyone catching any fish!"

David put his pole down and ran up the gravel path. "It's those skinny worms, Mama."

Tess put the poles away and joined him. "It's good to see you two talking."

Denver waved them up the steps. "Come on up. Want a sandwich?"

Tess and David came up the steps. "I'm good, but this hungry monkey might want a banana if you have one. He loves bananas."

Eliza patted his back. "That's because I made him banana pudding."

"It was good too, Mama. I never knew nanners made puddin'."

Denver held in a laugh. "I like nanner puddin' too."

Tess took David to the kitchen. "I see bananas some on the counter."

Watching them, Eliza smiled and then faced Denver. "Tess and I kind of lied to you about her staying at my house to be alone. She's been watching David and taking him to Mama and Papa's to play with Ivy."

Tess and David came over. "I need to drive up to Ezra's for a few days. Can this monkey join your zoo until I get back Friday? That'll give you some more time to ... well, you know."

Denver knelt beside David. "Why not? I'll take this monkey out on the pontoon boat fishing."

"You can show him how to paddle the canoe too," Eliza said.

"Cool," Tess said. "I'll get his clothes and books and come right back."

Denver followed her down the hall and outside, where he hugged her. "I miss you, sunshine."

She pulled away to look into his eyes. "I miss you too. Do you have any idea what you'll do?"

"Eliza said you don't mind if I adopt David."

"Not at all. If the situation were reversed, wouldn't you adopt my children?"

"In a heartbeat."

Tess kissed him. "Look, no matter what you do, I'll always love you."

"I know," Denver said, placing his palm to her cheek and kissing her. About to go inside, he ran to her car door as she was opening it. "Why are you going to see Ezra?"

"I told you I might. We'll talk guitars, and I'll check out Monticello and pick up some more books about Sally Hemings."

"You really admire her, don't you?"

"I sure do. If I were her back then, I like to think I would be as strong as she was, being with a man she couldn't marry and having his children, especially the part about making that deal in France with Jefferson to have him free them from slavery. That's one tough woman." Tess got in the car. "I love you, baby. I'll be back in a minute with that monkey's clothes."

Denver waved as she drove away. Although he couldn't wait to be with her again, he looked forward to spending a few days with David. It would give him a chance to experience being a dad, especially if he adopted him.

fatherhood

Leaning back on the sofa, Denver yawned. The hamburgers and fries for supper, along with the endless cartoons Tess had accustomed David too, were making him sleepy.

Sitting between him and Eliza, David looked up at him. "Are you ready for bed, Denber?"

"I used to have trouble making a V sound too," Eliza said. "Try again."

David raised his hands and signed each letter in Denver's name. "How 'bout that? Then I don't have to say it."

Denver grinned at Eliza. "He gotcha there, didn't he?"

"I told you how smart he is."

David looked at each of them. "You're like my mama and papa." He patted Denver's leg. "'Cept you're taller and fatter."

Eliza covered a giggle. Denver patted her hand on the back of the sofa. "It's not nice to laugh at Daddy, Mama."

Hands over David's head, Eliza signed, "Do you realize what you just said?"

"What about it? If I adopt him, I'll be his daddy."

David pulled their hands down and held them in his lap. "No fair signing where I can't see." He put Eliza and Denver's hands together. "There, now I can watch TV."

Eliza yawned. "Do you want me to help you get ready for bed?"

"Where will I sleep?" David faced Denver. "Your house if bigger than Mama's house. It's spooky."

"You can sleep with me," Eliza said.

"What about Denb—I mean Den-*ver?* He might get scared."

"That's true," Eliza said, winking at Denver. "His bed is big enough for all of us."

"Good, I like snuggling," David said. "Mama and Papa used to snuggle with me in bed when I was little."

Denver stood. "Well, Mama, I guess we better go to bed like this boy says. I'd like to get up early and take us fishing on the pontoon boat anyway."

"Yay!" David jumped from the sofa and ran toward the bathroom. "I get to brush my teeth fiiirrrssssst."

Eliza faced Denver. "Imagine that. I've been wanting to sleep with you and a five-year-old makes it happen."

"Behave, Mama. He means sleep and nothing else."

Denver brushed his teeth, put on pajamas and got in bed. David pattered in wearing pajamas too, and climbed in bed beside Denver with a book." Mama smells pretty. Will y'all kiss goodnight?"

"How does she smell pretty?"

"She sprayed some flower juice on her neck."

To keep from laughing out loud, Denver bit his lower lip until the urge passed. "Flower juice, huh? Is that what she calls it?"

"She didn't say, but it smells like flowers." David sat up against the headboard and opened the book. Eliza came in. She wore the same blue silk nightgown that she wore on their first honeymoon night, a hint of pink lipstick, a touch of mascara, and her shining black hair fell across her shoulders, bare except for the gown's two spaghetti straps.

Denver got up. "I better sleep in the guest room."

She stepped outside the door and waved Denver toward her. "We'll be back in a minute, David."

Denver grabbed her hand and took her to the kitchen. "What the heck are you doing?"

"What do you mean?"

"You know what I mean, you look amazing."

"Poor baby," Eliza said, running her fingertips along his arm. "Where's your self-control? Besides, you're marrying Tess, so you shouldn't be thinking about me like that."

"Well, I … I … I …"

Eliza licked her lips. "Do you need me to kiss that stutter away?"

Denver covered his eyes. "I don't know who's worse with the teasing, you or Tess." He lowered his hand. "At least David will be between us. Are you gonna behave?"

"I have to. You're wearing pajamas, so I can't rub my legs against yours." She raised the hem of the gown to the curve of her hip, revealing a long, slender leg. "I shaved them just for you. You can feel them if you want to."

Denver whirled away and hurried to the bed. This was gonna be the longest night of his life. He sat against the headboard beside David while Eliza did the same on the other side. "Show Denver how smart you are by reading us a story."

David closed the book. "Can I go to sleep? I had a dream last night about Mama and Papa and some other people. I hope it comes back."

"What other people?"

"It was a man with brown hair and a woman with red hair. A little girl with black hair was with them. She said she hopes her mommy and daddy will be happy again."

Eliza and Denver looked at each other. The people David was talking about sounded like his parents and Lily. He took the book and put it on the nightstand. "That sounds like a nice dream. You know they're just dreams, right?"

"Mama and Papa look like they did before they got sick. Mama can even hear and talk like everyone else does. She tells me how much she loves me and to be good for the people I'm with."

"But she doesn't tell you any names …"

"She doesn't have to." David took Denver's hand and Eliza's hand and pulled them together. "She means you."

"The little girl's hair is black?" Eliza asked.

"Uh-huh," David said, nodding. "Her eyebrows are black too. Her eyelashes are like the black butterflies we painted in Mama's flowers." He grinned. "Well, they're not that big, but they're pretty like yours, Mama."

Denver didn't know whether to laugh or cry. Not only did he have two miracles in bed with him, one of them had given him the best gift he had ever received: the gift of knowing his mom and dad and Lily were watching over him and Eliza. Although that was the case, he wanted the week to be over. The real miracle would be marrying Tess. Yes, he would adopt David and be a dad to him in every way possible, but that couldn't include being with Eliza. Too much had passed between them, regardless of how his heart—and David—told him differently.

David scooted down to the pillow and turned over to face Eliza, who was facing away too. He rubbed her shoulder. "Goodnight, Mama."

She patted his hand. "Goodnight, sweetheart."

Feeling the pain of being left out, a pain that made no sense since he was going to marry Tess, Denver turned the nightstand lamp off.

David's breathing soon fell into the steady rhythm of sleep. The house creaked as the night cooled. Off in the woods, far in the distance, an owl cried, *who-whoooo, who-whoooo.*

The bed shifted. Eliza passed through the moonlight pouring in the window and left the room. Denver went to the door, where the sweet aroma of her perfume filled the air. At the sliding glass doors, she placed her hands to the cool glass, evidenced by the haze gathering around her fingers. Her head lowered. Soft sobs shook her shoulders. Regardless of how much Denver wanted to comfort her, he couldn't. It would be better to finish out the week and make a clean break. Anything more would hurt Eliza worse than she was hurting now, and he couldn't do that to her even if he wanted to.

** * **

At the counter beside the stove, Eliza cracked eggs into a bowl. Like when her appetite had left her in those months after Lily had died, it had left her now. It had even left Denver in the last few days, but David needed to eat. She was grateful for how he hadn't noticed the growing distance between her and Denver since the night they all had slept in his bed.

With a fork from a drawer, she whipped the eggs.

As lovely as David's description of his dream had been, meaning Denver's parents and Lily were in Heaven, and they hoped love would rekindle its flame in this house, Denver saying it was only a dream had hurt her deeply. In all the months she had either sat on the dock or in the rocking chair, aching with the need to hold her daughter in her arms, she had never stood at the sliding glass doors like she had that night. Maybe it was from seeing Denver standing there at times. Maybe it was from the stars that drew her there, where their icy glare threatened to wrap itself around her heart again, to insulate her from Denver's growing indifference to her feelings.

Maybe it was the kinship she felt by placing her hands on the glass, hard and cold like the stars themselves. It was Friday, and Tess would pick up David. It wouldn't matter though, because in the days since they all had slept in Denver's bed, whether fishing on the pontoon boat, canoeing on the lake, or hiking in the park, his eyes had never held that sparkle of interest or attraction like they had before David had mentioned his dream.

A tendril of smoke drifted upward from the stove burner, where Denver had spilled eggs for french toast one morning, which they had both forgotten to wipe off. Eliza placed a pan there, let it heat, and cursed under her breath as she poured the eggs in, forgetting to add olive oil to keep them from sticking. She dumped them in the trash, wiped the pan, and started over.

Rubbing his eyes, David shuffled into the kitchen in his pajamas. "What's Denber doing, Mama? He's not in his room."

"He got up early and took the canoe out."

"I like fishing with him. And the pontoon boat. And the canoe."

"I can tell he likes fishing with you too."

"Me too. He smiles at me a lot, but ..."

Eliza stopped stirring the eggs. "But what?"

"He doesn't smile at you like he did before I told him about my dream."

"He's got a lot on his mind."

"Like what?"

Eliza knelt beside David. "It's complicated."

His blue eyes squinted. "What's that word mean?"

"You know how you sometimes want to read more than one book, or play with more than one toy, or watch more than one cartoon, and you can't make up your mind?"

"Uh-huh."

"It's like that."

David climbed up on a bar stool at the counter. "Are you and Denber married? You act like it sometimes, but sometimes you don't. You never told me, did you?"

"I told you how something made my husband and me sad."

"Denber's your husband?"

Eliza poured the eggs in a plate, turned the burner off, and sat beside him. "You know the little girl in your dream?"

"She looks like you."

"Denver and I had a baby, but she died when she was born. I think that little girl is her in Heaven."

"Why did she die? Was she hurting like Mama and Papa and Meemaw?"

"We don't know, but losing her hurt Denver and me more than we could stand. That's why I moved to the sign language school."

"But you moved here again."

"That's right, to be near my family."

"I like Ivy. When can I go to kindergarten like she does?"

Eliza got up. "Let me make you some toast before your eggs get cold."

David slid off the bar stool. "I can do it." He did so while Eliza plated eggs, poured a glass of milk, and poured herself a cup of coffee. They returned to the bar. David swallowed eggs. "Well, when can I go to kindergarten?"

"I'll check next week and see what the school says. I've never adopted a sweet boy like you, so I have to find out these things."

"Will we go back to your house? It's okay, but we don't have a dock or a boat or a canoe."

Eliza didn't say the obvious: *and it doesn't have Denver.* Still, he said he would adopt David, so that was something.

Footsteps thudded up the steps to the deck. Denver entered the sliding glass doors, and David waved. "Did you go to the goat island, Denber?"

Denver came over. "Not this time. I need to talk to Eliza a minute. She'll be right back."

She followed him downstairs to the basement, where he faced her. "You know Tess is picking David up today to give us two more days together. I don't see any need for that. I've changed my mind about adopting David too. I need to start over fresh with Tess, and I can't do that if I adopt David."

To hide her trembling chin, Eliza covered her mouth. "I never thought—" She turned away. "I never thought you could be so cruel to that sweet little boy."

"I'll still take him fishing, Eliza. It's not like I'm abandoning him like …"

"Say it, you know you want to." She whirled around. "Like I abandoned you. Thank God I didn't tell him you were going to adopt him. It would break his heart to find out you changed your mind." She paused to get her quivering voice under control. "Yes, I abandoned you, but you're doing that to me and David now."

"I love Tess. That'll never change."

"Has your love for me changed?"

"I …"

"Don't stand there with your mouth hanging open, Denver Andrews, it's time to be honest with me. Do you still love me or not?"

"It's not that simple."

"Then you do."

"I always will."

"What are you afraid of? I'll never hurt you again as long as I live. We can have the life we would've had if Lily hadn't died and this thing between you and Tess hadn't happened." Eliza paused. "I didn't mean that. I know you and Tess are in love, but I know you're in love with me too."

Denver went to the covered painting of Josh's family. "Have you showed this to David yet?"

"I was hoping I could hang it in his room here."

He raised the cover. "You did a great job."

Eliza strode over and jerked the cover down. "It's none of your business now."

Denver went to the sliding glass doors. "You might know it, but every time I look at the lake I see you. Tess figured it out, but I didn't tell her why. You're like a ghost who lives inside me. I see you kissing me on the dock for the first time. I see you watching the fireworks for the first time. I see you swimming in the lake after, when you cut the gas off on the pontoon boat to make us spend the night. I feel you wrapped around me when we went to sleep too, when I realized I had fallen in love with you." Denver shook his head. "And it's all gone."

Every fiber of Eliza's being ached to tell him they could have all that again. Instead, she let him stand there, remembering all the times they had shared. If anything could bring them back together, those things could. They were the most magical moments of their lives, and that magic needed a chance to work, both for him to realize they belonged together and for him to change his mind about adopting David.

She took a single step toward him, but no more. "I'll tell Tess to take David to Mama and Papa. We need to get this over with."

In her room, Eliza sent Tess a short text. She dressed David and told him Tess was going to take him to see Mama and Papa. Denver came upstairs to the sofa, and David went to him. "What's wrong, Denber, why are you sad?"

Denver took him into his lap. "Nothing's wrong a hug won't fix."

David wrapped his arms around Denver's neck and let go. "Is that better?"

A car door slammed outside. "Come on," Eliza said. "Tess is taking you to see Ivy." She took him to the door. Without a single word, Tess took him to the car and left, returning a few minutes later to sit beside Denver. Eliza joined them, hating the silence of the moment and what might happen in the next few minutes.

Denver faced Eliza. "I need to talk to Tess."

* * *

Tess waited until Eliza left before she faced Denver. "I'm sorry we're putting you through this."

"I feel like I'm being torn apart."

"None of this would have happened if Lily hadn't died. You and Eliza would be happier than you ever thought possible if that hadn't happened. You know that, right?"

Denver went to the sliding glass doors. Beyond them, sunlight sparkled on the lake. He placed his hands on the glass, watching … watching. "I know, and that makes it even worse."

Tess went to him, turned him around, and leaned her back against him. "Hold me," she said, raising his hands to her stomach. "I love it when you hold me like this. I feel like we'll always be together, no matter what."

She let the minutes pass, enjoying the growing warmth between them, the firm pressure of his hands to her stomach, the rise and fall of his chest against her back, his breath against her cheek.

"I want to be with you," Denver said. "What would you have done if I had chosen Eliza?"

"That's why I went to see Ezra. He offered me a job and the apartment over his workshop for as long as I need it."

"How long would that have been?"

"At least a year. I need time to get over everything, and you and Eliza and David need time without me around." She pressed his hands to her stomach. "Do you trust me?"

"Always."

"Do you trust me when I say we can have a happy ending if you choose Eliza?"

"I don't know how."

She raised his hands to her lips, kissed them, and lowered them to her stomach again. "Trust me, we'll be okay."

Denver turned her around. He held her face in his hands. "I know we'll be okay, because I'm not letting you go."

He started to kiss her but Tess pulled away. If she let him release all of his love now, it would ruin everything. She went to Eliza's door and knocked. They both returned to the sofa, but Denver stayed at the sliding glass doors. Eliza looked at Tess, then at Denver. "I need to tell you something. I only told Tess when—"

"Don't," Denver said, raising his hand. "After everything you've put me through, don't you dare say it."

"Don't say what?"

"There's only one thing you could tell me right now, right when I've got to choose. You never filed the divorce papers, did you?"

"I'm— I wanted to tell you at the hospital, but ..." Eliza looked away and back. "No matter how much I thought I should let you go, no matter how much I tried to stop loving you, I couldn't."

"It's just a piece of paper. I'm marrying Te—" Denver tilted his head to one side as if he heard something. He raised his palm to one of the sliding glass doors and turned to face the lake.

Tess waited. Despite her plans for a happy ending for the three of them, if he turned toward her, away from his memories of him and Eliza on the lake, she would accept his choice, regardless of her love for her sister.

But if he—

With both hands on the glass now, head lowered, shoulders shaking, he sank to the floor, where he rocked and moaned and cried huge gulping sobs.

And there it was—he had made his choice whether he knew it or not—and it was all Tess could do to not run to him and hold him. But that would ruin their happy ending, because the first person to him would claim his whole heart, and that person should be Eliza.

Yes, when Eliza had returned to explain everything, the first spark of Tess's idea of a happy ending had flared into life. Then, as she had considered it even more, resulting in their trip to Ocracoke, she had allowed the idea to transform from flare into flame. Of course, the guilt of leading him on during that trip had gnawed at the muscle of her heart, only relieved by late night tears outside while he slept. Regardless, here they were. Regardless, her idea was blooming into reality. Regardless, it would break her heart to do what she was about to do because it would also break Denver's heart.

She faced her sister. She loved her more than she could ever say, for showing her what love was on that day so long ago, when she and Denver had gazed into each other's eyes at Papa's house.

As a girl of thirteen, Tess had fallen in love with Denver like Eliza had fallen in love with him. How amazing to have him as her first love, but now, as a woman of eighteen, it was time to share that love.

She stood, took Eliza's hand, and pulled her up for a hug. "He needs you more than me now," she whispered. "Give him time. He's hurting like he did when you left him, but now I'm leaving him."

Tess released Eliza, gave Denver one last look, and strode from the living room and down the hall. She closed the door behind her and stopped.

"Teeeeess! Teeeeess! Don't go!"

In tears herself, Tess ran to her car and slammed the door to escape Denver's screams. The front door flew open. He ran to the car as she backed up, pulling the hood from beneath his hands. Eliza rushed through the doorway, reaching for him, her calls for him to come back drowned out by Denver's screaming for Tess not to leave him.

She whipped the steering wheel around to clear him and shoved the transmission in drive, hit the accelerator and looked into the rear-view mirror. Denver stood in the middle of the road with Eliza holding him. He pulled away and ran after the car, still screaming, still crying, still broken but on the verge of allowing Eliza to heal him again, but only as long as Tess kept going.

Driving to Eliza's house, she shoved the tears from her eyes with the heel of her hand. If there was one time in her life she would hate herself for, it was this one.

She packed her clothes and left Eliza a note, telling her to send a text about how she and Denver were doing in a few days, and threw it in the trash.

In time—however much time it took—they would be better than ever. After all, they both were broken when Lily died, and they both would heal as their old love grew into a new love— one they would have as long as they lived, both physically and spiritually, like the trillions of stars, warm and glittering in the night sky.

time

As Tess's car sped away, Eliza ran after Denver. The car paused at the end of the road and took a right, toward her house. Denver stopped. His sides expanded and contracted with heavy breaths. Eliza stopped too. He would either walk to her house, run back for his pickup and drive there, or come back and go inside, because he understood how Tess had made his decision for him.

A car like Tess's, a silver sedan, turned into the road. Denver ran toward it. The neighbor slowed and waved and Denver stepped aside. Eliza waved too and waited to see what Denver would do. He turned and came back, head down, chest still heaving from his run.

The next few minutes were critical. Be supporting but don't smother him. Be gentle but don't baby him. Be loving but don't swear to help him get over Tess—the other love of his life—which would be like slicing his heart in two and throwing half into the lake.

He silently passed her and continued to the house. She followed him in and closed the door behind her. At the refrigerator, he took out a beer and twisted the top off the bottle, poured it in the sink and threw the bottle in the trash, went to the sofa to sit with his elbows on his knees and his head in his hands.

Eliza sat on one of the bar stools at the counter. Let him rest. Let him think. Let him take all the time in the world. Not running after Tess, or driving after her, or drinking the beer, were all good signs. Still, he might need more time, so Eliza called Papa and asked if David could stay overnight. He said he understood, ending the call by saying he loved her and everyone hoped things would work out.

Thirty-seven minutes later, by the clock on the microwave, Denver went to the sliding glass doors. Eliza could barely make out the white shape of a boat motoring up the lake. The boat passed the doors, leaving nothing but the fading whine of its engine. Denver shook his head slowly, rubbed his neck, and returned to the sofa.

Eliza washed David's breakfast dishes. He was with Mama and Papa by now, who were wondering about the change of circumstances at the Andrews household. Tess was on the way to Ezra's, having told everyone her plans in case she had to leave. Then there was her idea of a happy ending, whatever that meant. The first idea that had popped into Eliza's mind—as ridiculous it had seemed—was for them to share Denver, which was why she had teased him by offering him her house key so he could sleep with Tess. Now, with Tess's plan underway, everyone would find out what it was eventually.

Eliza dried and put away the dishes. The microwave clock read 3:30. Where had the time gone? She returned to the counter where she could see Denver in the living room, now lying on the sofa.

On the lake, waves were building, driven by a wind she hadn't noticed. Dark clouds scuttled across the horizon, torn like her and Denver's souls soon to be mended. Goosebumps dotted her arms.

In the basement, Eliza gathered kindling, old newspaper, and three sticks of oak. A fire soon crackled and popped in the living room hearth, crafted from rounded stones and concrete. Denver's eyes were closed. As she well knew, mental anguish created physical anguish. Let him sleep. Drive to the grocery for something for supper. Wake him when it was ready. By then, maybe they could talk about everything that had happened and see where they stood, preferably together, or where their lives were going to take them.

* * *

The delicious aroma of roast beef in the oven, with potatoes, carrots, and onions, told Eliza supper was ready. She plated everything and took it to the table, including some dinner rolls she had bought, poured sweet tea with lemon, and knelt beside Denver to finger the hair from his forehead. "Hey."

He opened his eyes. "I'm not asleep."

"Are you okay?"

"I smell food." He sat up. "Did I sleep until suppertime?"

"You needed it."

"The fire's nice." He stood and stretched. "Where's David?"

"I asked Papa if he could stay with them tonight. Do you mind if I stay? I can leave if—"

Denver rubbed his eyes, lowered his hand, sucked in a huge breath and released it. "I guess I looked like a fool running after Tess."

Knowing it was too early to talk about what had happened, Eliza went to the table and sat. "Let's eat before it gets cold."

"I thought I smelled beef." Denver joined her. "I always loved this recipe."

Knives sliced the tender roast. Forks raised bites of beef, carrots, potatoes, and onions. Glasses were raised and lowered.

300

The embers of the fire popped. Burned wood shifted. A gust of wind moaned in the trees. Stars appeared and hid again behind the wisps of cloud.

Eliza ached to touch Denver's face, to gently thumb a circle on his cheek, to tell him how much she loved him and how she would never hurt him again. Too soon. Too soon.

He reached over and closed his fingers over hers. Such a simple thing, amazing yet astounding, the familiar warmth of their fingers joined like the first time they had held hands in Ohio, in Papa's yard when Tess fell in love with the idea of love.

Ages passed: seconds, days, weeks, eons of time it seemed. Despite the tears burning her eyes, Eliza couldn't bear not facing him.

He raised his hand to her face, cupped it in his palm, thumbed her temple. "Why are you crying?"

Eliza pulled away. "Because I'm a stupid woman."

"Don't say that, Eliza."

She hurried to the kitchen sink with their plates, her flats slapping the hardwood floor. Denver brought their glasses and the leftover rolls. "I'll get some more wood for the fire."

Eliza snatched a paper towel from the holder and wiped her eyes. Denver came back from the basement and went to the living room with the wood. She sat in one of the chairs near the fireplace, a huge upholstered thing, kicked her flats off and curled her feet beneath her. Wood in place, he adjusted a stubborn piece with the poker and took the matching chair across from her.

Another gust of wind moaned in the trees. Denver's eyes darted toward the sliding glass doors, then to her, then to the fire. "Before I wrecked my pickup, I saw you and Josh hugging outside. What was that about?"

"I was setting up the easel for the portrait. He was thanking me for painting it. I already told you how much his family meant to him."

"And I thought the wrong thing." Denver's chest rose and fell with a huge breath. "That's what happens when people don't talk, like how we didn't talk after Lily died."

A stick of wood shifted in the fire. Embers flared and sparked. Eliza rose to prod the wood back in place and returned to the chair. "I hope you know how sorry I am for not talking to you."

"I forgave you." Denver heaved another huge breath. "I hope you can forgive me for not trying harder."

"That's in the past too. Like you told me when I found the cast of Lily's hands and feet, her death devastated both of us. I'm sure we're not the first parents to go through that."

"Or the last," Denver said. "If we … no, I shouldn't say."

Eliza hoped she knew what he was going to say. Give him time and see if he said it anyway. If so, that meant he was considering a future together instead of apart. She looked away. Let him make this decision without her influence. Their future now lay in his hands, and in his hands alone.

Minutes passed, maybe hours. For all she knew, the earth could've turned a lifetime's worth of turns. She should face him, watch him, look to see if she could read his thoughts and dreams, hopes and wishes—and his prayers.

His elbow was on the arm of the chair, and he was rubbing his chin. The fire reflected in his eyes, coloring the single tear on his cheek crimson. He faced Eliza again. "I miss her. I mean, I know we never saw her alive, but I miss how she used to kick my hand on your stomach. I loved that. I loved how your face glowed when you watched to see the look on my face when she did that. Even though those times were the only times we shared with her—well, and listening to her heartbeat and seeing her on the ultrasound—I miss her."

He faced the fire again, fingered the tear away, and returned to Eliza. "I was wondering if you would want to start a family right away? You know, if we stay married."

And there it was, the bond of family they had once dreamed of, the bond still living in them as well as in an angel in Heaven named Lily. Refusing to allow relief to etch her face with even the hint of a smile, Eliza faced Denver. "Having a family with you is my dream, Denver." She stood, amazed at how far they had come in only a few hours. "If you don't mind me staying, I'll go to bed."

He nodded and faced the fire again, its red glow again reflecting in his eyes. "I'll wait until the fire burns down."

Eliza went to him, grasped his hand and let go.

Done in the bathroom, dressed in a simple white nightgown, she left her hearing aids on the nightstand, turned the lamp off, and rolled over to close her eyes. If she were blessed, Lily would send her a dream of Denver. He would come, only to kneel by the bed and study her high cheekbones, her strong nose, her dark eyelashes, maybe to hover over her pillow to take in the aroma of fresh air in her hair, still alive in their memories from all of those sunny days on the lake.

She would roll over and smile, reach out and take his hand, bring him beneath the covers and hold him—nothing more— the entire night through.

Yes, what a dream … one so perfect, one so amazing, one so astounding … it could only be sent from an angel in Heaven.

But for her, a better dream would include a single soft kiss. Then she would turn the lamp on so they could look into each other's eyes while lying facing each other. Between signing words and sentences, he would tease a tendril of hair away from her eyes, and she would run her fingers through his above his ear. Smiles would follow, a giggle here and there, and if one of them made a silly comment like they used to do, they would laugh until their stomachs ached.

Of course, the perfect dream would allow their laughter to fade, followed by dwindling smiles and more than one soft kiss. Hands would clasp. Fingers would entwine. Clothing would be thrown to the floor. Lips would join, firmer and firmer still. Necks, shoulders, and beyond would tingle with kisses and caresses, until finally, one of them would give in to the love that had been building against the dam of heartache built by Lily's death, to completely and utterly toss it aside.

Then they would lie in each other's arms, marveling at how the miracle of love, both from him and her—and especially Tess—had brought them together again.

* * *

Kneeling by the fireplace, Denver prodded the remaining three sticks of wood together and returned to the chair. The surfaces of the three sticks of wood, now consumed to the point of embers, shimmered orange and red and yellow, more alive than not, burning with flare and flicker like him, Eliza, and Tess had burned since Eliza had left him, when the union between all of them had been set in motion. Like those embers, the union between him, Eliza, and Tess was about to be extinguished, and he wasn't sure how he felt about it. After all, Tess had told him to trust her because they would be okay. Although she hadn't explained exactly how they would be okay, he assumed she had meant the happy ending they had talked about. Whatever it was, he couldn't imagine it. The only happy ending he could imagine is if he went to Eliza, gave in to his love for her, gave in to Tess's love for them both. If he did that, how would he do it? Oh, yes. Oh, yes. He would go to her, only to kneel by the bed and study her high cheekbones, her strong nose, her dark eyelashes, maybe to hover over her pillow to take in the aroma of fresh air in her hair, still alive in their memories from all of those sunny days on the lake.

Then, if they were meant to be together, she would roll over and smile, reach out and take his hand, bring him beneath the covers and hold him—nothing more—the entire night through.

No, not really. He couldn't do that and nothing more. Their reunion would include a single soft kiss. Then she would turn the lamp on so they could look into each other's eyes while lying facing each other. Between signing words and sentences, he would tease a tendril of hair away from her eyes, and she would run her fingers through his hair above his ear. Smiles would follow, a giggle here and there, and if one of them made a silly comment like the used to do, they would laugh until their stomachs ached.

Of course, their laughter would fade, followed by dwindling smiles and more than one soft kiss. Hands would clasp. Fingers would entwine. Clothing would be thrown to the floor. Lips would join, firmer and firmer still. Necks, shoulders, and beyond would tingle with kisses and caresses, until finally, one of them would give in to the love that had been building against the dam of heartache built by Lily's death, to completely and utterly toss it aside.

Then they would lie in each other's arms, marveling at how the miracle of love, both from him and her—and especially Tess—had brought them together again.

Denver rose from the chair, gave the glowing embers one last look, and went to Eliza's door.

* * *

In the apartment above Ezra's workshop, Tess put away the last of her clothes. He and Bertha were concerned about

Denver's absence, but she had assured them that things would work out for the best.

Ready for bed, Tess turned the nightstand lamp on and opened her latest Sally Hemings book. Regardless of her interest in this remarkable woman, her eyes closed and opened, closed and opened. She returned the book to the nightstand and turned the lamp off.

In about three weeks, if her hopes became reality, Eliza would run to Denver to show him the positive home pregnancy test. At eighteen weeks they would visit a doctor for a sonogram. Whether or not they wanted to know the sex of the baby was up to them. As far as Tess was concerned, surprises were a lot better, especially when those surprises included happy endings. Yes, a lot of things had to fall in place to create a happy ending for all of them. Mama and Papa needed to accept it, and Eliza and Denver needed to accept it too. Then again, it depended on what his version of a happy ending was.

Tess turned the lamp back on, took her engagement ring from the drawer, and slipped it on her finger. In her heart she was married to Denver and always would be. Without that belief she couldn't have a happy ending. She couldn't have it without Denver's love either, but he had already given her that and would never take it back.

Admiring the way the light reflected in the diamond, with blues, reds, and greens, she smiled to herself. Those three colors could be Eliza, Denver, and her, bound together forever inside this shimmering stone of hope.

The thought settled her mind. Yes, they would have their happy ending, starting with Eliza's positive pregnancy test and the sonogram.

Tess opened the nightstand drawer and took out a book about pregnancy. It never hurt to learn more about a subject, and she would be able to talk to Eliza about it.

She opened the book, decided to get some sleep instead, and turned the lamp off again. Although she looked forward to working with Ezra, plus getting to know both him and Bertha, what she really looked forward to was returning home in a year.

With her hands pressed to her stomach, where she had held Denver's hands, she imagined him holding her. His steady strength would get her through the coming year, but she still would miss him terribly. He would miss her too, but he would have his hands full with planning for his and Eliza's baby to be born.

What a miracle to happen, the miracle of love and family, but especially the miracle of their happy ending to come.

miracles

Denver made a face as the doctor squirted clear gel on Eliza's slightly rounded tummy. "You said that stuff was cold with Lily."

"It is," Eliza said. "Hey, no pain no gain."

"That sounds like something Tess would say."

The doctor started the exam. "So, do you want to know the sex?"

Denver glanced at Eliza. "Right now we want to know if everything is okay."

The doctor stopped. "Hmm, that's interesting."

"What is?" Eliza asked.

"Just a little more and we'll see." Done with the exam, he removed his gloves. "Everything looks great, not a single anomaly. "I'd say you're on your way to having a healthy pregnancy."

"What was so interesting?" Denver asked.

"Are you interested in the sex?"

"I'm not," Eliza said.

"We didn't know with Lily," Denver said. "Are you sure?"

"This time is different. You've got to have faith, Denny."

"Have you been talking to Tess? She used to call me that all the time."

"We keep in touch."

"All right," the doctor said, taking a seat on a stool, "the sex will be a surprise." He faced Denver. "What about multiple births? You might have quintuplets and have a heart attack."

"Sheesh," Denver said, shaking his head, "is this mess with Denver day?"

The doctor faced Eliza. "Your husband doesn't like jokes, does he?"

A nurse cleaned Eliza's tummy. The doctor made the next appointment, saying he looked forward to seeing the progression of her pregnancy.

Dressed and on the way home, Eliza patted Denver's knee. "Are you ready to be a daddy, Daddy?"

"I'll be a double daddy when David's adoption comes through."

"That's true. All we need to do now is have this baby."

* * *

Denver gripped Eliza's hand. Sweat beaded her forehead. Her breaths hissed in and out. She raised from the pillow, moaning in pain until a shrill scream of effort burst from her clenched teeth.

"Here we are," the doctor said. "Let's suction her nostrils and get a cry out of baby Andrews."

"Waaahhh-waaahhh-waaahhh!"

"Way to go," Denver said. "She didn't even need her bottom popped." He started to kiss Eliza, but couldn't because her teeth were still clenched. She raised up like before, groaning in effort.

"Waaahhh-waaahhh-waaahhh!"

"Welcome to the world, baby Andrews number two," the doctor said. "That's what your mommy and daddy get for not wanting to know if there was more than one of you."

Denver's mouth fell open. "Please tell me that's all."

"That's all," the doctor said. "Two healthy girls."

Eliza pulled Denver's hand. "Come here and kiss me, Daddy, because we won't have much time for more than that any time soon."

"Six weeks is a good guideline," the doctor said. "Do you plan to have any more soon?"

"We'll see," Eliza said.

"Four's a good round number," Denver said. Grinning, he kissed Eliza. "Besides, David and me can't let you girls outnumber us guys."

* * *

Denver took the bottle from the warmer, dotted his wrist with milk, and went to the sofa, where Eliza held Abi, short for Abigail, and Anna. He loved both names. The traditional Amish name Abigail meant "father's joy," and Anna had been Eliza's dear friend, never to be forgotten.

He sat beside Eliza and took Abi into his arms. Eliza unbuttoned her blouse, lowered the nursing bra flap, and raised Anna to her breast. Both babies grunted with satisfaction, lips working in and out, fingers curling and uncurling.

"We sure have ourselves a couple of cuties," Denver said. "Will they get to have cereal in their milk soon?"

"Next month," Eliza said. "The doctor said three months is a little early." She kissed Anna's forehead, smoothed her dark hair, gazed into the blue eyes, and faced Denver again. "Did you realize Tess has been gone a year?"

"I know."

"Do you miss her?"

Denver paused. Be honest or not?

"I understand if you do," Eliza said. "I think you should see her."

"You know she hasn't called me since she left. That doesn't sound like someone who wants to see me."

"She called me before you got up this morning. She said you could come anytime."

"Maybe I'll drive up tomorrow. I need to pick David up from the bus stop before long."

"That's in an hour and a half. You can walk to Tess's house in five minutes."

"Do *what?*"

"I sold her my house. I couldn't let it sit forever."

Denver lay Abi on his shoulder and patted her back. He had thought about Tess every day since she had left, remembering how she had said she would come back from Ezra's after a year. Yes, he missed her, because he still loved her and always would.

Abi burped, but he kept patting. She had inherited his appetite, enjoying her meals enough for several burps afterward.

Eliza lay Anna over her shoulder and patted her back too. "If you go see Tess, you'll find out if we all have our happy ending."

"We have ours, but I hope she's happy too. You know how much she means to me."

"To me too." Anna burped, but Eliza kept patting. "To say I'm grateful for everything she did for us is an understatement. There's nothing I wouldn't do for her." Abi burped again, followed by Anna. Eliza placed Anna in a bassinette by the sliding glass doors and went to Denver. "Give me that monkey for a minute. Then you can go see Tess before you pick up David."

Denver stood. "All right. Be back in a little bit."

Choosing to walk, Denver picked up his pace. Being a full-time dad to David, Anna, and Abi kept him from walking often, and he enjoyed the cool October air, tinged with the spicy aroma of leaves turning yellow, red, and orange. Five minutes later he knocked on Tess's door. How they would react after not seeing each other for a year was anyone's guess. He knocked again, tried the knob, and opened the door. "Tess? It's—"

"Over here." Tess rounded the corner of the house by the driveway and stopped. "I was in the back yard."

She was just as Denver remembered: auburn hair in a ponytail, snug-fitting jeans, heart-shaped face, full lips he loved to kiss, eyes so green he saw them in his dreams more often than he should, being married to Eliza.

She took a step, another, another, and ran to hold him, laying her head on his chest. "I missed you so much."

He rubbed slow circles on her back. "I missed you too, angel."

She pulled away. "I guess we better go inside before we give the neighbors something to talk about."

In the living room, she hugged him again. "Remember all those nights I walked to your house?"

Letting her go before more happened than a hug, Denver laughed. "As you well know, Tess the Mess, you did a lot more than walk to my house." He sat in a chair across from the sofa. "Eliza said you're buying her house."

"Interest free payments. Considering how I got you two back together again, she should've given it to me."

"I guess you made a good salary working for Ezra."

"He and Bertha are generous to a fault. They gave me an acre of land on the lake, no questions asked. I think they wanted me to stay. When I told them I was selling it and moving back here, they actually paid me for it because they wanted to keep the developers from getting it." Tess paused, eyes lowering.

Seconds later she wiped a tear from one cheek, then faced Denver again. "The hardest thing I ever did was to leave you. I hope you can forgive me."

Denver fought tears himself. He waited until the urge passed. "That's all in the past."

Her eyes brightened. "Good. Like I always told you, you and Eliza belong together, and that's the only reason I left like I did." Sighing hugely, she stood. "Want some coffee?"

Denver followed her to the kitchen. At the open back door, he pointed. "What are those ribbons around the trees in the woods?"

"That's where my new guitar shop is going. Will you have time to help me build them when it's ready? You're just a short walk away."

"We'll see. I do have three kids and a wife to keep me busy."

"When you have time." Tess gave him a mug. "I watched Eliza getting bigger with Anna and Abigail. Talk about a belly."

About to sip coffee, Denver stopped. "Sheesh, I forgot all about those game cameras. You've been watching us all this time?"

"Eliza changed the batteries for me. I may have been away, but I wanted to be part of your lives. That poor sister of mine had walking like a duck down to a science."

Denver sipped coffee. "How did you explain being at Ezra's without me?" He pointed at the engagement ring on her finger. "Especially while you were wearing that?"

"I told him and Bertha I still love you and always would, that we would have a happy ending regardless. Do you mind if I wear it?"

"To be honest, after all the time we spent together, I feel like we're married."

"My thoughts exactly."

"You don't want to find someone else?"

"I won't say it's impossible, but I'll never find another you. Anyway, like you said, I feel like we're married."

From toward a hall that led from the kitchen, what sounded like a cat meowed.

Denver nodded toward the hall. "I hope you don't mean that about not finding someone else. If you do, does that mean you're turning into a cat lady?"

Smirking at him, Tess took his mug. She left both on the counter and pulled a chair from the dining room table. "Shut up and sit your fanny down so you can meet the newest member of my family."

Denver sat. She returned with something wrapped in a blanket, placed it in his arms, and uncovered the end resting in the crook of his elbow. "Meet your son, Drew Andrews."

Denver blinked and shook his head. "My *what?*"

"Your son. He looks just like your baby pictures you showed me that time."

Denver wanted to jump up, but he didn't want to upset the sleeping bundle in his arms. Yes, with brown hair and the same facial structure, the baby resembled him perfectly at that age. He looked up at Tess. "Is this why you wanted to spend a week together in Ocracoke before my month with Eliza, to get pregnant? He looks about the same age as Anna and Abi."

Tess pulled out a chair and sat across from him. "What do you want to believe?"

"What do you mean?"

She got up. "Be right back." She returned to place a Sally Hemings book on the table.

"What the heck is going on, Tess? Are you trying to say our happy ending is going to be with you as my concubine like Sally Hemings was Thomas Jefferson's concubine and Drew is our first child?"

"No, you idiot." Tess opened the book and took out a business card. "This is from a sperm donor clinic in Charlottesville. I went there when I visited Ezra during your month with Eliza. I knew you would choose Eliza, so my happy ending is to have my own baby."

In Denver's arms, Drew squirmed. Denver waited until he stopped. "Look, Tess, there's no way you knew I was going to choose Eliza."

"You didn't, so don't worry about it."

"Are you sure about his sperm donor thing? He looks just like me."

"The clinic let me look at pictures of the donors. I chose one who looked like you."

"C'mon, Tess, you really expect me to believe that?"

Drew squirmed again. Tess took him. "Let's go to the living room so I can feed your son."

Following Tess, Denver scratched his head. As much as he wanted Drew to be his son, it would create all kinds of problems, like explaining him to Absalom and Oneita and Eliza. He took the same chair as before, while Tess settled down on the sofa. She unbuttoned her shirt and lowered the nursing bra flap, exactly like Eliza did earlier. "Remember when we talked about this?" she asked.

"Uh-huh, something about me wanting to watch."

"'Uh-huh' is right, like you're watching now."

"It's not that kind of watching. It's still weird since we're not together."

"Weird or not, I want him to be your son. You didn't have a problem adopting David, so I expect you to adopt Drew. Then he'll be your son anyway."

"What about—"

"I've already told Mama and Papa and Eliza. They understand."

"Are you sure he's not mine?"

"Like I asked you a minute ago, what do you want to believe? Or rather, what happy ending do you want Eliza and you and me to have? It can be anything you want."

"What if I want a DNA test?"

"That's up to you. If you adopt him, he's yours anyway. I know it's not the same, but if you know he's ours, would that make it harder or easier on you?"

Denver sat back in the chair. What a mess, straight from the intriguing mind of Tess the Mess. "Well, I'll adopt him, that's for sure. I'll help you build guitars when I have time, so I'll get to see him and you almost as often as I see Eliza and our kids. Do you think they'll understand how I have another child from another mom?"

Tess moved Drew to her other breast. "David will understand because you adopted him. Anna and Abigail and Drew will grow up together, and we'll explain it to them."

"Do you think you'll visit the sperm donor clinic again?"

Grinning, Tess cut her eyes at him. "That depends on the version of the happy ending we want for ourselves, doesn't it? Like we talked about in Ocracoke, I want a girl with my auburn hair and your eyes, and you're only a short walk away."

"Yeah, but I can't cheat on Eliza. You know that, right?"

"I'm not asking you to. As far as I'm concerned, Drew's biological dad is a test tube in a sperm donor clinic in Charlottesville. All I want is a happy ending for all of us, and that depends on what we want it to be."

Denver rubbed his eyes. Since Tess hadn't given Drew his name like they had discussed on Ocracoke, he might not be his son anyway. Then again, since she *had* named him Drew, similar to Andrews, that could be a hint that he *was* his son.

Tess—sweet, amazing, and sharp as a tack Tess—had crafted a happy ending for everyone concerned. The funny thing was, he couldn't be sure how happy it was for him, not unless he asked for a DNA test. Regardless, it really was a happy ending. Drew was theirs because he would adopt him. Oneita and Absalom had accepted him as another grandchild already, another plus. David, Anna, and Abi would know Drew as their brother, plus number three. Eliza was the key in all this. She could choose to believe whatever she chose as the perfect happy ending too. Denver almost laughed. Before he had walked over here, Eliza had already hinted at her happy ending, saying there's nothing she wouldn't do for Tess because of how she had helped them find each other again.

Tess giggled. "I think I see smoke coming from your ears."

Denver joined her on the sofa. "You've got our happy ending all figured out, don't you?"

She kissed his cheek. "Like we say in the south, baby, 'my mama didn't raise no fools.'"

family

enver left the kitchen with a platter of steaks, hamburgers, and hotdogs. On the deck outside the sliding glass doors, he set the platter on the patio table and went to the railing.

In the yard below, Absalom and Oneita were sitting at one of two huge picnic tables he had built for the occasion. On the table in front of them, a plump baby named Alan, Denver's dad's namesake, cooed and grinned. At six months old, he was the latest edition to his and Eliza's family, and David, now nine, and Abi and Anna, now four, adored him. Right now, however, they were adoring the lake. On the end of the dock, David was teaching four-year-old Drew how to cast a fishing rod, while near the front of the dock, Ivy, Anna and Abi played in the sand. Normally they played in the water, but since it was October, the cool air had them wearing jeans instead of swimsuits. The only person who could make this day better was Lily. Still, he could imagine her, either on the dock with the boys or playing with the girls, as sweet and as endearing as she could be, now an angel in Heaven instead of a ghost from his and Eliza's past.

The sliding glass doors swished open. Eliza placed a covered bowl of tossed salad on the patio table and joined Denver at the railing. "Are you surveying your domain?"

"I'm admiring our family. Ten years ago today, when we got married, who would've known it would be like this. "That reminds me." He turned toward Eliza. "When Tess left us alone for a month, why didn't you tell me you never finalized the divorce?"

"Would it have made any difference if I told you then instead of when you had to choose one of us?"

"Well, it worked out. Now I'm a busy dad with a bunch of kids to raise."

"That's right, along with Liza."

Denver chuckled. "I never thought Tess would name her that."

Eliza slapped his arm. "What's wrong with Liza?"

"I thought you might be jealous of us building guitars together."

"No, you thought I might be jealous because her kids might be yours instead of a sperm donor's."

"Like she told me," Denver said, his voice teasing, "which one makes you happier?"

"I trust you," Eliza said, hugging him. "Besides, after everything we've been through, I trust Tess too. As far as why I didn't tell you how we were still married, I didn't want that to affect your choice between Tess and me."

"It didn't." Denver kissed her. "Because Tess sort of chose for me by leaving."

Eliza pointed to the yard. "The grill is smoking. You better get our food on the fire before we have a revolt."

Denver left with the platter. Eliza went to the guest room, where Tess was nursing Liza. "How's it going in here? Is my namesake almost done with her supper?"

Tess frowned. "I should've named her Nibbles, she bites."

"Gums."

"It still hurts."

Eliza sat on the bed beside Tess. "That's what you get for naming her after me. She knows you and my husband are more than friends."

"We sure are. It isn't just any man who would adopt his sister-in-law's kids."

"I haven't asked you lately. Are you still happy with our situation?"

"Are you?"

"You first."

"I'd be happier if Denver were mine all the time instead of just in the guitar shop."

"But he spends time with you and the kids. After all, he's their dad."

Tess moved Liza to her other breast, kissed her cheek, and faced Eliza. "I'm happy. I'd be a fool if I weren't."

Eliza smoothed Liza's red fuzz down over her head. The green eyes peered up at her, as if to say, *Hey, Aunt Eliza, don't mess with my hair while I'm eating.*

"She sure is a cutie," Tess said. "I wonder if Denver would've chosen me if he had known he would have six kids if he chose you?"

"Great question," Eliza said. "One we'll never know the answer to." She stood. "Come out whenever. He's just putting everything on the grill." She left the guest room, closing the door behind her.

Tess frowned again. "Hey, Nibbles, take it easy on Mama. I might need those for your daddy's seventh kid." Liza waved her hand at Tess. She placed her finger within the tiny palm, and Liza gripped it firmly. The tiny pink lips grinned, then went back to nursing. Tess kissed the soft forehead. "What a smile. Your daddy and I will have to chase the boys away with a stick when you get older."

Liza's lips slowed, nursed again, slowed again. The green eyes blinked once, twice, and closed. Tess placed her in the crib, turned the baby monitor on, and took the receiver with her to the backyard, where she sat beside Mama. Alan faced her and held out his hands. She took him into her lap. "Hey, you chunky monkey. Are you ready for a hot dog?"

"It won't be long," Mama said. "He's about to chew his fingers off from teething."

Tess bumped Mama's shoulder with hers. "I hope you know how much Eliza and Denver and me appreciate you babysitting all our kids when Denver and I are working and she's painting."

"I wouldn't have it any other way, Tess."

"I help when I can," Papa said.

"True, but we moved here for Eliza and our grandchildren," Mama said. "Now we have all the love we can handle."

Denver closed the grill lid and sat beside Papa. "David wants me to teach him how to water ski."

"I wouldn't mind trying that myself," Papa said.

Mama rolled her eyes at him. "Denver would need a stronger motor for the pontoon boat to pull you up, you big old bear."

Eliza brought two pitchers of tea to the table and filled five glasses. Absalom took his and raised it. "A toast to family."

Denver raised his glass. "And a toast to Willow, plus her husband and their new daughter."

"I wish they could've been here," Tess said. She faced Eliza. "But we know how we feel the day after having a baby."

"We sure do." Eliza raised her glass. "A toast to Lily too. God bless you, our sweet angel."

Everyone clinked glasses and drank. Lowering his glass, Papa eyed Denver. "Oneita and I were talking the other day. We're not sure how we feel about this sperm donor thing."

"Don't look at me," Denver said, tipping his glass toward Tess. "She's *your* daughter."

"Well?" Mama said, cutting her eyes toward Tess.

"Don't look at me, look at Eliza. I might not have done it if she hadn't agreed to let Denver adopt Drew and Liza."

Sipping tea, Eliza lowered the glass. "Oh, so now it's all *my* fault."

Alan blew a raspberry. "Ma-ma-ma-ma-ma-ma!"

"See there," Tess said, giving him to Eliza, "your son agrees." She got up and went behind Denver to wrap her arms around his neck. "Don't you think so, baby?"

"Hey, I'm just an innocent bystander with six kids. What do I know?"

"See all that smoke?" Papa said, pointing toward the grill. "What I know is you better not burn our supper."

Denver went to the grill. Tess joined him, facing away from everyone else. "What a life, huh?" she asked, keeping her voice low.

"One I wouldn't trade for anything." He flipped the burgers and steaks, rolled the hotdogs over, and closed the lid. "How about you?"

"Like I tell you all the time, I'm happy. Are you walking over later to help me with that special-order guitar? I'll give you a bonus if you do."

"Sure. I can always use more cash to buy food for this hungry crowd of ours."

Eliza came over with Alan. "I heard that, Tess. What's this about a special-order guitar?"

"A new customer ordered it. I need Denver to help with heating the sides and clamping them to the form. It's a cutaway, so it's harder than a regular guitar."

"How late are you keeping him? It *is* our tenth anniversary, you know."

"I'm sorry, Eliza, I forgot."

"I think you forgot on purpose. How much money's involved?"

"Wait a minute," Denver said. "Don't I get to decide whether I work on the guitar or stay home with you?"

Grinning, Eliza poked his chest. "It sounds like you forgot our anniversary too."

Papa shook his head. "Now I know why I like Charlie Brown—good grief."

Denver raised his hands and signed to Eliza, "I'm staying home, and you know why."

She raised her hands. "Good. I bought a new nighty downtown and can't wait until you see it."

"That's not fair," Mama said. "I forgot most of the signs I learned."

"Me too," Papa said. "Do we get to know what you signed?"

"I know what they signed," Tess said. "It means I'll take a break from that guitar and keep the kids tonight."

"Ahh," Papa said, winking at Mama. "I know what that means. Maybe we should do the same thing."

Mama winked back. "I might just take you up on that, you big old bear."

* * *

At home, after feeding Alan and Liza, Tess settled them down in the two baby beds in her room. David and Drew shared the other bedroom, while Anna and Abi shared the other.

She peeked into each room. Papa had made two bed frames for each, and Tess loved having her extended family sleep over like this.

The boys, both with brown hair to their ears, slept soundly. The girls, with black hair past their shoulders, were whispering and giggling. She silently told them goodnight, adding a special good night to Lily, the entire family's sweet angel—never, ever, not in all their lifetimes put together, to be forgotten.

Tess went to the kitchen for a glass of wine. She had bought a bottle from a local vineyard last weekend, intrigued when she overheard the owners, a couple who appeared to be their early thirties, with two kids about the same age as Anna, Abi, and Drew, having supper at the brewery in town. Although the couple spoke softly, Tess could hear the undercurrent of an argument in their voices. Why some couples couldn't take the time to understand each other, she didn't know. After all, she, Denver, and Eliza understood each other perfectly.

Done with the wine, Tess took the baby monitor receiver and walked the moonlit path through the woods to the lake. On her new dock, she sat on the wooden bench she and Denver had built. A soft breeze blew, dotting her arms with goose bumps. Anyone else might need a jacket, but the cool night air made her feel alive, like when Denver used to run his fingertips along her body, both before and after they made love.

Love, what an intriguing thing. Ethan was dating a woman he had met in church, and she was learning sign language. Akina was engaged to a fellow sign language teacher she had met in D.C. And Jan—even Jan—had gotten married last year, to a sculptor who, because of his strong hands she had said, gave great massages. Then there was Beth, Willow and her husband's new daughter, the latest addition to the family, named after Denver's mom.

The breeze gusted and lulled. Waves lapped against the dock. Air, crisp and clean, filled her senses. The only thing that would make this moment any better was if Denver walked down the moonlit path, leaves crunching beneath his footfalls, and sat beside her, saying how much he missed her when they were apart, and how he loved her as much as the first time he told her.

Yes, it was a dream of sorts, created when they fell in love, but dreams sometimes came true despite whether they should or not. And too, true love reached infinitely deeper than physical love, like when she used to lean back against him to feel as if she were a part of his soul.

The moon rose higher. The stars dimmed further. The breeze died, replaced by a stillness that hovered over the lake, leaving nothing but the crunch of footsteps in the leaves along the path and the black slash of his shadow coming closer through the trees.

And closer still.

Yes, what a life.

What a *wonderful* life.

Readers: please find the first chapter of the author's next book, *The Coincidence of Hope,* after the book club questions. It is due to be released in the spring of 2022.

Book Club Questions

1. In the first chapter, although Tess loves Denver, she still hopes he and Eliza will have another chance to be together. How does this make you feel about Tess and her conflicts?

2. Eliza is considering painting again, and Anna seems to be waking from her coma. How do these occurrences affect the story?

3. Denver has second thoughts about a relationship with Tess because of her age. Do you think it's that, or does he still hope to reunite with Eliza?

4. As Eliza grows closer to David, is it clear she loves him, or do you think he's still a replacement for Lily?

5. How do you feel about Leah when she and Denver have their one date in Washington? Do you think she could be a match for Denver?

6. Did you think David saying Josh and Anna might be better off in Heaven if they were hurting would affect the story?

7. What did you think when Denver changed his mind about having a relationship with Tess, along with him seeing her supposedly dating Mark, and Tess thinking he and Leah were sleeping together?

8. Did you enjoy Tess's birthday party scene and the subtext between Denver and Mark?

9. Were you glad when Tess and Denver made up at Willow's wedding reception?

10. Did it surprise you when Eliza showed up at the reception?

11. At the reception, was it clear how Absalom still felt guilty about Eliza losing her hearing?

12. When Anna wakes from the coma physically impaired, did you think she might die?

13. As Josh complains of aches and pains, do you think he might die?

14. Did it make sense how Denver reacted to seeing Eliza in Raleigh, then in Ohio when he had his accident?

15. When Eliza decided to buy a house near her family and Denver, did you have any idea if he and her would reunite?

15. Why did Tess force Denver and Eliza to stay together for a month?

16. What did you think of Tess and Denver's trip to Ocracoke and how they planned for children and talked about family?

17. At the end of Denver's month with Eliza, he planned to be with Tess. Why do you think he broke down crying at the sliding glass doors?

18. Were you happy when Denver and Eliza reunited? How did you like the scene where they were thinking of how it could happen?

19. Were you surprised when Eliza and Denver had twins and when Tess returned with her own baby?

20. In the last chapter, what is your version of Eliza, Denver, and Tess's happy ending, and what hints in the last few chapters did you use to decide it? Are her kids from a sperm donor, or is she and Denver having a physical relationship? Which version makes you happier, and is it possible for a person to love two people at the same time?

Please enjoy this selection from *The Coincidence of Hope*, to be published early in 2022.

Visitors

The Ardennes American Cemetery
Neuville-en-Condroz, Belgium
December 6, 2011

Surrounding Joe Matthan, hundreds of white crosses fill the vast cemetery. Beyond them, in front of a backdrop of leafless trees, each bone-gray in the dawn, an American flag hangs from its pole. The sun rises. Through the trees its light slashes the crosses with crimson, followed by orange, followed by yellow. Each cross is a reminder to humanity of the offerings beneath them, many forgotten. The sun climbs. The shimmering globe bursts above the trees. Frost sparkles on the brown grass. Here and there, patches of snow glitter with rainbow hues. Another day is born. Another day to live. Another day to die. The stone crosses now reflect the light, white and crisp, and Joe is on the way to find his own grave.

For decades it's the same thing: wake up inside a body not his, muscles not his, bones not his. Even the brain isn't his, nor the touch, nor the vision or hearing, nor the taste or smell. Although he shares them all with each body's owner, he is unable to control a single muscle. He is a ghost, a spirit, an essence clinging to this strange existence. He has no idea why, yet it is so. Each host either eats breakfast or doesn't, dresses or doesn't, or puts on a robe and stares in a mirror or out a window. Sometimes they don't get up. Sometimes they cry. Sometimes they smile. Sometimes they marry. Sometimes they divorce. Of all the things they might do, most vary. Some go to work and some don't. Some kiss a significant other and some don't. Some wake their kids for school and some don't. Joe prefers the hosts in a happy marriage. Kids are a plus.

He hates how it doesn't always happen that way.

A few days ago, when his last host, a fifty-eight-year-old plumber—he loved running a model train around the Christmas tree for his grandkids—died from colon cancer, he found himself within the body of a young man dressing in a United States Army uniform. This morning the young man is miraculously looking for Joe's headstone in the Ardennes American Cemetery in Belgium. The memorial center's chaplain said some people are coming to see Private Matthan's grave for the first time, and it's the young man's job to attend them during the visit. Although Joe is excited to see who's coming, he's afraid to see his own grave. Death isn't fun, but living this way isn't fun either. He's gotten tired of it over the years, although bored is a better word.

Within the multitude of white crosses—5,329 to be exact, 792 of them unnamed— the young man searches. His breath plumes. Sunlight melts the frost, and the droplets dapple his black shoes. The air is fresh and clean. The crisp smell reminds Joe of mid-winter snowstorm blanketing his parent's farm; the young man's musky antiperspirant does not.

He turns, takes a few more steps, and stops at a cross to lean closer.

Joseph S. Matthan

PFC, 106th Infantry Div., Nebraska

Dec. 17, 1944

Joe nods his phantom head. *That's me all right. I wonder why I my body wasn't shipped back home. It isn't like my injuries were bad enough to keep anyone from seeing it.*

Nodding as if acknowledging either the location of the grave or the sacrifice, the young man stands.

It's then that Joe sees a freshly dug hole, small and rectangular, in his grave. The young man scratches his head as if he doesn't know anything about it. The chaplain didn't mention it, so it must be a mystery. He and Joe see something in their peripheral vision, and the young man turns.

In the distance, leaving the huge memorial building constructed of gleaming marble, three figures enter the morning sun. One, an elderly woman, walks slow and a bit stooped over. The second, a middle-aged man with blond hair, carries what resembles a small chest made of dark wood, wrapped in clear plastic. The last is the uniformed Army chaplain.

The three people come closer. The elderly woman's face grows clearer, along with the face of the blond man.

Then, like the exploding grenade that ended Joe's dreams of life and love so long ago, the ghostly remains of his heart bursts with astonishment as he recognizes who these two people are.

About the Author

J. Willis Sanders lives in southern Virginia, with his wife and several stringed musical instruments.

With several novels published and more on the way, he enjoys crafting intriguing characters with equally intriguing conflicts to overcome. He also loves the natural world and, more often than not, his stories include those settings. Most also utilize intense love relationships and layered themes.

His first novel (not this one, but he plans to publish it) is a ghostly World War II era historical that takes place mostly in the midwestern United States, which utilizes some little-known facts about German POW camps there at that time. It's the first of a three-book series, in which characters from the first book continue their lives.

Although he loves history, he has written several contemporary novels as well, and some include interesting paranormal twists, both with and without religious themes.

He also loves the Outer Banks of North Carolina, and has published three novels within different time frames based on the area, what he calls his Outer Banks of North Carolina Series.

Another genre he enjoys is thriller novels, so he has launched a series with a main female character named Reid Stone.

Other hobbies include reading (of course), vegetable gardening, playing music with friends, and songwriting, some of which are in a few of his novels.

If you're interested in Clarksville, Virginia, the main setting for this book, it is a real town in southern Virginia, and you can check this website: https://clarksvilleva.org/#/

To follow the author's work, please visit any of the following:

https://jwillissanders.wixsite.com/writer

https://www.facebook.com/J-Willis-Sanders-874367072622901

https://www.amazon.com/J-Willis-Sanders/e/B092RZG6MC?ref_=dbs_p_ebk_r00_abau_000000

Readers: to help those considering a purchase, please consider leaving a review on Amazon.com, Goodreads.com, or wherever you purchased this book.
Thank you.